1/4

DEATH
COMES TO
DARTMOOR

ALSO AVAILABLE BY VIVIAN CONROY

MERRIWEATHER AND ROYSTON MYSTERIES

The Butterfly Conspiracy

CORNISH CASTLE MYSTERIES

Rubies in the Roses

Death Plays a Part

COUNTRY GIFT SHOP MYSTERIES

Written into the Grave

Grand Prize: Murder!

Dead to Begin With

LADY ALKMENE CALLENDER MYSTERIES

Fatal Masquerade

Deadly Treasures

Diamonds of Death

A Proposal to Die For

MURDER WILL FOLLOW MYSTERIES

Honeymoon with Death

A Testament to Murder

DEATH COMES TO DARTMOOR

A MERRIWEATHER AND ROYSTON MYSTERY

Vivian Conroy

CROOKED
LANE

NEW YORK

Published in the United States by Crooked Lane Books, an imprint of The Quick Brown Fox & Company LLC.

Crooked Lane Books and its logo are trademarks of The Quick Brown Fox & Company LLC.

Library of Congress Catalog-in-Publication data available upon request.

ISBN (hardcover): 978-1-64385-009-2
ISBN (ePub): 978-1-64385-010-8
ISBN (ePDF): 978-1-64385-011-5

Cover design by Mimi Bark
Book design by Jennifer Canzone

Printed in the United States.

www.crookedlanebooks.com

Crooked Lane Books
34 West 27th St., 10th Floor
New York, NY 10001

First Edition: August 2019

10 9 8 7 6 5 4 3 2 1

CHAPTER 1

"What on earth are you so busy with, Merula?"
Merula Merriweather shocked upright, her pencil scratching across the paper she had been completely engrossed in. She blinked as she stared at the dark chiseled features of Lord Raven Royston sitting opposite her in the coach that rattled its way along a country dirt road.

Raven's expression was cynical as usual, but a genuine interest sparked in his eyes, and his slightly provocative look reminded her of the first time they had met, at a zoological lecture where Merula's uncle was to present the novelty he had been toiling on, which had in reality been Merula's work. Raven had at once seen through the ruse of letting Uncle Rupert take credit for her achievements, challenging her to prove to him what her work was really about.

"Are you making notes about the journey?" Raven asked, nodding at her notebook that she had rested against her small case of personal belongings so he could not see what she was writing, no matter how he craned his neck.

"The only thing I've observed about it so far," Raven continued, "is that it is taking far too long."

Bowsprit cleared his throat. He was seated beside his master and displaying, as usual, an odd combination of impeccable manners and a total freedom that betrayed he had not been born into service or trained to obey orders and fade into the background. In his quiet but emphatic tone he declared, "A few decades ago it would have taken much longer, as the railway didn't reach Paignton yet, my lord. I heard there are plans to create more routes, also inland. All the villages are vying to be along a route and have their own station. The railway brings the tourists and the money they might spend here during their stay."

"Don't people object to the arrival of the railway?" Merula frowned. "A lady in my aunt's acquaintance is certain that railway travel leads to moral decay and even causes illnesses. She claims the human body wasn't created to move at the speed a steam engine can reach."

Bowsprit nodded with a serious expression. "The illustrated news magazines bring the most lurid stories of fights breaking out among passengers and decent ladies being attacked by men who are driven to insanity by the train's movement."

"Really, Bowsprit . . ." Raven shook a reproving finger at his valet.

Bowsprit pulled an innocent expression. "There are several recorded cases of perfectly respectable gentlemen behaving in a less than appropriate fashion as soon as they are on a moving train. What else could have caused their lapse but the train's motions, the magazines argue."

"You should stop reading these sensationalist accounts. They try to convince one that even the most common things make people mad." Raven shifted his weight. "Sometimes I wonder what people are more afraid of: death or madness. Judging by all these reports, one would think the latter."

Merula studied his expression more closely, as she was aware that the subject touched upon a sore spot in Raven's own past: his mother's death after she had been sent off into the countryside to recuperate from nervous strain.

She knew the unsolved mystery surrounding her death—a drowning in a pond behind the family country estate that had been deemed "accidental" by the investigating authorities—weighed heavily on Raven's mind, as he wasn't certain whether his mother had really been unbalanced or, in fact, had been driven to distraction by a malignant person who had consciously persecuted her.

"I could have sat on the train forever," an excited voice spoke up from beside Merula.

Simply called *Lamb* in Merula's family's household, where several maids had the first name Anne, she had recently been promoted from mere maid to Merula's personal attendant, an impromptu solution to give Merula's journey—as an unmarried young woman with a likewise unmarried, and unfortunately somewhat ill-reputed, lord—a veneer of propriety.

Merula guessed that most of their acquaintances would still have gossiped about it, had they known, but Aunt Emma, ever eager to avert any possible damage to the family name, would no doubt have told them merely that Merula had left London to recuperate in the countryside with some obscure family member no one had ever heard of. After Uncle Rupert's arrest for murder and the relentless campaign in the newspapers to accuse him of being the key figure in a huge "butterfly conspiracy," the acquaintances could understand that Merula was in need of rest and a care-free time away from the city where it had all played out.

Although Aunt Emma despised lying and considered it a sign of a sloppy upbringing with low morals, she didn't hesitate to revert to a little white lie herself whenever she deemed that it served a greater good. And restoring the family name after the intense scrutiny it had recently been under because of the murder accusation was, in her eyes, the greatest good there could possibly be.

Lamb sat with her nose pressed against the cold glass pane of the coach and stared with wide eyes at everything outside. Her narrow shoulders were tight with excitement in her new deep-red traveling ensemble, which had once belonged to Merula but had now been given to Lamb to make her look the part of a lady's companion.

Poor Lamb had been divided between bliss that she'd been chosen to accompany Miss Merula outside of London and pure terror that she'd have to perform the duties of a servant far above her usual station. Merula had reassured Lamb that she'd do fine, as she knew the girl to be both eager to please and intelligent, a combination that ensured she'd adjust to her new role quickly.

"Everything is gray here," Raven complained, only half hiding his yawn behind a politely raised hand. "I should have remembered this is a land of endless rocks and moors. Nothing to excite or cause wonder. Perhaps this meteorite shower Oaks mentioned to me in his last letter could be of some interest. The Perseids may only recently have been named as such, but I'm certain that these showers have been observed for many centuries."

He added with a grimace, "Probably as some omen of impending doom. It's beyond me why people always view natural phenomena as signs of destruction. Why can't they simply be part of the grand workings of the universe? In the same manner as the seasons come and go, we see phenomena in the skies such as these meteorites or lunar and solar eclipses. They tell us everything has a course, they are evidence of structure and design. Not of chaos and disaster."

"I'd like to see a solar eclipse sometime," Merula said. "I've read that everything changes when it happens: the shadows, the light, and that even the animals know that something strange is afoot, as the birds keep quiet and the deer and foxes hide deep in the forest."

Raven peered at Merula with tilted head. "You still haven't told me what you're so engrossed in."

Merula held her hand over the notebook, even though she knew Raven couldn't see what she was doing. "I'm drawing some scenes of what we see on the way. Just a little exercise."

"You draw as well?" Raven pursed his lips. "There seems to be no end to your talents."

Merula tried to determine whether he genuinely meant this or was pulling her leg and decided that she wasn't sure. As was often the case with this strange man.

Knowing of his bad relationship with his sister-in-law and his disregard for women in general, Merula had difficulty believing that Raven would truly value her, and yet it seemed so, if only because he was a rational man who accepted facts when they were laid before him. And he had been able to see with his own eyes how Merula had borne herself in the murder case in which her uncle had sat in the shadow of the gallows. How she had gathered information, observed, deduced, and in the end, even risked her own life to unmask the true killer.

Whatever Raven thought of her, he'd have to admit her brain was as astute as his and her courage never lacking. Yes, she had been afraid and about to give up, but she had pushed through. He had come to know her in the best possible way you could ever come to know someone: by being in trouble with them and seeing how they respond.

Raven knew her in a different way than anybody else in the world, and it had given her a strange thrill of pleasure, of accomplishment and self-confidence, to be singled out by him to accompany him to Dartmoor, where he had an acquaintance. And not just any acquaintance, but a man living on his own with a house full of zoological specimens that he kept under close guard, as he seemed to be quite the hermit who disliked human company and spent his days among his animals and his books. That Raven was allowed to come and bring her with him was a treat.

"I don't pretend that I can draw well," Merula said, "but to get better I must practice. I'm not using any colors, just my pencil to make little sketches of the land."

Raven smiled, that slow sardonic smile that merely turned the corners of his mouth up a little. "Two women and two men on a journey. The men are bored out of their minds, and the women find fascination in every little thing. Lamb is looking as if she's in the heart of Paris seeing fashionable ladies walk by on the boulevard in their pretty dresses with their hats full of feathers and pearls, and Merula is drawing the sights as if they are not all the same, just rocks and moors devoid of life."

"If you call them devoid of life, you haven't been paying attention," Merula protested. "I've seen countless birds and a man on horseback." As she said it, she realized that such trivialities probably didn't interest Raven, who spoke of Paris as if he had been there many times.

Did he miss it? The grandeur of the city, the liveliness, the nights out with acquaintances, the company of admiring women?

Raven always acted like he didn't care what people thought of him and the string of failed business investments that had left his purse empty and his reputation in tatters. But Merula firmly believed it had to be gratifying to be admired and smiled at and spoken to with deference instead of scorn. For herself, though, she wasn't quite sure what people should admire and respect: as an orphan with a shady past, having been abandoned and left in her uncle's care, she didn't have a family name to lean on, something so important in the circles in which her uncle and aunt moved. Her looks were tolerable, she supposed, but nowhere near the great beauty that could attract a well-positioned husband.

And Merula wasn't even certain that having a well-positioned husband and receiving invitations from the most influential families would satisfy the need inside of her to do something meaningful and be someone in her own right.

"And have you drawn all of these scintillating sights?" Raven's eyes dared her to affirm it. For some reason he seemed eager to argue, restless, as she could see by his lean, suntanned fingers constantly moving to rub a stain on the hat he had put in his lap or trail along the edge of it.

"To me they are new and interesting." Merula held his gaze. "And besides, I'm just looking for objects to draw, whatever they are. They need not be fashionable or charming, as long as I can capture them and make them look true to life."

"Show them to me." Raven extended his hand.

Merula tightened her grip on the notebook. She knew Raven wouldn't just look at the current page she was working on, outlining the landscape they traveled along with its cliffs that plunged sharply to the restless sea. No, he would leaf through it, going backward through time, and then he'd also find the drawing she had made of him, during their train journey as he had sat staring out the window, his face relaxed but for a slight tension around his mouth, the hint of a frown over his eyes. He had a great face for any artist to try to capture, but she was uncertain whether he would see her effort as mere artistic practice.

Before Raven could ask again and make things awkward, they heard a voice yell something, and the coach came to a jerking halt. Sitting up, Raven reached for the door and opened it a crack, allowing a stream of furious words to rush in: ". . . out of your mind! Jumping into the middle of the road in front of my horses. They might have reared and kicked in your head. Not that you don't deserve it for being such a fool."

A voice about as agitated and ferocious replied, "You're not allowed to pass here. Turn back."

"Are you mad? Turn back? We're on our way to Cranley. Now out of my path!"

"This road is blocked. You must turn back. You can drive to Cranley by another way."

"That roundabout way? That will take hours. Get out of my way, man, or I'll drive right across you."

Raven threw the door wide open and leaned out, resting his leg on the coach's step so he could maintain an upright posture. "What is the matter, coachman?"

"This idiot here is telling me to turn back."

"It's not my orders," the voice called out. "The wreckmaster decided it."

"Who is the wreckmaster?" Raven asked.

The coachman, in a begrudging tone, said, "He sees to the coastline, the beaches, and the estuary, that what ships lose and is found is divided fairly among the beachcombers. He goes out on stormy nights and saves people in danger. He has a flock of helpers and he believes he about owns the area."

"You better believe it," the man in the road called. "If the wreckmaster says you can't pass, you can't pass. Now turn back."

Raven asked, "How long is this road obstruction going to last?"

"Until dusk. Then they will stop searching."

Raven pulled himself back into the carriage and said to Bowsprit, "You have a little conversation with the coachman to draw him out about this wreckmaster. I'm curious as to what exactly they are searching for. Ply him with these cigars." He took a beautiful silver case from his pocket and handed it to Bowsprit. "Divert him so he doesn't notice or mind what we're doing."

"And what will you be doing?" Bowsprit asked with a dubious expression.

"Nothing much," Raven assured him. "My legs are stiff from sitting for far too long. I need to stretch them. Merula, you come with me. Lamb can stay in the coach and mind our belongings."

Merula closed her notebook and clutched it, with the pencil, as Raven helped her out of the coach. Her legs were also stiff, and it took her a moment to steady herself, lock her knees, and roll back her shoulders.

A strong wind blew the scent of the sea into her nostrils. The dull drone of the waves was ever present like a hum in the distance, a vibration on the air, a warning signal almost that the ear strained to detect and tune in to. The landscape had a wild and untamed character, like the man who had blocked their way. He was now striding off, dressed in dark clothes, a woolen cap pulled over his head. He was a giant of a man, at least six feet tall, with thick arms dangling by his side and huge reddish hands.

"Is he a fisherman? What are they searching for?" she asked Raven softly.

Bowsprit had turned to the coachman and was offering him a cigar from Raven's case. The coachman seemed pleasantly surprised by the offer, or perhaps by the good quality of the cigars and the expensive case they came from, because he was studying Bowsprit with a new respect, oblivious to his surroundings.

Raven nodded in satisfaction and drew Merula along. She was glad she was wearing sturdy shoes, as they left the road immediately and beat their own path across sandy patches to where they could see more of the estuary below. Something dark slithered into a clump of grass. A lizard, perhaps? Or even a snake?

A chill went down Merula's back. Had she not heard once it was unwise to just charge through grassy land, as there might be adders hiding there? Disturbed, especially almost trodden on, they could get vicious and bite. They were venomous, she recalled.

Raven didn't seem to think of snakes or poison as he strode on, his eyes on where the rocks began. "That should give us an admirable view of the estuary," he muttered. "I wonder what they are doing there. Did the hard wind drive a ship onto the rocks? Are they recovering the cargo?"

Or dead bodies. Merula swallowed as she pictured a gruesome sight marring the first day of her exciting vacation with Raven. But she didn't want to appear timid in his eyes and walked on beside him, ignoring the twinge in her ankle as she misstepped.

The wind drove tears into her eyes, and the roar of the sea became more powerful. The notebook's pages flapped as the gusts tried to get at it and tear it from her hand. She clutched it so hard she could hear her pencil creak in protest.

Then they stood on the edge of the rocks and could see the full expanse of water and beach below. Broad and sandy, the beach stretched ahead of them, not deserted and forlorn as you'd expect on a day like this, but full of men in dark attire. Some were searching in the sand, overturning it with shovels, while others were checking piles of driftwood that lay scattered.

"See." Raven pinched her arm. "There must have been a sea disaster this night. They are looking for valuables that were washed ashore on the tide."

Merula took in all the details of the little scene, determined to draw it as soon as she was away from the hard wind that might tear apart her notebook. The men looked completely in their element here as they worked, strong and silent, each knowing what to do.

Despite her fear of dead bodies, she didn't see anything of that kind to trouble her. Maybe the people aboard the vessel had been saved?

Hadn't the coachman mentioned to them that the wreckmaster also went out to save people? A courageous man. The sea had awesome powers, and no mere mortal could withstand it. Still, if the story was true, he went and snatched people about to die from its grasp. She wondered if he was down there now helping the men.

"What are you doing there?"

They both turned to face the harsh, accusing voice. The man who had stopped them in the road had apparently not gone straight back to his mates but had lingered, watching them. His icy blue eyes flashed across them.

Raven shrugged. "Just admiring the view. You told us we can't go on, so we will wait here until you are done. Taking a roundabout route will also take time. We might as well wait."

"Wait you can, but in your coach. Not here. It's dangerous. You could just . . ." He took a step forward. "Tumble over the edge."

Merula gasped for breath at the implied threat. Suddenly she sensed the depths behind her, the countless feet until her falling body would hit the rocks and sand below. She'd be dead or seriously injured for certain.

"You have an odd way of expressing your concern for our safety," Raven said. "The way in which you are crowding us, we might well fall down that same drop you're warning us against."

"Accidents do happen," the man said.

Merula had the impression his eyes were sparking indignation at them, but behind them there didn't seem to be anything. They were sort of empty and dead. She shivered.

Raven gripped her arm firmly. "We will return to our coach. Good day." They passed the man, but they had barely gone two more paces when he was at Merula's side and snatched the notebook from her hand. He opened it, glared at the drawings, and tore out the sheets with his coarse hands, tearing loose several more pages and then stuffing the sheets into his pocket.

"What are you doing?" Raven roared. "That is the lady's property. Return it to her immediately."

"We don't like snooping." The man leaned down to stare Raven in the eye. "Accidents do happen, remember that." And he turned and walked away.

"Odd people," Raven said slowly. "Apparently they take their beachcombing very seriously. He must have thought you had drawn their work." He met her eye, a frown furrowing his forehead.

Merula tried not to show how much the man's violent action in taking her drawings had shaken her. She looked down on the plundered notebook. "He took everything I made. And they weren't even pictures of this beach or these people."

"He didn't like us, and my idea to take a look at the work rubbed him the wrong way. I'm sorry about your drawings. Nothing you can't draw again, I hope?"

Merula doubted that she'd get another chance to catch Raven unaware of her scrutiny and sketch his likeness as she had on the train. Her sense of loss was sharp and acute, but she pushed it away as a silly notion. He was right, she'd have many more chances to draw while they were here.

Quickly they returned to the coach to await the moment they might continue their travels to the village of Cranley and the house of Raven's friend that lay a few miles beyond.

CHAPTER 2

After two more cigars and a drop of the finest brandy from Bowsprit's pocket flask, the coachman decided begrudgingly that it would be best to take the roundabout way anyway. Waiting too long and then traveling along a darkening road would pose an extra danger to the horses, so, resigning himself to the inevitable, he climbed the box and took the reins to hand.

The horses, eager from having to stand still, broke into an energetic trot, and soon they had left the estuary behind and were traveling through farmland and woodland, sometimes crossing an age-old stone bridge, until they passed through the hamlet of Cranley, which consisted solely of a few houses of gray stone with low roofs, small gardens in front holding both flowers and vegetables for the family's daily needs.

In the middle was a stone church with a sturdy square tower, and its bells were tolling, the vicar standing in the door to receive his flock with a word of welcome. There was a sorrowful expression on his face, and the people arriving at the church all looked solemn as well.

"Judging by their appearances, they could be going to a funeral," Merula observed to Raven. "Still, I don't see any stone crosses or tombstones around the church. There doesn't seem to be a graveyard."

"Not all communities on these wide-open moors have their own cemetery." Bowsprit leaned forward, apparently eager to explain. "Sometimes the coffin bearers have to walk for miles to the nearest church that does have a grave-yard. There's this very interesting story connected with a huge stone along the way to such a church . . ."

But Merula wasn't really listening. She stared in fascination at the people walking to the church, even the children who refrained from pushing each other or pulling faces at one another behind their parents' back. The despondent mood seemed to have affected them all.

But if they weren't gathering for a funeral, weighed down by grief for the loss of one of their own, then what could this meeting be about? Why was everyone looking so serious and almost . . . afraid? Of what?

Unsettled by the idea there could be something to fear here on the moors, Merula dismissed the thought with energy, forcing her mind to focus on the arrival ahead. Their host had to be looking out for them already, awaiting them with a hot meal and perhaps a first quick look at his collection.

Would there be any recently discovered species among them, like the emperor penguin they had encountered in their adventure surrounding Lady Sophia's sudden death? Perhaps she might sketch some of the rare animals, not just in black and white but in color. She had brought both her pencils and her watercolors.

Beyond Cranley, the moorland was wide open under the summer evening skies, dotted by tors and a standing stone in the distance, a ragged shape pointing up like a bony finger.

Taking in the wild untamed land, Bowsprit leaned forward again with his elbows on his knees. "All of those tors have names. Some quite normal, others stemming from local lore attached to them. Their shapes inspired it, I suppose. They do look a little like stacked bread or a dog's head."

"A dog's head?" Merula echoed.

"Yes, there is talk of a giant hound roaming these moors at night. Not only does it bay and howl at the moon, but it also hunts people. It appears out of nowhere and follows them, chasing them until they either collapse with fatigue or run into a bog and drown."

"And why would this giant hound do this?" Raven asked, hitching a brow.

Bowsprit seemed taken aback by the question. "Well, uh . . . that is what creatures of legend do. They are mean-spirited and murderous. Like the sirens who lured sailors to their deaths with their unworldly voices."

When Raven didn't respond, Bowsprit continued, "Devonshire has many legends, and Dartmoor has more than any other place. About all kinds of creatures who haunt the moors. I also read about this woman who went missing along a coastal path, and everyone who later traversed it claimed they could see her walking ahead of them in a white gown that floated on the breeze."

"Probably wisps of fog moving to and fro and people immediately seeing ghosts." Raven shook his head.

"But it happens even in London." Lamb sat up with an earnest expression. "There was a coachman years ago who always drank before he went taking charges through the city. One night he fell off the box and broke his neck. One week after he died, when he was fresh in the grave . . ."

She shivered as she spoke the words. "His coach, which had been given to another, was stolen. The police couldn't find it anywhere, but people have sworn that on foggy nights, he rides through the streets at a murderous pace, whipping up his horses and cursing everyone who gets in his way."

"And have you ever seen this ghostly coachman yourself?" Raven asked.

"No, and I'm glad for it." Lamb crossed herself. "I want nothing to do with creatures from the other side of the grave."

"Ah." Raven's tone suggested he was far from convinced that such creatures did indeed walk among the living but didn't want to argue the point with someone who was clearly convinced that her spooky coachman existed. Or at least that there was a possibility he did.

Turning to Bowsprit, Raven said, "Something to put into a detective story, then. Strange killings, a murderous hound on the loose. I think that if someone with a talent for words put his hand to it, it could become quite a good tale. Might sell some copies here and abroad."

A few crooked trees stood close to the metal gate through which they whirled onto the driveway leading them up to the house. With bright light burning behind every window, the house seemed to welcome them from afar. Even up in the tower on the left, a light flickered and wavered, as if the flame struggled against a draft.

"Perhaps our host has been expecting us for hours," Bowsprit conjectured.

"He must be cross," Lamb added, "because his dinner has gone to waste. If you leave soup too long, it loses its taste. Not to mention veal." Her eyes went wide at the suggestion of such luxury in which she might partake. As a lady's companion, she might be allowed to eat with her mistress instead of being relegated to the kitchens with the other servants.

Raven laughed softly. "I doubt very much that the man I know will have thought about dinner. I wager Oaks hasn't had any prepared and will ask us to hunt for cheese and dried sausage in the pantry."

Merula shot him a quick look to see if he was joking, but he seemed to be in earnest. "How well do you know this man, anyway?" she asked curiously.

"Not well at all, to be frank. I know he has traveled extensively, to Asia, South America, and Canada, and from these latter shores he carried home the kraken. Word has it he keeps it draped across a stand in his bathroom."

Merula cocked her head. "You're jesting."

"No, that's what they say. But we'll soon see it all for ourselves."

The carriage halted in front of the house, and Raven opened the door and got out, reaching back in to assist Merula. As she glanced up at the house, she detected the inevitable gargoyles, gaping otherworldly faces staring down onto the beholder, as if to say they were guarding the keep and didn't like intruders.

But where other houses had just a few of these creatures, on a corner, under a turret, or supporting a balcony, here there were rows and rows of them, grinning with malevolence. A shadow seemed to move between them, and just as Merula was about to walk up the steps with Raven, the shadow fell down at them, spreading into twice its shape.

Merula shrieked, and Raven gripped her arm, then laughed. "That's a bat, silly girl. Have you never seen one?"

"Of course, in the summers in the country. But I didn't remember them being so large." She shivered as she watched the monstrous shape whirl around the rooftops.

"The strain of a long day traveling is getting to you," Raven concluded. "It's no larger than bats usually are."

The door opened, and on the doorstep a haggard man appeared. His face was pale, his hair stood up as if he had raked through it countless times, and his eyes stared at them with the frantic intensity of a man in the desert eyeing a sudden expanse of water. "You have her?" he asked, peering at the carriage where Lamb stood. "You recovered her safe and sound?"

"I'm Raven Royston." Raven extended his hand. "We corresponded?"

The man stared at him as if he had been addressed in a foreign language.

"You invited us here?" Raven pressed. "This is a friend of mine with a zoological interest, Miss Merula Merriweather. Her maid and my valet are over there at the carriage."

The man wet his lips. "Yes," he whispered, "yes, of course." The desperate need in his eyes faded to make way for sadness, and his shoulders sagged. "Come in."

Raven hitched a brow at Merula at this lukewarm reception. Perhaps he had expected their host to grab his hand and drag him upstairs right away to see the kraken in the bathroom?

For her part, Merula would be grateful if they could have some kind of warm supper and sit for a while at a fireplace, stretching their legs and sipping coffee or wine.

Their host stood in the hallway, looking about him as if he was lost in his own house. "Yes," he said, "Yes . . . I . . ." He fell silent and studied the floorboards.

Merula glanced around briefly, taking in much dark oak, oil paintings, deer antlers, and a knight's armor with a long sword strapped to the waist. It looked like the entry hall in any old country house, and she was a bit disappointed that there were no mementos of Oaks's exotic travels in view. She had expected to find birds of paradise with their dashing tail feathers, turtles, and beetles the size of her palm. But there were no animals around. Or perhaps they were higher up, where the shadows seemed to move. For a moment she was certain another bat would drop itself upon them, but she tried to laugh at her own nervousness.

Still, when something touched her sleeve, she almost jumped.

"I'm sorry, Miss," Lamb whispered as she came to stand beside her. She didn't seem to know quite how to carry herself, wringing her hands in front of her and glancing nervously at their host.

Bowsprit brought in the luggage. "I gave the driver money," he announced, "to spend the night at the inn near Cranley, so he can travel back at leisure in the morning."

"Very well," Raven said. "After all, it wasn't his fault that the road was blocked."

Their host was still standing with his head down as if he wasn't conscious of the presence of other people in his hall-way. Suddenly, however, he jerked his head up. "Cranley? You've been through Cranley?"

"Yes. A charming little place. There did seem to be a sad mood upon it. People going to the church with long faces. Like there's a disease or something and they're holding prayer meetings to avert it taking more lives."

Merula studied their host while Raven spoke, looking for acknowledgment of some serious matter in his response.

"Disease . . ." Their host repeated the word in a strange tone. "Disease. No, it is not . . . or perhaps it is. Is madness disease?"

His eyes met Merula's, and she was taken aback by the fierce glow in them, almost of fever.

Raven clapped his hands together as if to break the strange atmosphere. "Some meal would be grand. And perhaps your butler can assist my valet in bringing the luggage to our rooms?"

Their host sighed. "I have no butler, not anymore." His gaze wandered through the hallway. "All gone. All gone but her. Now she's gone too."

Raven glanced at Merula. She read concentration in his eyes, an attempt to understand what was going on here. Was their host merely peculiar, like some people who were alone often, speaking to himself about topics they had no notion of?

Bowsprit offered, "I can take up the luggage. Lamb can help me. You'd better sit down and recover from the journey."

Their host seemed to break to sudden life. "Yes, yes, of course, how inhospitable of me. Do come in." He pointed to a door to their right, then seemed to change his mind. "Why don't we all go up and we can sit in my library? Yes, a better idea, much better."

He dashed ahead of them, taking the steps two at a time. Near the top he tripped and fell, his knee hitting the wood of the step hard. Merula flinched, imagining the sharp pain.

Raven asked if he was all right, and he responded that he was, pulling himself upright and walking on, albeit slower.

On the landing, light came from several lanterns along the wall, illuminating an array of odd objects. Where downstairs every reference to a life abroad had been absent, here traveling souvenirs crowded each other: framed hand-drawn maps, wooden clubs, a bow and arrow, a long javelin with a vicious metal tip, and a shelfful of skulls, some clearly animal, others almost human.

Merula stared at the latter in fascination, wondering how Oaks had come by them. Their host had already entered the library, where all lamps were lit: on the desk, on the mantelpiece. Fire blazed in the hearth, and Raven walked over and stood in front of it, stretching out his hands and rubbing them as if he were cold.

Merula looked at their host while he closed the door. She thought for a moment she saw the glimmer of tears in his eyes. Perhaps he had really hurt himself with his tumble on the stairs?

She didn't dare ask, however. She didn't know him, and he was a man, after all. He could take care of himself.

"Merula . . ." Raven waved her over and directed her into a chair. "Here's an extra pillow for your back." He handed her a faded green velvet pillow with gold tassels on the four corners.

He didn't sit down himself but walked past the bookcases, studying the volumes on display and remarking about some titles he seemed to find particularly fascinating. "Ah, Jenner's treatise on the behavior of the cuckoo. I want to do a field study like that myself sometime. Just haven't decided yet what bird or mammal to focus on. It has to be something extraordinary. One or two such treatises can propel a man to sudden fame. Have you considered writing about your travels? There must be periodicals interested in publishing such accounts. I for one would gladly read them."

Their host had seated himself at his desk and was rearranging objects on it, transferring his ink bottle from left to right, his stand with pen, his paper weight. He smoothed his blotting paper and then began putting everything he had just transferred back in its original place.

Merula was almost certain he had no awareness of what he was doing and wasn't listening to a word Raven had said about his books or his traveling and the prospect of writing about it.

Suddenly a sharp sound invaded the quiet room. A woman's terrified scream.

"Tillie!" their host cried as he rose to his feet so fast his chair fell over and crashed to the floor. He rushed to the door and opened it, stormed into the landing toward the stairs. "Tillie!" he yelled again.

Raven followed, while Merula rose and stood at the door, gripping the doorpost to calm her staggering heartbeat. The female scream had died down, and the sudden silence seemed to be trembling with anxious expectation. What had happened?

Looking down the well-lit landing, she could see their host being met by Bowsprit, who excused himself in a loud emphatic tone for the fact that Lamb had cried out because she had believed she had seen a monstrous spider. "It was just a botanical sketch on the wall," Bowsprit said. "In the dim light, Lamb took the spider for a real creature. I'm very sorry for any disturbance this may have caused."

His formal tone was perfectly polite, but knowing him better than their host did, Merula could detect the hint of disapproval of Lamb's behavior. Bowsprit himself would probably not have made a sound even if the spider had been real. His sailor's years had taken him all over the world and put him in the strangest places and circumstances where his ability to keep calm and collected must have saved his own life and perhaps even that of others. During the search for Lady Sophia's killer, his quick thinking had kept them out of the hands of the police so they could complete their investigation and unmask the real killer.

Waving off Bowsprit's explanation, their host nodded and returned to them, a deep disappointment etched in his face. He passed Merula without even seeing her. She made eye contact with Raven and formed *Tillie?* with her lips.

Raven shrugged to indicate he had no idea who Tillie was.

Merula frowned, her thoughts racing to deduce something from what she did know about their host and his household. Uncle Rupert had confirmed for Aunt Emma that the man they would be visiting was a lifelong bachelor— another reason why Lamb's presence as a companion for Merula had been deemed essential—so Merula concluded that the female name couldn't refer to a wife or even to a deceased wife.

Besides, why would their host call out for her just because he had heard a terrified cry in the night?

"So how have you been since your return?" Raven asked, seating himself opposite Merula but half turning in his chair so he could see their host, who had returned to his desk. "I realize now that you have not been properly introduced to each other yet. As I said, this is Miss Merula Merriweather, and my acquaintance here is called Charles Oaks. A well-traveled man who can show us many interesting specimens from other countries. Also butterflies. These latter are," he added to Oaks, "Merula's specialty. She bred some herself in her uncle's conservatory."

After the disastrous lecture where Lady Sophia had died, though, Aunt Emma had forbidden Merula to pursue her passion for butterflies any longer. A stab of pain shot through Merula at the idea that she would never see one of those gorgeous creatures hatch again, climb carefully out of the cocoon and unfold its wings for the very first time. The stunning metamorphosis from hairy caterpillar to fairytale-like creature with delicate wings, which could even contain see-through patches, was something Merula could have witnessed time and time again. But that was all over. She had to reinvent herself somehow now. Keep science and discovery in her life, even if it wasn't through butterflies anymore.

"Pleased to meet you." Merula smiled at their host. His pale face with the fervent eyes was uncomfortable to look at, but she forced herself to ignore his agitation and keep the polite conversation going. "I'm delighted you agreed to receive us here. If you have traveled for so long and are just recently returned, your household must still be in disarray. It's very kind of you to receive guests at all."

She hoped this would hand Oaks a convenient excuse for the lack of servants and the other rather peculiar circumstances in which they had found him there. Aunt Emma had taught her always to avoid social disgrace and embarrassment for other people.

"It must be hard under any circumstances," Raven added in turn, "to get reliable servants in such a deserted place. I daresay that the men we saw on the beach are excellent fishermen and farmers, but I doubt whether they could run a household. A first-class butler has to know a little bit of everything and have a strict hand with the other servants at that. Not too strict a hand, of course, as he might drive them away."

Merula wondered if Raven was just trying to make conversation or was rather following her lead to offer their host an excuse for his apparently empty house.

"Yes," Oaks said. "Yes, it has been very hard. It's superstition, you know."

"Excuse me?" Raven sat on the edge of his seat, his lean hands tightening on his knees.

Merula also believed she mustn't have heard Oaks properly. He couldn't have said *superstition*, could he?

"These people have lived all of their lives with tales of white women on the moors and ghostly hands of dead sailors reaching out from the sea to drag you down with them." Oaks spoke slowly, thoughtfully. "They believe in the unexplained as firmly as they do in the tides and the seasons. They believe and they act on their beliefs. I can't blame them for it. It's the same in every culture. In South America, it was the spirits of the jungle. Here it is the dead sailors. Yes, I can understand."

Raven tilted his head. "Are you trying to say that superstition has something to do with these people not wanting to work for you?"

"Of course. It was so hard to get guides, you know. We were after a ruin. Not even a temple. At least, I don't think it was ever a temple. Just an old building in the jungle. Perhaps a palace? Or a plantation building? I don't even know. But nobody wanted to take us there. And when one man offered, he was dead the next morning. The anaconda had slithered through his window and wound itself around his neck. Choked to death in his own bed."

Merula suppressed a gasp. At the estuary, she had been afraid of an adder hiding among the grass, but adders were relatively small. Snakes that killed by suffocating their victims were often as thick as a man's shoulder and long enough to wind themselves around their prey in endless coils. Having seen a watercolor of an anaconda at a lecture of the Royal Zoological Society, she had immediately dreamt about it lowering itself from a potted palm in her conservatory and grabbing her arm, fixating her with its vicious little eyes.

Their host stared ahead. "An anaconda in the heart of a village. I've always wondered if . . ."

"Someone let the snake through the window? Because they considered the offer of their fellow villager to guide you to the ruin a betrayal?"

Raven had spoken softly, and for a few moments Merula thought Oaks might not have heard him. He just sat there with that faraway look on his face, as if he were back in the heat of the jungle where such assassin snakes lived and could lower themselves from a tree to choke him to death.

Then Oaks said, "Of course it was a betrayal. I should have understood that. People get killed for betrayals."

He hid his face in his hands and tried to breathe deeply.

"It's all my fault," Merula thought she heard him mutter, "all my fault."

Raven looked at her and narrowed his eyes, as if to convey he wasn't sure about the man's mental state.

Bowsprit entered the room with Lamb, whose cheeks were very red, probably because she was still embarrassed by her screaming about a painted spider.

Bowsprit said to Oaks, "The botanical drawing which includes the spider is very well done. May I ask where it comes from and who made it?"

Oaks sat with his head in his hands, not stirring, a picture of defeat.

Bowsprit looked from the man's slumped form to his master, his half frown silently asking what was wrong and how he might be of assistance.

Raven said briskly, "Well, uh, if you don't have staff, Bowsprit can make us something to eat. You help him, Lamb. Off you go."

Lamb looked doubtful, and when the two left, Merula thought she heard the girl whisper to Bowsprit that the kitchens had to be full of rats and that, if she saw or heard any, she'd scream again. "So loud they can hear it all the way in Cranley!"

Merula suppressed a laugh at the idea of what the impeccable Bowsprit would have to say to that. Coming from a poor background in Rotherhithe, Lamb was used to critters and didn't lose her nerve easily, but Merula now realized how much the excitement of all these new things must have gripped her. Perhaps Lamb wasn't so much afraid of the darkness and what lurked there but of her new position and how she might possibly lose it again if she wasn't good enough at the tasks ahead of her.

Merula decided she'd address the matter with her in a roundabout way as soon as she could to take some of the pressure off the poor girl. After all, this was supposed to be a pleasure trip for all of them.

But now returning her attention to the still library, their distracted host and the strange atmosphere all around them—the search on the estuary beach, the confiscated notebook pages, the grim faces of the villagers on their way to church—she doubted there would be much pleasure in store for them here.

CHAPTER 3

When Merula awoke, she believed for a few moments she was in her bed at home. The blankets were warm, the mattress soft and comfortable, and the yelling voices outside had to be those of coachmen in a fight over a lack of space granted or peddlers who each claimed the same spot to sell his wares. That was the way of London.

But slowly she became aware that these voices didn't belong to just two or three men but to a whole throng of people, and that they weren't arguing either—the voices rising and falling as they yelled insults or threats at each other—but chanting something, repeating it again and again: "Come on out. Come on out so we can hang you."

What on earth was this? A bad dream?

Merula widened her eyes and pinched her own arm.

Ouch! That hurt.

Touching her face, she felt the familiar features, and slapping her cheek gently hurt as well. She was apparently wide awake.

Her hands now ran across the blanket while her eyes

searched the ceiling above her head. This wasn't her bed. This wasn't her room in her uncle's house.

And those voices . . .

She got out of bed quickly and put on a dressing gown over her nightdress. When she was nearly at the door, someone knocked on it, a sharp urgent rap with the knuckles.

She called out, "Who's there?"

"Raven. We're in trouble."

She opened the door a crack and peeked out. Raven was dressed in a shirt over trousers that were half tucked into boots. He caught her glance and explained with a gesture across his attire, "I was going out riding. Our host has a few horses here, I know. But before I was even into my boots, I heard those voices. There's a mob outside."

"A mob?"

"Come on, then, and you can see for yourself." Raven gestured for her to follow him, and she closed her bedroom door behind her and tiptoed after him. At the window looking down on the gravel in front of the house, Raven halted and slipped the heavy green curtain to one side. He nodded down.

Merula came to stand beside him. The voices were louder now, their chanting a roar like the sea's. There had to be about twenty of them, all carrying burning torches. Mostly men, but also one or two women among them with their hair loose and their faces streaked with dirt. They were wailing, raising their hands to the skies above. With dawn breaking, the deep blue was invaded by orange and red, mirroring the flickering torchlight.

Merula's mind raced to make sense of all of it. "You said the people looked so grave going to church last night. You mentioned prayer meetings in cases of disease. Do you think there is a contagious disease in the village?"

"I'm sure we would not have been allowed to drive through it then. No. It's not a disease. It's something else. Something they blame Oaks for."

"Oaks?" Merula repeated. "Why? If what Uncle Rupert told me is anything to go by, he lives like a hermit, not associating with other people. Even if something befell the village, why would they blame Oaks for it?"

"He said something last night about superstition." Raven stared down on the shouting mob. "Such beliefs are strong in this region. People hang plants above their doors to ward off evil influences or have community bonfires. Perhaps something befell the village, as you so aptly put it, and they think Oaks somehow brought this bad luck upon them. By moving here. He's not one of them."

"An easy scapegoat," Merula agreed.

The villagers brandished their torches and cried, "Come out now! Come out now!"

The flickering light cast distorted shadows, hollowing their frantic eyes and widening their screaming mouths. A shiver went down Merula's spine.

Raven dropped the curtain in place. "I'll go and talk to them."

"No!" Merula grabbed his arm.

"Someone has to calm them before they do something rash. I'm not Oaks. They're not after me."

"You have no idea how violent these people really are. They might grab you anyway and hurt you, just to satisfy their blood thirst. There's twenty of them, and you're alone."

"I'll ask Bowsprit to come out with me. He's an able man; he can fight."

"He can defend himself when attacked by two men, three at most. He can't handle a raging mob who are carrying torches. If you open the front door and they throw a torch through the opening, the hall will be on fire. What then? We have no servants to help us douse it."

Raven held her gaze. "What's your solution? They're furious and they won't just leave. They'll just get more and more angry as time goes by and no one shows themselves."

Without waiting for her reply, he added, "I'll go ask Oaks what he thinks."

Raven went down the corridor and knocked at a door. No answer.

He knocked again, leaning toward the door to listen. Then he glanced at Merula. "I'm not sure he's even in there."

He opened the door a crack and peeked in. Then he came over to her with long strides, anger flashing in his eyes. "He's not there. The bed hasn't been slept in. He ran. Leaving us to face the villagers. He must have suspected something like this was hanging over his head. That explains his distracted mood last night. Why didn't he just tell us? We could have prepared. Now we're defenseless."

Raven raced downstairs and threw open doors, bellowing for Oaks.

Merula went to the library, vaguely hoping that he might

be hiding in there. But there was no sign of Oaks there either.

She heard Bowsprit's voice below for a moment, talking to Raven; then the sounds were drowned out by banging on the front door. Voices cried out in a surge of abuse.

Lamb rushed up to her, eyes wild with fear. "What's happening? Are they going to kill us?"

"Hush now; nothing is going to happen to you." Merula arrested Lamb's arm. "Stay calm. Take a deep breath."

The banging on the door grew louder. Were they trying to break it down?

"They're going to kill us!" Lamb wailed.

Merula's own heart was thumping under her chest bone and her mouth was dry. She had no idea what was wrong here, and even if she did, she doubted she could explain it to the mob out there. They didn't want to listen. They wanted a victim.

Raven came running back up. "Lock yourselves in the bedroom," he said, his breathing ragged. "Stay there and don't come out, no matter what happens."

"What are you going to do?" Merula grabbed his arm before he could run off again. "Raven, tell me."

"This is no situation for women to be in. Lock yourselves up and . . ."

"And what if they set the place on fire?" Merula held his gaze. Lamb whimpered by her side. "Then we're caught in a trap."

Raven exhaled in frustration but didn't deny that she was probably right. "Let *me* talk to them," Merula continued.

"I'll tell them Oaks has gone. They will not hurt me. I'm a woman."

Raven shook his head, but Merula had already let go of him and rushed down the stairs. Raven shouted, "Merula, no! I forbid you to do it."

Merula was at the front door. It was splintering under the weight tossed against it. She dragged it open.

Two men who had been banging it with a tree trunk rolled into the hallway. They landed flat on their faces in front of her feet and stared up at her with bewildered looks.

Outside, the yelling had stopped abruptly. Everything was deathly quiet. Like silence before the storm.

Merula felt the curious gazes on her disheveled hair, her dressing gown, her bare feet. Using this moment of surprise, a lull in the rush of their anger, she said, "What are you doing, breaking down the door? Mr. Oaks is not here. He went out horse riding. I'm sure that if you come back later, he will talk to you."

"Talk to us?" A man came up to her, spitting tobacco on the clean steps in front of the door. "We want his head. He's the cause of all of it. The animal lives here."

"What animal?" Merula asked. For a moment she wondered if Oaks had a dog and it roamed at night and killed sheep. Perhaps the villagers were angry because they had lost valuable livestock? For a family with little means, the loss of a sheep or two could mean that hunger invaded their lives.

But the man continued, "The creature that dragged the ships down into the sea."

Another man appeared behind him, adding, "And killed the girl."

"Girl?" Merula echoed, perplexed. Her heart started to beat even faster. What creature would kill a girl?

The man shook his head. "It's no good talking. We'll burn this whole place down."

Merula's spine tingled with cold, and her feet seemed to sink through the solid floor beneath her.

She had once before been confronted with men who sought to destroy something they did not understand with fire. They had been city men, perhaps more reasonable than these frightened, superstitious country people. But they had done it. And these people would do it as well. She saw it in their quietly watchful faces as they stood there in the flickering torches' light. That was what they had come for.

The man who had spat on the steps moved. Merula knew he was going to throw up his arm as a signal. Then the mob would push forward, the men would rush in, they would drop the torches on the floor, and the flames would start to lick at everything they could grab.

But a voice called out, loud and hard across the villagers' heads, "Are you all mad? What is this? Stand back!"

A well-dressed man on a big black horse forced his way through the crowd. The villagers made way for him, suddenly shrinking back, looking at each other as if unsure. The man halted his horse at the steps and jumped down. He eyed Merula.

For a moment she believed she saw a lecherous gleam in his dark eyes, and then he roared at the mob, "Are you mad? To set fire to this house?"

Merula expected him to go on and explain that guests were staying here and they could have killed innocent people. He would calm them down, make them see reason. They would disperse and it would all be over. She could barely believe it, and clenched her hands by her side to will it to be so.

But instead the unknown man said, "If you burn this place, the creatures will survive. They are not human, not flesh and blood. They are immaterial. They will rise again from the ashes to haunt you even more. They will come at night to the village to skulk through the streets, watch through the windows to wait until someone ventures outside. They will grab them and strangle them . . ."

One of the two women screamed and fainted. Nobody bothered to catch her body as it slipped to the ground. They all stared at the man on horseback, appalled and entranced by his words.

He continued, "By burning this house, you will simply multiply the creatures. They will come at night to take vengeance on you. They will kill every last one of you before you have even wounded them."

"He is right," one man called. He wore a blacksmith's leather apron, his bare arms thick with cords of muscle. "These beasts are not material. They can't be killed. Only driven away."

"I'll make sure they are driven away," the man on horseback said. "I've promised you that. I'll keep my promise."

"After how many deaths?" someone called from the back of the crowd.

"It will stop. I promise. Now go home. There's nothing to do here except make it worse."

The villagers stood and watched with wide eyes, unde-cided. The man in the blacksmith's apron raised both of his hands over his head and made a gesture to push them back. His quiet emphasis brought a change to their faces. Fanaticism made way for dejection. They turned on their heels, shuffling away without looking at each other or speaking.

With their heads down, they walked off, leaving the fainted woman lying on the grass alone.

Their fervor had been terrible to behold, but this dejec-tion was somehow even worse.

Merula looked at the man on horseback, anger rushing through her veins. "Why on earth did you say that? Why did you pretend there are creatures here that can kill people? That will come out after them?"

"I hadn't exactly expected a hug and a kiss," the man said, letting his eyes run over her at leisure, "but a thank-you would not go amiss. I helped drive this mob away. Else the house would now be burning, and I don't think your dainty little hands could have put out all of those flames."

Merula took a deep breath. Part of her knew he was right, but she couldn't agree with his way of handling the situation. "Perhaps it is true that you prevented the arson, but you shouldn't have acted like their fears are justified."

She looked at the collapsed woman on the grass, won-dering if she should go to her and help her. Then she noticed that the other woman and a young man hadn't followed the dispersing mob but hovered some fifty yards away, watch-ing like skittish animals for a chance to approach.

"I tend to agree with Merula." Raven appeared out of the house and eyed the man. "Instead of disarming the situation, you have only fed their fears. You sent them off like a pack of hungry wolves whose appetite has just been whetted. They will be back, and what then?"

"I intend to solve it all. And you can help me. I assume you are friends of Charles Oaks?" The man let his questioning gaze dart from Merula to Raven and back.

Raven leaned back on his heels, jutting his chin up. "Who wants to know?"

"Oh, excuse me, but there was hardly time for a proper introduction." He reached out his hand without bothering to take off his glove. "Bixby. I live nearby at Gorse Manor. I look in on poor Charles on occasion."

"Poor Charles?" Raven queried, ignoring the outreached hand.

"Yes, his nerves are completely shot. He should be tended by a professional. Not just a doctor, but someone who knows about abnormalities of the mind. I tend to think his problems started in childhood. His constant traveling, the need for a change of surroundings, supports the assumption that he's running from something. Perhaps the memory of some traumatic childhood experience?"

"Are you an expert yourself?"

"No, just an interested amateur. I daresay my collection on mental illnesses is the most extensive in the region. Specialists come to consult me."

"To consult the books, you mean," Raven corrected.

"Whatever you like." Bixby smiled, patting his horse

on the neck. Impatient with having to stand still, it scraped its hoof in the gravel and snorted. "I didn't catch your name."

"I never offered it," Raven rejoined. "What do you want from Charles? Are you some quack who will talk him into believing he has a nervous condition so you can dip into his purse for extravagant treatments that have no scientific basis or proven purpose?"

Bixby shook his head. "You're sadly deceived. Your friend needs help. If not, he'll soon be dead. Either because these people will kill him or because the police will come for him to charge and hang him."

"Hang him?" Raven echoed, puzzled. "You mean lawful execution after a trial?"

Bixby nodded with a grave expression. He looked at Merula as if he wasn't sure how much he could say in front of her. Then he seemed to make up his mind and continued to Raven, "I take it you are a rational man. I won't try to delude you with tales of creatures who rise from the sea or from the ashes of a burned-down house."

"Finally you're beginning to make sense," Raven said, but the man raised an imperative hand to cut him off.

"I spoke to these people in a language they can understand. You may disagree with me, but I'm certain that I *did* disarm the situation. I saved all of your lives. But I cannot save poor Charles. Because he is guilty. He is . . . shielding a murderer."

CHAPTER 4

Merula gasped, staring at this oddly commanding man who had ridden in and taken charge of the explosive situation. He had to have come from the city with his book collection on mental abnormalities, and therefore must also be an outsider like Oaks, but still the locals seemed to respect and believe him.

"Shielding a murderer?" Raven repeated with a frown. "How do you mean?"

Bixby gestured up at the house's upper story. "Hasn't he shown you? How long have you been here, anyway?"

"We arrived late last night," Merula said. "As dusk settled in. We didn't have time to get into any real conversation."

"Or assess the gravity of the situation," Bixby added. He smiled at her. "I don't blame you. Few people understand what is going on here. But I will show you."

He jumped down from his horse and pulled the reins over its neck, tying them to the steps' railing. Then he took the steps in two long strides and entered the house. "Follow me."

Merula noticed that, as soon as Bixby had gone inside, the woman and young man approached the collapsed woman on the grass and leaned over her. Relieved that she was being cared for, Merula entered the house herself.

Bixby was already at the stairs, intending to go up, but Raven caught up with him and blocked his path. "I don't remember asking you to come inside. You're acting like this is your house."

"Excuse me, but I'm on friendly terms with Charles. I've been here many times. Besides, do formalities really matter when lives are at stake?"

Bixby looked over his shoulder at Merula. "There will be more deaths. Either in the village or . . . Charles himself will die. They'll hang him. That's not an idle threat. They're terrified, and I want to show you why. Then you can fully grasp the seriousness of the situation."

Merula couldn't deny that the villagers had repeatedly threatened Oaks and that they had been extremely violent in their behavior in general, so clearly Bixby wasn't exaggerating. Perhaps whatever he wanted to show them could shed light on this whole confusing episode?

"Take us to whatever you want us to see," she encouraged him, walking up to Raven quickly and signaling him with her eyes to get out of the way.

Raven obeyed reluctantly, letting Bixby race up the steps ahead of them. Leaning over to Merula, Raven whispered, "I don't like his attitude. He made the villagers even more afraid, and now he's strutting about here as if he owns the place. He's taking control of the situation, and we don't even know who he is. Bixby, Bixby, I've never heard the name before. And if his collection is so important to specialists, why hide it out here in Dartmoor? Why not stay in London?"

"I don't know, but Bixby obviously knows more about why the villagers were here to demand Oaks's death. We have to get some answers from him. After all, Oaks isn't here to give them to us."

Raven couldn't deny this and followed her with a grim expression.

Upstairs, Bixby didn't turn left to where the library and their bedrooms were but to the right, taking them to a broad door at the end of the corridor. It was decorated with metalwork in the form of leaves and branches spreading across the entire door.

Bixby opened it and gestured for Merula to go inside. The curtains were open, and the light of the early-morning sun streamed in, playing across the objects sitting on the many shelves along the walls. The rays glinted off the tall, juglike containers made of glass. They were full of clear liquid, and in that liquid sat animals. The curve of the glass deformed their heads, giving them bulging eyes or even the impression that the creatures had five legs instead of four.

Merula had heard of conserving animals in a chemical substance, an alternative method to mounting them, but she had never actually seen it. Right after the strange confrontation with the enraged villagers and talk of Charles Oaks possibly being mad and shielding a murderer, the sight of this uncommon collection raised the hair on her neck.

"When Charles came to live here and started employing servants, they also got a glimpse of this room," Bixby informed them. "They started to spread stories that he conducts gruesome experiments on dead animals and even on corpses."

Merula thought of the shelf with the skulls, some of which looked uncomfortably human, and shivered.

Bixby continued, "Charles laughed it off at first, saying people were always afraid of the unknown and the rumors would die down. They might have if nothing further had occurred."

"Nothing further?" Raven frowned at the cryptic reference. "You mean, something happened that convinced the villagers that Charles was indeed experimenting?"

"It was his latest purchase." Bixby pronounced the latter word as if it was somehow despicable. "I assume you have heard of the kraken?"

"That is what we're here for," Merula said. "It's a huge sea monster, isn't it? Able to drag whole ships down into the depths of the sea."

"I doubt it could do that," Bixby retorted with a strange smile. "But it has other properties. Through there." He pointed at a smaller door in the back of the room. There was a key in the lock.

As Bixby didn't seem eager himself to open the door for them, Raven walked over, turned the key, and pushed the door slowly inward. It creaked on its hinges.

Merula held her breath as she approached and glanced in. Beyond the door was a room, probably once an antechamber or dressing room. It had just one narrow, barred window, and there was no carpet on the floor but tiles. In the corner was an old cracked bathtub and beside it stood a wooden rack for clothes. Across this rack lay the strangest creature Merula had ever seen.

It seemed to be made of soft pliable material like jelly, but still it was solid because it kept its shape. It was not quite blue or gray or brown or pink but seemed to have shades of all these that kept changing in the dim light. It had long tentacles that hung down, reaching all the way to the floor.

If this was the kraken, it was much smaller than Merula had imagined. Still it projected a strange, otherworldly presence that pushed goose bumps out on her arms. Her gaze slipped away from it across the tiles, and she noticed wet traces on them. She followed the trail to the bathtub. It seemed to be full of water. The water even seemed to move as if some invisible breeze stirred it. But the air in the room was perfectly still.

Shivering, she stepped back, almost colliding with Raven behind her. "I don't see," he said to Bixby, "what this creature has to do with the village or its inhabitants."

"They believe it is alive."

Merula turned to look at Bixby. "Excuse me?"

"They believe it is alive. That it crawls through the bars of that window at night and goes out to look for prey."

Raven held his head back and laughed. "We are in Dartmoor, aren't we? Bowsprit mentioned a huge hound hunting people across the moors, so this must be its marine counterpart. The vicious kraken who slithers out of its prison at night to find prey."

"You wouldn't be laughing," Bixby said tautly, "if you had seen the victims."

"What victims?" Raven's expression changed from suppressed mirth to utter seriousness.

"The victims of the shipwrecks that occurred recently."

"Shipwrecks are not uncommon along the coast of Devon and Cornwall, I've heard," Raven retorted.

"No, but there were a huge number close together. People started whispering that it was the kraken."

"You can't believe such a thing. Look at it. It couldn't drag a ship down into the depths of the sea."

"No. I agree with that. But this morning a girl was found by the riverside. Strangled. Not by human hands but by some other . . . thing."

Bixby pointed at the kraken. "Have you looked closely at his tentacles? They are covered in suckers. If attached to skin, they'd leave marks. And those marks were on the neck of the girl who was found strangled. The kraken killed her."

Raven made a scoffing sound, then studied Bixby with narrowed eyes. "You seem like a reasonable, educated man. You believe this nonsense? You believe that this clearly very dead creature slithers through those bars at night and travels all the way across the land to the beach to kill girls? We came from Paignton yesterday. It is a long journey. How could this beast even make such a trip? It's aquatic, it . . ."

"They believe it follows the river," Bixby retorted.

"The river comes from the moors and goes past Cranley, through the woodland, to flow into the estuary. An open connection with the sea. Besides . . ." Bixby shrugged. "It doesn't matter what I believe. The villagers believe it. When the shipwrecks increased, the whispers began, over ale at the inn. That something not human was at work here, a strange creature from the depths of the sea. These are superstitious people who believe the sea hides many secrets. And now with the death of this girl . . ." He clicked his tongue.

"So it was a funeral last night," Merula said, remembering the sad faces of the villagers walking out to the little church in the heart of their town. Perhaps they had conducted the service in their own church and then carried the coffin with the dead body to a church that did have a graveyard? Though it had been rather late in the evening for that.

"No, the girl was still missing then. They went to pray that she would be found. Alive. Found she was, this morning at the break of dawn. But not alive and well. Very dead. Strangled, the reddish blots of suckers clearly visible on her neck."

Raven studied the kraken as if he wondered if the suckers would really leave impressions. But he didn't reach out to test with his finger. He said slowly, "So there have been both shipwrecks and a strangled girl by the river this morning, and the villagers blame Charles for it. They believe he brought the kraken, the killer, among them."

"Unfortunately, yes." Bixby consulted his watch, a fine golden timepiece kept on an elaborately decorated chain.

"I'd better be going to look for him. I have to find him before they do. They'll beat him to death. Or take him to the coast and throw him down the cliffs. To give him to the sea, as a sacrifice, to appease the creature."

Without waiting for Raven's response, Bixby pushed past Bowsprit and Lamb, who hovered at the door.

"This is terrible," Lamb wailed, her hands up to her face. "That creature! I can't bear to look at it. I want to go away from here."

"Hush, you silly girl," Bowsprit remonstrated her. "That kraken is very dead. Whatever killed that girl, it wasn't the thing you see hanging there."

"How do you know for certain?" Lamb backed up two paces. "First that horrible spider last night . . ."

"It was in a drawing on the wall."

"It had a bird in its grasp. A grown bird!"

Bowsprit sighed. "That drawing was made in Suriname. Tropical spiders are larger than the ones who live here." He explained to Raven and Merula, "I discovered that it is a drawing by a Mrs. Merian, who traveled to Suriname about two hundred years ago."

"A woman?" Merula was intrigued. "Could she just travel there by herself?"

Excitement caught her that something like that was even possible. Could she travel to see animals in their natural surroundings? A whole flock of parrots flying across the Amazon River. A troop of monkeys jumping from tree to tree, screeching to one another.

Lamb cut across her hopeful thoughts, wailing to

Bowsprit, "But just look at all those jars. What if they can come out and attack us? I want to go back to London."

"Well, you can't." Bowsprit glowered at Lamb. "You're Miss Merula's personal maid now, and you go wherever she goes. Do you see her sobbing and crying that she wants to go back to London? No. She wants to get to the bottom of this mystery. A girl died, and an innocent man is blamed for it. We have to find out what is really going on here."

"You call Charles innocent." Raven raked back his hair with both hands. "But do we really know for certain that he is? I mean, I don't believe for one moment that this kraken killed anyone, but Charles was acting very peculiarly last night. He is under nervous strain, and you never know what people might do then."

"You think he could have killed the girl?" Merula asked with a frown. "But what for? And why leave strange marks on her that point at the kraken that is at this house and thus indirectly at himself?"

"That does seem illogical and unwise, but if he's truly out of his wits . . ." Raven sighed. "Bowsprit, you and I are going out on horseback to look for Charles. Merula and Lamb must stay here."

He met Merula's gaze. "I can't guarantee it will be safe. The villagers might come back. But you can't ride a horse, and . . ."

"Who says I can't?" Merula protested. "You never even asked me whether I could."

Raven waved impatiently. "Perhaps you rode once or twice on a quiet sunny day, down the driveway of your uncle's country home. That's not the same thing as a ride across rough terrain on a horse you don't know. I'm not risking an injury. Bowsprit . . ."

"Coming." The valet shot one last warning glance at the sniffling Lamb before leaving the room after his determined master.

"I want to leave," Lamb said again.

Merula shook her head. "We can't."

"Just look at all of those horrible things." Lamb gestured around her at the glass containers with the dead animals. "They might all come alive and try to devour us."

"They are dead and locked up in jars. They can't get out."

"And why is that one empty, then?" Lamb pointed at a huge container in a separate alcove high in the wall.

Merula squinted. Indeed, the container seemed to be empty, but the lid was on and there was a label on it, designating the contents.

She grabbed a small stool, dragged it over to the appropriate spot, and clambered onto it to see the jar better.

Lamb cried out for her to be careful or she would get hurt.

The container was indeed empty save for the clear liquid inside.

The label read TASMANIAN DEVIL and a Latin designation containing the words *meat* and *eating*. So it was a creature that devoured flesh . . .

Merula had no idea what a Tasmanian devil was exactly, but she didn't think it would help Lamb's current mood to tell her what the label said or suggest that the unknown creature could indeed be on the loose, looking for a bite to eat.

She stepped down and realized she was still in her dressing gown. "We have to get dressed and find some breakfast," she decided. "With hot food in our stomachs, we'll see things in a different light."

"I'm not moving even two feet away from you," Lamb whispered right behind her. "Or one of us might get strangled."

CHAPTER 5

Doing purposeful things always made Merula feel better, and today was no different. She dressed, explored the kitchens, found biscuits, bread, and cheese, had Lamb prepare coffee, and then they sat together in the large dining room, eating their morning meal.

The sun streamed in through the windows' colored glass, turning the plain carpet into a pattern of red, blue, and yellow. Dust danced on the rays, and wherever the light drove away the gloom, Merula detected cobwebs and signs of silent decay eating its way into the furniture and the wallpaper. The house needed servants and a lot of them too, to preserve everything that was here. But with the rumors about the murderous creature coming from here, no one would want to come work there.

"I hope they find this strange Mr. Oaks and bring him back here and then we can leave. It's none of our business whether he's innocent or not." Lamb nodded firmly. "I don't think Lord Raven knows him very well. Else he would have realized the man was somehow not right in his head."

"We don't know whether he is right in his head or not," Merula rebuked gently.

"He has to be peculiar, living here all alone with all of these creatures in jars. I even saw a calf among them with two heads. That isn't natural."

"Animals can be born with deformities. Natural historians study those to learn more about the animal kingdom. It's just for the purpose of scientific progress."

Lamb pushed her plate away. "I can't eat thinking about it. Those eyes looking at you through the glass. Wherever you stand in the room, they seem to be looking at you. As if they can follow you around. And the girl being strangled. A cold wet tentacle grabbing your neck." She shuddered, wrapping her arms around her shoulders. "I won't sleep another wink in this place."

"I'm sorry you don't feel well here. But in London there is crime as well. Killers on the streets."

Merula wasn't really convinced by her own argument and also pushed her plate aside. "Let's put together what we know. A girl was killed. If we ignore that she might have been killed by some sea monster, we must accept that she was killed by another human being. Most likely a local. Why would he kill that girl? Just because he's a madman? Or because he has a reason for wanting her out of the way? Motives for murder can be revenge, greed, or jealousy."

Merula wondered briefly if the killer could have been a woman who disliked the girl for being young and pretty. She was simply assuming it had been a man because strangulation seemed like a man's action. So physical and violent, forcing direct confrontation with the victim. Would a woman be cold-blooded enough to go through with it as, under her very hands, the victim struggled for survival? Wouldn't she resort to other, more indirect means, such as poison?

Then again, a terrible rage might drive a person to act out of character, not caring for the consequences. She had to keep an open mind and consider all the possibilities. "We should know more about the victim. Who was she, where did she live, what did she do? I guess that in a small village, people know things about each other. Too bad there is no housekeeper here who might prove garrulous."

"I did see a boy," Lamb said.

Merula blinked at her. "Excuse me?"

"A boy. At the stables. I think he cares for the horses. Brushes and feeds them and takes care of the saddles and the carriages if Mr. Oaks has some. He might know things."

"Excellent." Merula rose. "We'll go to the stables to see what he might tell us."

Lamb followed her like a shadow as she strode out of the dining room, through the hallway, then out of the damaged front door.

Just seeing the splintered wood made Merula's throat constrict again and her heart pound violently. They had escaped disaster because of Bixby's timely arrival.

Perhaps they should have expressed more gratitude? He did seem to have a way of convincing the villagers to listen to him, which had not just saved them now but might also prove useful in the future. They couldn't afford to alienate someone whose help they might need later on.

At the stables they found the door open and sounds of shoveling coming from the inside. As Merula walked in, she had to halt a moment to allow her eyes to adjust from the bright sunshine outside to the dimness within. Vaguely she detected movement to her right. A figure was raking the straw on the floor. As she began to see more, she spotted a wheelbarrow by his side stacked with dirty straw. The sharp scent of dung was in the air.

Wrinkling her nose, Merula approached two more paces. "Good morning."

The boy dropped the shovel, which clanged to the floor. He stood looking at her, his eyes wide. Then he exhaled. "For a moment I thought you were Tillie."

Merula recognized the name as the same one their host had mentioned the previous night when he had heard a female scream. "Does she work here?"

The boy nodded. "She cleans and cooks. She vanished two nights ago."

"Vanished?" Merula asked.

"Yes, she went to the inn to give her wages to her father. She always does that on the night he plays cards with the other men. Ever since her mother died, it's just the two of them. She didn't want to go into service at first, leaving him alone. But she couldn't help him at the smithy either. It's not a girl's work."

"The local blacksmith is her father?" Merula asked. She

remembered having seen the man among the locals with the torches. He seemed to have some influence over them, as he had gestured at them after Bixby's orders to retreat and they had obeyed him.

The boy nodded. "She made it to the inn, for she did give her wages to him. But she never came back here. They looked for her everywhere. On the moors and the beach."

"The beach?" Merula echoed. "We saw a huge party on the beach of the estuary yesterday. We assumed they were combing the beach after a sea disaster."

The boy shook his head. "They were looking for Tillie. The wreckmaster promised her father he'd find her."

Merula tilted her head. "But the beach is miles from here. Why would they assume she had gone there? Was she running away from someone?" Had she agreed to meet someone there? Who could take her further away? Across the water? Or by railway?

The boy shrugged. "The wreckmaster and his henchmen never say what they are going to do. It's a man's job, they say, nothing for boys. I can't help them. I have to stay here and care for the horses."

He lifted his head and looked at them from under his wild brown hair. "Tillie has to come back. It's her birthday soon. I got her a present. Something she'll like."

Merula felt a shiver go down her spine. Bixby had told them about a dead girl, found only that morning. Was that the girl who had worked here? The one this boy was obviously so fond of? Might even be a little enamored of?

Dead? Murdered?

"Were there other servants here beside you two?" she asked. She needed to form an opinion of the household and its workings.

He shrugged. "In the beginning. A housekeeper and a coachman. But they left. I don't mind working here. I wanted to keep an eye on Tillie. I did a good job too, I did."

He sounded a bit overemphatic, as if to convince himself that he had not failed now that his charge was gone without a trace.

"Of course you did." Merula forced a smile. "Is there someone we can talk to? About Mr. Oaks? Do you know who lived here before? Or who arranged for Mr. Oaks to buy this house when he came to live here?"

Perhaps the former owner or a legal person who had taken care of the house's sale could throw light on Oaks's reasons for moving here, to a remote area where the people were wary of strangers?

The boy's expression changed. "Mr. Oaks is gone," he said in a tone as if this was the best news in ages. "He won't be back. He didn't deserve her. He never did."

Merula narrowed her eyes, trying to gauge the sentiment behind the boy's words. "Do you know where Mr. Oaks went? Did he tell you?"

Had he run? Afraid of what people might say after the girl's death?

But how had Oaks even known there had been a death? Unless, of course, he himself was the killer . . .

"He told me nothing." The boy looked distant now, unaccommodating.

Lamb suddenly spoke up. "Come now, of course he told you something. You care for his horses; he trusts you."

The boy stared at her as if he wasn't quite sure whether to believe her.

Lamb continued, "Horses are valuable and they can be nervous. Only special people can work with them. Mr. Oaks recognized you as such a special person. You have a way with horses. I saw you this morning from the window, with the chestnut stallion. You could master him. Not many can, I bet."

"Nobody but me." The boy stuck out his chest.

"There. I thought so." Lamb leaned over and assumed a confidential tone. "Mr. Oaks lets no one handle his horses but you. He trusts you. He must have told you where he was going."

"He was in an awful rush. Breathing fast. 'They are after me,' he said, 'they are after me.' He didn't give me time to saddle the horse properly. He pulled the reins from my hand before I was even done. He was sweating, and his face was pale. He kept looking about him as if he was afraid of someone jumping him. But there was no one here but the two of us."

The boy frowned, apparently considering the strangeness of his master's hurried departure, then shook himself. "I just want Tillie to come back. I can take care of her. I know where the master's money chest is. I can pay her her wages even if the master doesn't come back."

Lamb glanced at Merula with a disappointed expression. She had tried her best to get him talking, to find some major clue to Mr. Oaks's whereabouts, but he didn't seem to know anything.

"Did Mr. Oaks have a favorite place he liked to go?" Merula asked. "Some hideout on the moors? Or farther away toward the coast? Or did he have a second house nearby?"

The boy shook his head. "I don't know if he has any house beside this."

"But he was friends with Mr. Bixby, wasn't he? They visited each other. Might he have gone to Mr. Bixby?"

The boy shook his head with determination. "I don't think so. Not after they fought."

"They fought?" Merula echoed. Strife between the men would be at odds with Bixby's affirmation that he and Oaks had been friends. That he had even taken care of Oaks in his way, visiting him and expressing concerns about his health.

"And when was this fight?" she asked the stable boy.

"Last week, I think. Mr. Bixby dined here and the master saw him off and I heard him saying, 'You have to stop mentioning it to me. I won't be pressured into it. I won't.'"

Merula chewed on her lower lip. Had Bixby discussed his concerns about Oaks's mental state, and had Oaks refused to listen to it again?

Had Bixby advised him to consult a specialist, a psychiatrist, for instance, and had Oaks refused, claiming he wouldn't be 'pressured into it'?

That seemed most likely, given the things Bixby had told them that morning.

So Oaks wouldn't turn to Bixby if he believed he was being hunted. But to whom would he turn?

"Did he have any other friends here?" she pressed. "Who came to visit him?"

"No one really. The villagers didn't like him. There was a gentleman once with a very nice carriage. But he didn't stay long. Tillie had to announce him and then Mr. Oaks said he didn't want to see him, and he left again."

A doctor from the city? Sent by Bixby, dismissed by Oaks? "Did Tillie tell you what that gentleman's name was?"

"He gave her his card to take up to Mr. Oaks. Tillie can't read, so she didn't know what it said. She just took up the card, and Mr. Oaks looked at it and said he wouldn't see the gentleman. Then Tillie had to tell him so. She said it was terribly rude. Turning away a fine city gentleman like that."

"A city gentleman? So it was no local man?"

The boy shook his head. "We had never seen him before."

Merula wondered if the card presented to Oaks might still be in the house so she could go and look at what it said, but Lamb poked her with an elbow. "I hear horses' hooves outside. Lord Raven must be returning."

Merula couldn't deny that a rush of relief flooded through her upon hearing this news. The place was rather eerie in its loneliness and with the strange events that had taken place. She'd feel better with Raven around and Bowsprit, two able men who weren't influenced by talk of creatures slithering around in the night.

They walked out of the stables and saw Raven and Bowsprit approaching, each on a horse. Raven had something in front of him, a large dark mass. As horse and rider came closer, Merula determined it was another man slumped against Raven.

"Mr. Oaks!" she called to them as they drew even nearer. "What happened to him?"

"We found him under the trees near the river. He was unconscious." Raven reined in the horse beside them. His expression was grim. "His heartbeat is very erratic, and he mutters as if he's in a delirium. I can't find wounds on him or bruises, so it doesn't seem like the villagers have beaten him."

"And his horse?" Merula asked. "He left here on horseback, didn't he?"

"Yes, but we didn't see his horse anywhere around. We'll have to look for it later. First he needs to be put to bed."

Bowsprit had jumped down from his horse and was now standing beside Raven to help him lower Oaks to the ground. Raven then dismounted, and between them, Oaks's arms slung over their shoulders, they half carried, half dragged the man to the house.

Inside they labored to get him up the stairs. Merula opened the door to the sitting room, urging them to put Oaks on the sofa for the time being, but Raven insisted it was better to put him into bed where he could properly rest.

Merula wondered if Raven was also worried that Oaks

would try to flee again and hoped that by putting him in his bedroom upstairs, they would make that a little more difficult. Did the bedroom door also have a lock so that Raven could trap the man inside?

She sent Lamb into the kitchens to make more coffee and to look for brandy or another strong liquor. She herself followed the men. "How far away from the house had he got? And why would he go to the river? I just talked to a stable boy who was certain he was on the run. Oaks would have ridden fast then, away from the area, trying to reach a railway station."

Raven didn't respond. He grunted under the weight of their uncooperative charge.

Bowsprit halted a moment to hoist the man's limp form better onto his shoulder, and then they continued, their shapes oddly reflected in the huge brass samovar that stood against the wall. It was flanked by two mounted animals that looked like fluffy little deer but had vicious fangs sticking out from under their upper lips, giving them a vampiric appearance. Merula wondered if they were a real species or the invention of a creative taxidermist. Combinations of skin, ears, tails, and teeth could lead to creatures from the realm of nightmares sooner than from the real natural world.

At last Raven and Bowsprit had wrestled Oaks into the bedroom and onto the bed. Heavy green curtains hung from the four posters, echoing the colors used in the wallpaper and the painted windowsill, which also served as a seat with a view of the garden. A stack of leather-bound books suggested Oaks liked to sit there and read.

Bowsprit tried to pull off Oaks's boots while Raven wiped the sweat off his own face. Looking at Merula, he said softly, "Oaks might have ridden to the river to throw himself into it."

"To kill himself, you mean?" Merula's mind raced. "In a state of despair? Or because he was mad with fear? He did mention to the stable boy that 'they' were after him."

"You talked to the stable boy in detail?" Raven studied her. "What did you expect to learn from him?"

"Where Oaks might have ridden out to so early in the morning. I also asked what people came to visit him here. Bixby, of course, but they did argue just last week. And a gentleman in a very fine carriage."

She told him everything the stable boy had told her and Lamb, including his rather cryptic references to the missing servant girl who might very well be the dead girl found that morning.

While she spoke, Bowsprit was busy undressing their host and putting him into bed.

Raven picked up one of the man's boots and studied the soles. "No peculiar red clay here that can give us a decisive clue," he said with a wry smile. "Nothing much here but a bit of dried mud holding some stems of grass or other leaves. Must have picked it up at the river. I should know more about plants, really. It might prove to be useful someday."

He put the boot down and looked at Merula. "You just said that the stable boy mentioned he knows where Oaks's money chest is."

"Yes, he claimed to be able to pay Tillie's wages even if Oaks wasn't here."

"How would he know that? He doesn't come into the house."

"Perhaps he did come into the house. Oaks might have paid him his wages in the library or his study. The money chest could be on or in a desk there. Perhaps the boy saw where he got it and remembered its place."

Raven stood with a pensive look on his face, staring toward the window seemingly without seeing anything. He spoke slowly, as if to himself. "Oaks mentioned the girl's name last night. He seemed to be upset about her. About the disappearance? Did he fear she'd be killed? But why? There had been shipwrecks, yes, and whispers that some creature was behind them, but Oaks had no reason to think a girl, on dry land, would be hurt by this same creature."

He suddenly turned to Merula, fixing her with his intense eyes. "Or did Oaks already know what had become of her? Did he kill her? You can't deny he was in a state of great distress when we met him. And why leave this morning insisting 'they' were after him? The death wasn't yet known."

"I have no idea." Merula looked at the man on the bed. "I had hoped you'd find him quickly so he could enlighten us, but he doesn't seem able to tell us anything. And even if he does come to and can speak with us, will he tell us the truth?"

Bowsprit said, "Will he even know what the truth is? I've seen men in a state like this, and they couldn't remember what had happened to them. Sometimes a blow to the head can do that. Or intoxication."

Raven strode to the bed. His lean fingers examined Oaks's head, running over the back of it. "I can't feel a bump here. I had already ascertained there was no damage to his face. No black eye or bruised lip. No signs anyone punched him. Intoxication . . ."

He leaned over and sniffed the man's breath. "No alcohol as far as I can tell."

His gaze ran over the face resting on the pillows, then to the side table. "Wait, what's this?"

He reached behind the lamp that stood on the side table and produced a small glass bottle with a stopper on it. He opened it and sniffed. "Odorless. Might be laudanum. Oaks might have told Bixby he needed no doctor, but he did take some kind of drops."

"We could send them to Galileo in London to have him find out what they are," Bowsprit suggested. "I'm sure he will be happy to help out."

"Excited to be part of a new investigation," Raven said with a sour half smile. "He was actually quite jealous that we left the city to come here. But he could hardly have accompanied us, with his creatures to take care of. They may all be still alive, but servants are just as eager to stay away from them as they are from Oaks's dead specimens. Besides, he wanted to try some obscure experiment he had found in an old manuscript. I do hope his house is still standing."

Merula couldn't help smiling at the memory of seeing Galileo for the first time through a haze of pungent fumes wafting from a test tube and wondering if those fumes were somehow explosive, as a Bunsen burner was flaming nearby. Once the need to complete an experiment was upon the eager scientist, he forgot about everything else. Including his own safety.

Raven continued in a grim tone, "I was just thinking as we rode back here how we went on a vacation to Dartmoor to recuperate from our last adventure. Now it seems we have run headlong into new trouble."

He turned to Merula. "How do you feel?"

"Fine, actually. My ribs haven't hurt at all, and we have been rather active." She smiled at him, trying to convince him that the injury she had acquired in her confrontation with Lady Sophia's killer hadn't worsened. "I think sometimes that being active helps to keep one's mind away from things that are painful when one has too much time on one's hands to think about them." If she had remained in London, she might have been tempted to dwell upon those fearful moments when she had been face-to-face with someone who had already killed and wasn't afraid to kill again to stay out of the hands of the police. Here in Dartmoor, confronted with yet another puzzle, she had to direct all of her mental energy to that.

Raven shook his head. "I don't agree. This should have been a nice quiet time for us. Some walking by the sea, on the moors. Visiting a country house that is open to the public. You could do some sketching, I some horse riding.

We'd go see the Perseids shoot across the night skies. Nothing to do with crime. And now it appears there have been deaths here, of sailors on wrecked ships and this strangled girl, and our friend Oaks is involved in them. Or at least implicated in them."

"It would be useful," Bowsprit observed, "to know more about these marks on the dead girl's neck. I do know that strangulation leaves discoloration, bruises, but I'm not sure what they mean about the marks. Strange marks, suggesting that the perpetrator wasn't human."

"Bixby said something about red blots," Merula said. "He referred to the suckers on the kraken's tentacles." She looked at Raven. "Do they actually suck? I mean, if the tentacle was thrust around the neck of a living girl, would those suckers have left red blots on her skin?"

"I doubt it. But then, I don't know much about tentacles. I do know that some animals kill with their touch because there is poison in their skin. For instance, in hairs on their skin. I wonder if those suckers are poisonous somehow."

"That is why you didn't touch them," Merula said. "You looked at them as if you wanted to test them but didn't."

"Well observed." Raven laughed softly. "I did indeed want to test them, but I can hardly sling such a tentacle around your neck and pull to see what it does. If it is poisonous, my little experiment could prove to be the end of our vacation." His tone was light, but Merula sensed he was genuinely worried about her being there, caught up in another crime.

The door opened, and Lamb carried in a tray holding a coffeepot, cups, a crystal carafe full of a brownish liquid, and glasses. She seemed to be concentrating completely on balancing the heavy tray, and Merula was glad she hadn't seen the odd deer in the corridor and dropped the tray, smashing everything on it.

Raven gestured for her to put the tray in the window-sill. "Put it beside those books. I'll pour."

Bowsprit caught Raven's eye. "If I have to send off a parcel with that bottle of drops to Galileo in London, I could go to that inn near Cranley and have a talk with locals, try to find out more."

"Yes, but you should disguise yourself a little. Some of the people who were here this morning to burn down the house might have seen you and know you're with us."

Bowsprit nodded. "I can dress up like a sailor. I've brought my old things with me." He rolled up his sleeve and showed them a tattoo just over the elbow. "Such signs always inspire confidence. I've been across the world, can tell my tales of storms and dangers. Foreign ports, foreign markets. Things they've never heard of out here."

"Just as long as you don't mention sea monsters." Raven wagged a finger at him. "You've seen firsthand how the mood heats here and how the mob is ready to attack and hang a man. If your cover isn't convincing, they might—"

Lamb gasped.

Bowsprit cast her a cool look. "I've done this before," he assured them, and left the room.

Raven rubbed his hands. "He should turn up something.

He's good at what he does." Reaching out to pour the coffee, he froze, staring at the books beside the tray. "What's this?"

He picked the top book off the stack. "A history of grave robbery?" He looked at the next book. "Kistvaens? What on earth are those?"

Oaks groaned from the bed. They all looked at him, Raven closing in quickly and touching his hand. "Charles? Are you with us? Say something."

"I saw it . . ." Oaks's bloodless lips barely moved as he whispered in a croaking voice. "I saw it. The ship never had a chance."

Raven looked at Merula. *Kraken*, he formed without making a sound.

Merula shrugged.

Oaks sighed deeply. "She should have . . . left. She should have gone away."

His hands grasped across the blanket Bowsprit had put over him.

Merula stared at the fingers tensing and relaxing like animal claws. Could this man be a killer? Had he strangled the girl? Perhaps under the influence of the strange drops they had found in this room?

Opium gave people terrible visions of things that were not real.

"No!" Oaks pushed himself up on the pillows, his face a contorted mask, his eyes open wide. "Take it away from me. It's gruesome. Take it away!" he screamed, then fell limply back.

Raven hurried to feel for his heartbeat. He sighed in relief. "Beating strong. He seems to have fallen asleep now."

"He is mad," Lamb proclaimed firmly. "We have to call a doctor and leave him in capable hands. Then we can go back to London."

"If he took drops of some kind, their influence will wear off. We have to speak with him and learn all we can about the strange happenings here. Bowsprit will also bring news of his time at the inn."

Raven paced the room. "While we were out looking for Oaks, I asked Bowsprit what he had learned about the wreck-master. You will recall he was supposed to ask the coach-man a thing or two while sampling my expensive cigars."

Merula had to laugh at his sardonic tone. "And did it pay off?"

"I'm not sure. The coachman repeated much the same things we had heard already. He's in charge of the search parties when ships get wrecked and their cargo washes up along the shore. He also saves people. But that doesn't explain why his helper was so eager to keep us away from the beach yesterday or why your notebook was seized and the drawings he assumed you might have made of the beach torn out of it. They must be hiding something."

"Smuggling!" Lamb cried. She walked up to Raven and gestured at him. "Everyone knows that in Cornwall and Dart-moor, they're all smugglers. They have boats coming in and then they take off the cargo and they trade it themselves. Liquor foremost, but also other things. They must be hid-ing that from the local law."

"Possibly." Raven knotted his fingers. "I've heard of hides on the moors where the liquor is stored until another person can come by to take it away. Did the girl know about the smuggling? Perhaps she saw the people involved? Had she threatened to tell? But why? Villagers stick together. They don't betray one another."

Betrayal, Merula thought. Their host had mentioned that topic the night before, speaking of his adventures abroad and the guide he had wanted to hire to take him to some ruin in the jungle. The guide had been considered a traitor by his fellow men and had been murdered. Or at least there was a possibility of that. A possibility that the anaconda hadn't come into his room by accident or coincidence.

Betrayal. Why had Oaks felt it necessary to talk of that? Had he known that the missing girl had been too talkative? That people might have thought she had betrayed the secret of the wreckmaster at the estuary and his helpers in Cranley and beyond, and that she had to die for that reason?

Had Oaks feared that his servant girl was already dead as he spoke to them?

Raven gestured at the bed. "I'll stay with him for a while, see if I can get some liquor into him, some coffee to clear his mind. I'll call you in when he's fit to speak with. You go and sit for a while, rest. Once Bowsprit is back from the inn, we'll have more to discuss."

CHAPTER 6

Bowsprit didn't return until late in the afternoon. He came in with an unsteady pace, and Merula wondered for a moment if he had drunk too much. But as she saw the keen light in his eyes, she knew he was still sober and probably just stiff from walking or riding.

Bowsprit gestured for her to come along with him up to the room where Raven was still tending their unwell host. "I had to wait a while for any men to come into the inn at all. The morning is quiet. Lunch pulled some merchants from a neighboring town who knew little about the deaths and even seemed reluctant to discuss anything unsavory over their meal. Then, around two, some men came in, and I recognized the one who had blocked the road."

Merula's heart skipped a beat. "He saw all of us well. Did he recognize you?"

"I don't think so. I was quite close to him, sitting beside him and drinking ale, and I never saw a flicker of recognition in his eyes. But these are sly people, and they don't let you see what they think or are up to."

While speaking, they had reached the landing, and Bowsprit went ahead of her and opened the door into Oaks's bedroom with a flourish. "After you, my dear lady."

Merula walked in and found their host sitting up against the pillows, having regained a little color in his face. His eyes were still dazed but no longer darting around the room, and he seemed to have been talking, for he was suddenly silent, nervously knotting his fingers on the blanket in front of him.

Merula felt a moment's stab of disappointment that Raven hadn't kept his word and hadn't called her up the moment their host started talking and revealing telling information. Had he never meant for her to be present?

Or had their host suddenly started pouring out his heart such that Raven felt that breaking the flow of his story might send him back into silence?

Bowsprit gestured to Raven to go on and went to sit in the windowsill while Merula stayed near the door. Still their host seemed to be bothered by the disruption. "I have a terrible headache," he declared suddenly, and reached to his bedside table. His eyes narrowed, and he half twisted his upper body to run his hands across the stand. "My drops. Where are they?"

"What drops?" Raven asked in an innocent tone. "Are you ill?"

"It's just a simple sedative I take. The bottle should be here." Oaks's gaze darted from the side table to the windowsill, as if he hoped to discern the bottle there.

"Since when do you take a sedative?" Raven asked. "Who prescribed it for you?"

"I've been taking it for years now." Oaks shrugged. "I'm a light sleeper, which isn't convenient while traveling."

"And you never suffered any ill effects from it? Delirium, not remembering what you did or where you were?"

"Not at all." Oaks ran his hands over the blanket. "Just the past week . . ." He reached for his head. "These terrible headaches. I can't think."

Raven sighed and told him to lie down and have some more rest. "It's very quiet, so I'm sure that even without the drops, you will sleep." He then walked to the door, leading Merula out into the landing.

Bowsprit didn't follow, so it seemed that he understood it was now his task to guard their host.

Outside the door, Merula said, "If Oaks has been taking those drops for a longer time, his recent errant behavior can't stem from those."

"Still, I would like to know what the drops consist of. A simple sedative, Oaks says. I've heard people say the same about laudanum. But it has addictive properties, and in larger doses it can even kill. Perhaps over time Oaks started taking more and more drops, and what had first been harmless then started to cause delusions? At any rate, he can't take more of them now. The bottle is on its way to Galileo. I am anxious to hear what his analysis turns up. Did Bowsprit mention to you how he got on at the inn?"

"He did seem to have spoken to some people involved. Including the man who blocked our way yesterday."

"Ah, the wreckmaster's right-hand man. How interesting."

Merula didn't feel like talking about this. Fixating him, she asked, "What did Oaks tell you?"

Raven's keen gaze darted across her face as if he searched there for something. She also glimpsed the indecision in the tightening of his jaw before he spoke. "He wasn't fully coherent . . ."

Merula drew in breath. Was Raven hiding the worst from her? Better to put it into words right away. "Did he confess to the murder?"

"No, definitely not."

"Then what are you hiding from me?" Merula held his gaze, lowering her voice even more although there was no risk of them being overheard. "You're hiding something, I can see it in your eyes."

Raven exhaled slowly. "I have no idea if I can trust what he told me."

"With that caution, tell me what he said."

"He repeated several times that we have to save the girl. The servant girl who used to work here. Tillie. He repeated her name as if convinced she was in danger. He doesn't seem to know she's dead. He told me to go out and find her and save her. Because . . . she loves him."

"She loves Oaks? They had an affair?" Merula wasn't quite sure how old the girl had been, but judging by the age at which girls usually went into service, she couldn't have been very old. Oaks was past forty at the least. An unlikely pair.

Merula swallowed. It was common knowledge that often in households, males—whether within the family or the servants—might cast an avaricious eye on the maids, promising things like presents or money to get favors from them. When maids were young and naive and the suitor in question was wealthy, handsome, or had a way with words, the maids fell for this, and more often than not, a pregnancy threw their entire life into turmoil. They might be cast out of the house, forced into the street, afraid to return to their families and admit to their condition.

Even if the affair didn't have such consequences, it might lead to other troubles, such as the lady of the house discovering that her husband or son was carrying on with a maid and the maid being blamed for it and dismissed or cruelly punished with extra hard work or, in severe cases, beaten.

Some maids used their bond with a high-placed male in the household to boast or make others feel inferior, and if those others banded against them, they might end up constantly targeted and humiliated until they fled and ended up on the streets anyway.

The position of a maid who carried on with someone above her station was precarious at the best of times, as the favor of the man she sought to please might shift to another at any moment.

But did a naive young woman from a country village know all that?

Raven stood studying her. "What thoughts are racing through your head? You look very worried."

"The girl is dead, and if there was something going on between her and her employer, that will give people all the more reason to suspect Oaks. They might think he tired of her and wanted to end the affair, that she threatened to speak of it publicly, or . . ."

Raven shook his head. "Oaks assured me that nothing happened between them. Nothing but a kiss she forced onto him one day as he came back from a walk and she came to ask him something. She kissed him and said she loved him and wished him to marry her so she could escape her father. It seems she had a hard time at home."

Merula remembered the stable boy saying that the girl hadn't wanted to go into service at first because she had wanted to stay with her father. That after her mother's death they were left to depend on each other. That didn't agree with what Raven was telling her now. Was Oaks lying? Devising a sad situation at home for the girl so he could explain that she had wanted to be with him? Or had the girl lied about wanting to get away from her father to explain her sudden interest in Oaks? Did it even make sense to assume a servant girl would dare to kiss her employer, a much older man?

Raven said with a sigh, "Oaks was in tears about it. He refused to marry her, even urged her never to approach him again about this subject. Then she vanished. He was afraid he had hurt her feelings and driven her to run away, perhaps even kill herself in despair because she felt rejected. Oaks believes he drove her away from here, but what will happen when he hears she's dead? He will surely blame himself."

"That was why he said they'd be after him. Because he blames himself that the girl ran. But did she really run because he rejected her? Or was there another reason? Do you know any more about her?"

"No, but perhaps Bowsprit can throw light on that."

Raven tapped his foot impatiently. "I want to believe Oaks when he says he turned her away, also because he understood she was merely clinging to him because she didn't have anybody else. But how well do I know him or his behavior around women? What if he first encouraged her and then turned her away?"

"Even then, he need not have killed her. Rich men can simply dismiss a girl they no longer like. He need not have murdered her, I presume."

"Except that the strange markings on her neck were supposed to have been made by his kraken."

Merula glanced down the corridor in the direction of the room with the specimens and the adjacent bathroom where the dead kraken hung on display. "I can't deny it looks rather creepy and might provoke superstitious thoughts in local minds. It's a creature from the sea, and all these people grew up with the sea nearby and listened to local lore."

"Yes"—Raven pointed a finger at her—"and that is our problem. For if we assume that Oaks has nothing to do with the murder and that someone else killed the girl in a way that suggests that Oaks's kraken is behind it, then what is the motive of this killer? I don't suppose he wants to see that specimen on the clothes rack on trial."

"Drive Oaks away from here? Perhaps people are afraid of his house, his beasts, his presence, and they want to terrify him into leaving."

"By killing one of their own girls? I can hardly believe it would have been a local."

Merula bit her lip. "How about the gentleman in the

very nice carriage who visited this place? Who was he and what was he here for?"

She studied Raven's tight features. "Was he a nerve doctor? Was he sent by Bixby? The stable boy told me they quarreled before Bixby left here last week, and Oaks was heard to repeat that he wouldn't be pressured into it. Did he resist treatment?"

Raven pursed his lips. "It's possible, I suppose. Do we have to invite some specialist of our own to come assess Oaks's condition?"

"If Oaks doesn't want to cooperate, will the specialist even be able to ascertain anything?"

"I don't know really."

With a heavy sigh, Raven opened the door and peeked in. Then he gestured to Bowsprit, who came over to the door and out of the room at once. "Oaks is sleeping," he reported. "His breathing sounds rather labored, as if he's dreaming about unpleasant things."

"I can imagine," Raven said, "as he obviously blames himself for his servant girl's disappearance."

Bowsprit said, "At the inn, I got a few men to talking. They told me that the girl, Tillie, had worked at the inn. That she had been a pretty little thing—excuse the wording, my lord, but that is what they said."

"Yes, tell it in their words so we may get an idea of how this girl Tillie lived and what she might have been involved in."

"The innkeeper doesn't mind when the customers take an interest in the girls. The man I talked to pointed out a blonde girl to me, telling me her name is Fern and she is friendly with a few of the men. He said with a sneer that, if she turned up dead, one of them got into a row with her and strangled her in anger or jealousy. He even had a name for me of the man who could have done such a thing. Ben Webber, son of the local greengrocer. It seems he liked Fern and wanted to marry her. He claimed he could offer her a better life than serving at the inn, as she could come and work in the shop. But Fern didn't like Mrs. Webber, Ben's mother. Her husband made provisions before he died that the son will become owner of the store when he turns thirty. Until that time his mother is in control of everything, and she lets her son work for her like a hired hand. Again: their words, not mine."

Bowsprit grimaced. "Mrs. Webber has strong opinions about everything and isn't afraid to voice them. Fern believed that the woman would be commandeering her, sending her here and there to do errands for her, and so she would rather stay at the inn. She was close to Tillie when Tillie still worked there, but it seems that they got into some kind of argument after Tillie left to work for Oaks."

"So Tillie had an argument with a friend of hers?" Merula repeated slowly. "We should talk to this girl Fern to find out what the argument was about."

"It's a shame they had an argument," Raven said pensively, "as one could assume girls amongst themselves might speak of men they are interested in. Fern might have known if Tillie took an interest in Oaks. But if they quarreled and Tillie left the inn to work elsewhere, that suggests they were no longer close and Tillie won't have told her anything."

He closed his eyes a moment as if to focus on his reasoning. "What made Tillie change her profession? You'd say the inn was a livelier place, and this house also has a bad reputation."

"It seems she was never quite equal to Fern." Bowsprit frowned, as if trying to recall what he had been told or what he had inferred from the remarks made. "Fern was prettier and wittier, with Tillie being more of a quiet girl. She disliked the customers getting too rowdy. Fern could joke with them and slap grabbing hands away, but not this girl. She thought it would be better to do something different, and so she came here. Also to support her father's household. When her mother died, the income she brought in from sewing ended, and he has to work hard to make ends meet. He travels the entire area to tend to the horses."

"Yes, the stable boy told me her father is a blacksmith," Merula said. "He was here this morning with the mob. The man in the leather apron. In the end he gave them the signal to go away. If Tillie was his daughter and he believes Oaks to be guilty of killing her, why didn't he try to have the mob burn the house anyway?"

"A fear of Bixby?" Raven shrugged. "Perhaps the blacksmith tends his horses as well and doesn't want to lose his business there. Go back in there and watch our host. Take note of everything he says, even if it's just mutterings in his restless dreams. I want to understand what has happened here."

"Very well, my lord. I can pass the time by reading some of the more interesting books Mr. Oaks put in the windowsill."

"Yes, that reminds me, do you know what kistvaens are?"

"Ancient graves on the moors. They're rumored to contain riches. But it's not wise to search for them. When violated, they might . . ." Bowsprit fell silent, grimacing.

Raven pressed, "Yes? Is there some curse attached to it? Like with Egyptian tombs?"

Bowsprit shrugged. "There are stories that those who once opened a kistvaen changed, and not for the better."

"Like Oaks," Merula said. "Can he have been looking into these graves?"

Raven eyed her. "Do you believe a curse fell upon Oaks after he discovered an ancient grave?"

"No, but I wonder if someone might have wanted others to believe that. Bixby, for instance, who is so eager to convince everyone Oaks is going mad."

"I'll keep a close eye on Oaks." Bowsprit turned to the door, then shook upright. "I remember now." He reached into his pocket and produced some folded sheets, holding them out to Merula. "I was close enough to the man who blocked the road yesterday to take back your belongings when he wasn't paying attention. I'm sure he doesn't need them. There you are."

He handed the sheets to Merula and entered the room, closing the door behind him with an impeccably soft click.

Raven shook his head. "My valet an expert pickpocket. I'd better not ask him where he acquired those skills."

Merula stared in amazement at the sheets in her hands. The pencil drawings on the top one were a little smudged from the paper having been tucked into the man's pocket, but otherwise it was all there.

"I'm curious"—Raven reached out to pull the stack from her hands—"what they were after when they took these from you. What you might have drawn that upset them."

"You know I drew nothing while we were looking at the estuary beach. It was impossible, as the wind was too strong. These are just sketches from the journey." Merula held on to them tightly.

Raven surveyed her. "You don't want me to see them?" He tilted his head. "I believed there were no secrets between us."

"There are none, but my sketches are not very good, and I feel awkward showing them." Knowing she was lying, her cheeks lit up.

Raven looked away. "Very well. There's nothing for me to do here. I might go into the village and see if I can buy some necessities at the greengrocer's. What better way to meet Mr. Ben Webber and his domineering mother? As Webber came to the inn often to court Fern, he must have met Tillie there before she took her leave and started working for Oaks. Webber might be able to tell us something worthwhile about the girl. He can certainly tell us where Fern lives so we can also talk to her and try to find out why Tillie left the inn and came to work for Oaks. Who knows what else we might learn just by listening well? For I'm sure the murder must be the talk of the town by now."

CHAPTER 7

Merula had insisted on going with Raven, and they had asked the stable boy whether there was a cart around. There was, and after he had put a horse in front of it, Raven drove them into the village. Merula had asked Lamb to come along, as she knew the girl was frightened in the house and still aching to get back to London.

It was sad to see how her excitement about this trip had died a sudden death and had turned her back into the shy, pale creature she had first been when Merula had come to know her. She liked Lamb inquisitive, talkative, and excited about the new things she might discover.

The village square had an old oak tree in the center, a place to put the cart, and directions on a wooden pole, pointing the visitor east, west, and south. "Town hall," Raven read aloud. "Well, well, how presumptuous for a little village. Newer, too, than the other directions, it seems."

He helped the ladies out of the cart, holding Merula's hand just a little longer and looking into her eyes with a probing intensity. She wished she had just shown him the sketches and been done with it, had him smirk about his likeness or wonder, anything better than drawing more undue attention to it. But it could not be helped.

At a shop with a small front window and a weather-beaten sign over the door, a young man was putting apples into a neat row. From inside, a voice called, "Make sure you put any black spots or bruises to the other side so the customers don't see them. They have to look their best."

"Yes, Mother!"

"Good afternoon," Raven greeted. "How delicious your apples look. They have that healthy country glow about them that you never see in the city. Might I purchase a few for my fiancée?"

Merula almost choked at being presented as Raven's fiancée, but the greengrocer's son looked them over, smiled at her, and picked up a brown paper bag. He had a nice symmetric face, strong jaws, and a hint of freckles over his nose. His deep-brown eyes seemed to twinkle as if he was pondering some secret only he was privy to.

If he had really loved the girl Fern and she had rejected him, there was nothing of sadness or grief in his demeanor.

Raven paid for the fruit and observed casually, "Such a lovely village, and still struck by misfortune. Didn't I hear that a serving wench from a tavern died mysteriously by the river last night?"

"She wasn't just a serving wench; she was a respectable village girl." The young man looked at Raven as if he suddenly discerned a poisonous insect.

"Forgive me if I'm misinformed," Raven said. "I'm a

writer for a London newspaper, and I've come here with the express purpose of writing on the mystery of the sea monster that strikes from the deep. Of course, no one is to know of this. I told my employer I was taking my fiancée to Devonshire for the sea air. She has been ill, haven't you, my dear?"

Merula nodded and tried to look as if she was tired and slightly bored, like you'd expect of a city-bred woman who enjoyed soirees with her fiancé's newspaper contacts and going to the theater or meeting with friends to gossip. Being shipped off to Devonshire, whether it be for the sea air or for invigorating walks on the moors, had to be dull to such a woman.

Raven continued to the young man, who listened intently, "I'm interested in reliable information from a good source. I'm willing to pay decent money for this information."

"Then you have come to the right man." The young man extended his hand. "Benjamin Webber. This is my store. I also deliver to people's homes, and I have been to the house where the sea monster lives. I can tell you everything about it."

Merula almost jerked upright with excitement but reminded herself just in time that she had to look like someone recovering from an illness. Someone who might smile indulgently at her fiancé's preoccupation with sea monsters but who would have no interest in such a subject herself.

Ben Webber put the last apples in place. "I'll tell my . . . uh . . . staff that I'll be away for a while. I can tell you all while we have a little stroll. No ears overhearing, you understand?"

Raven nodded, and Ben Webber popped inside.

"His mother," Raven whispered, "and he calls her the staff."

"He also lied that this is his store. It is not."

"At least not yet."

Merula grimaced. "Do you have any idea how reliable his information will be?"

"None at all, but I guess that, even if he's lying, we'll get some kernels of truth. He visited the house, and that may prove to be—oh, here he comes."

The four of them walked away from the square through a narrow street with cobbles and children playing with a dirty puppy, until they came into a broader street where a moss-splattered bench beckoned from under an apple tree. Raven suggested they sit down to speak of the matter. He spread his handkerchief out for Merula to sit on.

Lamb had to stand behind them, and it didn't escape Merula's attention that Ben Webber cast appreciative looks at her. Lamb's pale cheeks suddenly gained some color.

Well, well . . .

"The gentleman who lives in the house is very strange." Ben Webber began his story in a low, confidential tone. "He has been all over the world looking for animals, and he brought home trophies of his travels. Not skins or things, like you might expect, but whole animals in glass jars. They look like they are staring at you."

So he had actually seen the specimens. Had Oaks shown

them to him? Why? He had just delivered food to the manor, hadn't he?

Ben Webber shifted his weight. "They are all from far-away places, and he even got one from Canada. The sea monster they call the kraken. It's a huge thing with long arms. It can easily wrap itself around you a dozen times. It has a strange luminous skin like it is reflecting light. And it makes the sound of splashing water."

Raven's muscles twitched as if he was about to burst into laughter at these fanciful details, but Merula kicked him in the foot to warn him, and he kept himself in check.

Ben Webber continued with a perfectly serious expression, "It leaves the house at night to search for the sea from which it came. It goes via the river to the estuary, from which it can access the sea. As it swims, it surprises bathers and strangles them."

"Bathers?" Raven echoed. "In the depth of night? You mean to say that the girl who died was bathing in the river when she was strangled?"

"The body lay upon the riverbank, they say. Half in the water. That must mean she tried to flee from the monster, but it grabbed her from behind."

Merula listened intently. If the girl had been strangled from behind and she had fallen forward onto the riverbank, did that mean the killer had indeed come from the water?

Raven asked, "But were you there when the dead body was found? Were you part of the search party for it?"

Ben's expression tightened. "The wreckmaster only wanted his own men present. I wasn't allowed to help."

"But the wreckmaster's business is miles from here. He doesn't control the river, does he?"

"Oh, he'd want to. He is friendly with everyone who has some influence around these parts. The millers, the farmers, even the workers up at Powder Mills. Sometimes I think he believes himself to be master of the whole of Dartmoor."

Merula resisted the urge to poke Raven, as this seemed highly significant. If the wreckmaster was involved in smuggling, as Lamb had suggested, he would of course need to have people who helped him move the smuggled goods. What was more innocent than a farmer taking a cart full of what looked like sacks of grain to a mill and the miller then taking the flour farther? In reality, they might be moving smuggled goods!

"We should have been allowed to look for her as well," Ben Webber said. "I've known Tillie since we were both children. But that wreckmaster guards the beaches of the estuary like they contain a treasure."

Ben Webber made a disparaging movement with his hand. "He thinks he's something, but his days are past. The railway is coming, and the tourists want to be entertained. We need to start tearooms and souvenir shops where we can sell toby jugs and tin ornaments. The village should be ruled by merchants like me."

"You seem like a very intelligent young man. Please tell me more about the kraken and the murdered girl."

Ben Webber reddened with pleasure at the compliment from the alleged London newspaperman, and he made a sweeping hand gesture. "I haven't seen the body myself, as I wasn't allowed to look for her. But I've heard it looked really odd. That you could see on the neck exactly where the kraken had gripped her and cut off her air. They have these things on their tentacles that leave traces."

"Indeed." Raven studied Ben Webber closer. "It's a shame you live in such a small village and have a shop to tend. You'd make an excellent reporter. You know all the interesting tidbits. I'm glad we came here. Aren't you, my dear?"

Merula smiled languidly. "If it pleases you, my dear."

Raven had already turned back to Webber. "This owner of the house the kraken steals away from at night, can you tell me more about him? I think his name is Oaks?"

Webber's eyes betrayed a moment's panic, as if he had just become aware, so soon after the flattering compliment that he knew all the right details, that he could hardly confess he knew next to nothing about this man. He drew breath slowly. "Well, I've always heard that it's not right to tell tales about people, but then again, once there are deaths . . ."

Raven nodded encouragingly.

Merula felt as if her loud heartbeat could be heard in the silence. People from this very village had been to the house that morning, had seen them, might recognize them sitting here with the talkative greengrocer's son. What if they came out and threatened them again? Drove them out of the village?

Ben Webber continued, "Tillie was always a wild one.

Her father didn't have the time to look after her, and her mother died years ago. She was always determined to become something special. I guess that's why she had to go and work for him. A stranger who had traveled wide and far. She told all kinds of fancy tales about her work there. That she was allowed to clean the silverware, which was very valuable, or that she had seen cups and saucers that came all the way from China. She even claimed that Mr. Oaks had asked her to marry him. We never believed her. She was a poor deluded girl."

His hands in his lap clenched into fists. "Her death is on his head. He drove the creature to kill her. He had to cover it up."

"Cover up what?" Raven asked. "Their affair? The fact that he didn't want to marry her at all?"

Ben's hands relaxed. "Something like that, yes, I suppose. He had money, and when they do, they think they can cover up anything. He must think the police will not come after him now. Besides, if the kraken did the killing, what can they charge him with?"

"But Ben . . ." Raven smiled kindly at the young man. "You're such an intelligent young man that I can't accept you'd believe in a murderous sea creature. You have your theory who did the killing. You know. Please tell me what you think. I highly value your opinion."

Ben hesitated a moment. It seemed he was considering something, weighing his options. Then he said, "It was Oaks."

Merula narrowed her eyes. The young man's tone didn't convince her. It was as if he had been thinking about someone else. Had he then decided it wasn't safe to mention that particular name? Whom could he be suspecting?

Raven shook his head as well. "But if Oaks wanted to kill the girl who served in his own house, why not kill her and bury her somewhere and lie to the villagers that she had left? She might never have been found. Why leave her body along the river and contrive this farce with the kraken that points straight back to him and his collection? Wouldn't a smart man do it differently?"

"Who said he was a smart man?" Ben's voice was low and menacing. "He was stupid. A coward, too."

"How do you mean?"

Ben rose from the bench. "I have to get back to the shop. The staff can't do without me. I trust you will keep your word and pay me for what I told you." He suddenly sounded agitated and distrustful.

"Of course. But I don't have the money on me now. And I think you owe me just a little bit more about the circumstances of the death. Find out for me via the local coroner, or the morgue, or the doctor—whoever handles the dead bodies here—what the cause of death was, how the body looked when found, and other peculiarities. Then report back to me and you will be handsomely rewarded."

Ben Webber looked doubtful. "How may I reach you?"

"I'll stop by again. I don't want you showing up at my hotel. I'm supposedly here to rest." With a superior gesture, Raven waved the young man off.

Ben Webber went, but not before he smiled at Lamb.

Merula glanced up at the girl, seeing the redness in her

cheeks and the glow in her eyes. "I think you made a con-quest," she joked lightly.

Lamb flushed deeper. "Such a man would never look at me. He's dashing, has a shop, and . . ."

"He doesn't have a shop," Raven corrected. "It's his mother's until he turns thirty, and judging by his youthful features, that'll take at least another five years, more likely seven. He's trying to make more of himself, and that can be dangerous. I wonder how much he really knows. He has been inside the house, near the kraken. Did that give him the idea? What if he wanted to get rid of Tillie . . . ?"

"Why would he?" Merula objected at once. "Bowsprit told us it was Fern who Ben Webber was interested in, not Tillie. But before Tillie came to work for Oaks, she was at the inn. What if things are going on there, criminal things? Webber just told us Tillie liked to make herself special. Per-haps she witnessed something and spoke about it."

"You mean her talkativeness became her undoing?" Raven mused. "Not bad. Not bad at all."

"Smuggling!" Lamb cried triumphantly. "I said it before. An inn is a meeting place for many people. You can exchange things, make plans while looking innocent sit-ting over ale and cards."

Raven hushed her high-pitched tones. "If there are criminal activities going on, we must tread lightly and not make anyone suspicious of us."

Lamb hung her head, but her expression stayed lively and excited, as if she was working on a grand theory.

Raven said, "We have to talk to Fern right away. She

works at the inn and she used to be Tillie's friend. If Tillie saw something, she might have mentioned it to Fern. Not exactly what she saw, perhaps, but that she knew something that might prove advantageous to her. Wait a moment." He got to his feet and rushed after Ben Webber.

After a few minutes, he came back. "We needn't go far. Webber told me Fern should be at the church cleaning and refreshing the flowers. That way, then." He pointed in the direction of the church's square, sturdy tower. The sunlight reflected off the golden-colored weathercock on top.

In the small square beside the church, several weathered oak trees threw shade across a few children playing with clay marbles. The sharp ticks of the marbles hitting each other were still audible as they walked through the invitingly open door into the church.

Inside, all sounds were blocked out by the thick walls, and solemn shades hung between the pews.

A blonde girl sat on her knees, scrubbing the tiles to their left. She used so much pressure that Merula thought she was either remarkably thorough or upset about something.

When she noticed them, she jumped to her feet with a cry, raising a hand to her throat. "You'd drive me into death sneaking up on me like that. Are you here for the vicar? He had to go see a dying old man, won't be back for hours. I know old Thompson. He claimed to be dying last spring and then in October before that. He just needs a bit of attention, I wager."

She dried her soggy hands on her apron. "I can tell you

a thing or two about this church, if that's what you're interested in. The vicar has told it often to visitors while I've
been here, so I know it all."

Her mouth pulled tight a moment as if she remembered
something unpleasant. But she smiled again almost immediately, gesturing accommodatingly down the aisle.

"That's very kind of you," Raven said, "but we're not
here to learn about the church. We're here to talk about
your friend Tillie."

Fern's eyes widened a moment, in surprise or shock. She
dug in her apron's pocket and produced a handkerchief to
dab at her eyes. "That's something terrible, sir. I can't
believe it happened. Not here in our village. You hear of
killings in the city, but not here."

"Not even when a monster from the water does it?"
Raven asked softly.

Fern looked at him, again taken aback, it seemed. "You
believe in such things?"

"Don't you? I thought Dartmoor folk were superstitious."

"Some may be, but I'm not. I'm sure someone human
killed Tillie."

"There was a reason she had to die?"

Fern sniffed in the handkerchief. "I suppose it's hard to
believe. She was always kind to everyone, wouldn't hear a
bad word about anyone. You'd never think she'd have an
enemy in the world."

"But she did?"

"Well, I never believed her, sir. I wish now that I had.
Then I might have helped her so that she didn't get killed."

Fern burst into tears. She sank into a pew and sobbed in her hands.

Raven looked at Merula as if to goad her into action. Merula stood next to the girl and looked down on her narrow, shivering shoulders. "What did she tell you that you didn't believe?"

"That she would be rich soon. I thought she was just lying to make herself seem important. To show me she had gone up in the world now that she worked at a fine house. She never liked the inn, the men grabbing at her. She felt herself too good for that."

Fern wiped her eyes. "You have to slap at them when they get a little too persuasive. But she never did. She didn't dare. She was really a skittish little thing. Which is why I didn't believe she'd be rich. How?"

How indeed? Merula asked herself. Out loud, she said, "Did she not say any more about how she'd get rich? Didn't you ask her questions about it? If you were so surprised and didn't believe her at all, you must have—"

"Of course. I asked her how she'd ever get rich and if a man was involved. She blushed terribly. She told me not to breathe a word of it to a soul. It was a surprise for her father. She always wanted to help him get on the right track again. He wasn't well after her mother died. Not well at all."

"You mean he was ill?"

"He was drinking. He came to the inn every night. He made trouble sometimes. Tillie begged the innkeeper to send him away, but the innkeeper said he'd just go elsewhere. Wanted his money, the greedy old bastard."

"You don't seem to like your employer," Raven observed dryly.

Fern scoffed at him, "He may be my employer, as you call it, but I know what he's like. Taking money out of the till when he goes to market so he can bet on the horses. His wife is not to know. Well, she has to be blind as a bat not to know that. But then she's so busy collecting money for the tapestry."

She gestured to the far wall. "There was a tapestry there depicting the miracle of Moses producing water from the rocks. It was old and moldy, falling apart. She wants to have it repaired by a master artist. Someone from London, I think. It costs a lot of money and she's taking donations for it. We have nothing to spend here, so she's smiling up at wealthy people who vacation here."

"Or new residents, like Mr. Bixby and Mr. Oaks?" Raven asked.

"I don't think Mr. Bixby has money to spend. He put it all in his house. They say he spent a fortune to change Gorse Manor. It wasn't grand enough for him."

"And Mr. Oaks? Tillie must have told you a thing or two about him."

"Just that he was kind and that he had shown his books to her. I didn't believe her. She can't read or write, so why would he show his books to her?" Fern dabbed her eyes and took a deep breath. "Tillie was such a silly goose, believing everyone wanted the best for her. But she was just being used."

Her lips wobbled. "If I had believed her and pressed her

harder to tell me what it was all about, I might have saved her life."

"Tillie didn't drop any kind of hint, however small, as to how she'd get rich?" Raven pressed.

Fern shook her head. "She just said it was a perfect plan. That it couldn't go wrong." She laughed softly, a strange little high-pitched laugh. "Couldn't go wrong, huh? She's dead!"

Raven gestured at Merula that they should leave.

Merula smiled at the girl. "Thank you for speaking with us. We're really very sorry for your friend's death."

Fern nodded and sniffled.

Outside, Merula narrowed her eyes against the light, which seemed piercingly bright after the dimness inside.

Raven rubbed his arms. "Those places are always cold like dungeons."

Merula eyed him. "I think it was a lovely little church with that one colored glass window. Didn't you see it?"

Raven stared at the ground. He spoke so soft she could barely hear him. "It was always chilled in the chapel at Raven Manor. But never as chilled as during those days when my mother's body was laid out there. High summer, and still it was cold as the grave itself. I wasn't supposed to go there, see her after she died, but I went anyway. I hated them all for keeping me away from her. Especially my father. I sneaked down one night and went to the chapel, all alone. How I wish I hadn't."

Merula swallowed. She didn't know quite what to say.

Raven continued, still staring with eyes that seemed to

look back into the past. "The coffin stood in the center on two benches. It was too high for me to look into. I guess that was good. I never saw her face. I suppose it must have been contorted after the fear she suffered. I just remember the coffin and the light of the candles playing across the wood. Of feeling that terrible cold invade my body until I was like a lump of ice. I couldn't move anymore. Still I wanted to run away."

"Did your father ever find out you had gone there?"

"I don't know. I never told him." Raven clenched his hands into fists, then relaxed them again. Jerking his head up, he met her eyes. "Do you believe Fern that Tillie never hinted at how she was going to get rich?"

"Don't you?"

"I'm not sure." Raven pursed his lips. "They were friends, allegedly. They worked together at the inn, had to face the leering men night after night. They must have had some kind of bond. A bond that lasted after Tillie left to work for Oaks. They still lived in the same village, must have seen each other when Tillie came to the inn to give her wages to her father. Isn't it logical that Tillie would confide in Fern? Perhaps even engage Fern in her plans to get rich? Supposedly they had an argument; well, perhaps it was about these alleged riches. I didn't want to ask her explicitly about the argument, as it might have made her suspicious of us. It's better if she believes for the moment that we're sympathizing with her loss. We might have to speak with her again later. Once we know more, we might be able to corner her."

"It sounds like you suspect her of knowing something vital she won't reveal." Merula studied Raven's demeanor. "Something relating directly to Tillie's death? She seemed forthcoming enough, sharing her knowledge readily, of her employer's gambling, his wife's charitable work, and Tillie's plans to get rich."

"Indeed." Raven stamped his foot. "But she wasn't exactly forthcoming with details on the latter. Perhaps she really doesn't know them, but on the other hand, I couldn't help but think about the books Oaks had in his bedroom, referring to the old graves on the moors. Fern just told us Tillie claimed that Oaks showed his books to her. Perhaps Oaks told her about the kistvaens, and Tillie believed that she knew the location of such a grave. She grew up around these parts and must have heard all the old tales. However, it would be rather scary for a girl to locate a grave on her own."

Merula tilted her head. "You mean that Fern knows what Tillie was up to and is keeping her mouth shut because . . ."

"Of the supposed riches involved," Raven added. "This could turn out to be very dangerous if Tillie's death is somehow connected to what she claimed to know."

"You mean Fern could be next?" Merula glanced back at the church's open door. "We should warn her."

"I don't think she needs to be warned. Our sudden entrance gave her more of a scare than is normal when you don't expect company. I think she already knows she might be in danger now that Tillie is dead, but still she's determined to keep the secret."

"That would be very dangerous." Merula wanted to expound further, but Raven pointed at one of the oak trees beside the church. "Look at that."

The oak tree's rough trunk had been covered by a poster depicting something dark blue with silver. But the paper had been ripped apart as if animal claws had raged over it, leaving but shreds, faded in sunlight or rain.

"I can just read a few letters," Merula said, straining her eyes to make out something amid the damage. "*Per* and *met*. Do you think this was about the Perseid meteor shower you mentioned to me on our way over here? A public announcement of some kind?"

Raven looked doubtful. "In a small town like this? Then again, when Oaks last wrote to me, he did mention an invitation to come see the Perseids at a friend's estate. Perhaps this friend is a man of science who wants to interest local people for the phenomenon. It doesn't look, though, as if they can appreciate it. It has been destroyed."

He held out his hand to the poster, his fingers spread wide. "This wasn't done by a human hand either."

Lamb gave a little shriek.

Raven shook his head at her. "A pitchfork, I meant to say. Not the claw of some monster."

"Not taken down," Merula mused, pointing at the pins that secured the paper to the tree trunk. "Anyone who didn't like it could have removed the whole poster. But whoever did this damaged it and left it visible. Like a warning."

"A warning? For whom?" Raven frowned.

"For other villagers. To stay away from it. Perhaps the mysterious wreckmaster did it? People seem to stand in awe of him."

"And all of his associates." Raven touched a shred of blue with his forefinger. "Good thing that this poster reminded me of it. We should go there. The meteor shower should be spectacular, a natural wonder, and perhaps we can also learn something useful for the case."

"Why would you think so?"

Raven smiled at her. "Because now I recall what Oaks wrote to me, whose house this stargazing garden party is at. Gorse Manor. Bixby's house."

CHAPTER 8

That night Merula felt an odd sense of expectation as they left the house, all at their finest, as they had no idea what high-placed guests might be expected to attend the garden party. Raven had decided that Bowsprit had to stay with Oaks to ensure he didn't wander off again and hurt himself. Lamb, however, accompanied them, wearing her deep-red costume again and smiling from ear to ear. Her downcast mood and fear of the strange surroundings had vanished like fog under morning sunshine.

Gorse Manor lay ten miles across the moorlands, which glowed in the evening sunshine. Every now and then, small pools of water lit up among the clumps of heather, and in the distance the hoarse call of the raven resounded as his majestic black figure soared against the bluish skies.

At crossroads, piles of stones had been placed, and at some there were flowers, as if villagers came here to commemorate something. Or perhaps it had been done by playing children? But where had the flowers come from? Merula wondered. They didn't seem to grow on this land.

"There are some clouds, but they are thin and move fast," Lamb observed. "We should be able to see the shooting stars. I've never seen them before."

She scooted to the edge of the seat. "What kind of people are coming?"

"I have no idea," Raven admitted. "Perhaps men of science? I'm surprised, though, that Bixby is interested in phenomena in the skies. He seemed like a very down-to-earth and practical man to me. Besides, he also mentioned his collection of books on mental abnormalities and the fact that specialists came to consult him on the subject. How many fields can one man cover?"

"Perhaps Bixby only agreed to have this meeting at his house to get to know people," Merula suggested. "I think he likes to be influential, or at least believe himself to be so. The villagers listened to him when he appeared."

"Yes, but at the same time, someone destroyed the poster announcing the meeting here tonight. If they are all so fond of him or in awe of him, why did that happen?"

Merula shrugged. "The wreckmaster and his local allies consider themselves the leaders of these villagers. What people did Webber name to us? Tinners and millers?"

Raven nodded. "They've dominated this area for ages. The tin mines and plants like Powder Mills provided people with work and wages. Then the railway arrived; outsiders like Bixby bought houses here and introduced new things. Perhaps Bixby's influence on the villagers annoyed the wreckmaster and his cronies and they decided to damage the poster to show their disapproval."

Ahead of them they could see another carriage going down the road. And even farther than that, there seemed to be fires burning, small pricks of bright orange light.

When they drew closer, Merula discerned that these lights were braziers put along the road. More and more appeared as they came closer to the house. It lay somewhat higher than the rest of the land and was surrounded by what had to be an artificially created wood of trees and shrubs. Perhaps it was even an arboretum, a collection of indigenous and exotic trees, brought here by an ardent botanist.

Their carriage halted in front of the house, and Bixby approached to welcome them. As soon as they had alighted and Raven shook their host's hand, he explained in a soft voice, "You know full well we have been under attack from some villagers. Although we are not sure they might be here tonight, we would appreciate it if you would not announce our connection to Charles Oaks. Could you perhaps introduce us as guests from London? And Miss Merriweather here is my fiancée."

Bixby hitched a brow. "In truth?"

Merula vividly remembered that he had last seen her in her dressing gown and flushed. "It's just something we agreed on to be able to . . ." She glanced at Raven for help to smooth over this awkward moment.

Raven smiled at Bixby. "These country people are traditional and might not understand how a man and woman can travel together without being . . . attached. I don't want to offend them or cause any form of aggression. I saw in the village that your poster was torn apart. With a pitchfork?"

Bixby pursed his lips. "I'm a man of science. Of the rational mind. I have no sensitivity to what people consider . . . beliefs. There have been one or two who have stated that the study of the heavens is not for mortal men. There also seems to be a connection between the Perseids and some saint whose name day is celebrated around this date. Calling the meteors mere bits of rock which fall from the skies is blasphemous to these people. But I can't for the life of me describe them as saint's tears."

"There's still a lot we don't know and don't understand about the universe." Raven pulled Merula's arm through his. "Now, where are we supposed to look at these meteors?"

Bixby gestured to the wooded area around. "In my gardens. I do own a telescope, but it's of little use with the meteors moving quickly across the skies. You should take up positions in the gardens and let your gaze roam the skies to see the flashes. It's no more than that, flashes, but at the height there are dozens of them in quick succession. There are braziers here and there to make sure you can find your way back to the house. Oh, and don't be frightened by the animals. They don't bite."

"What animals?" Raven queried, but their host had already turned away from them to meet another carriage that came rattling up.

Lamb, who had stood beside them in silence, now grabbed Merula's free arm. "What animals does he mean? Are they dangerous? Is it even safe to be out here?"

Merula was sad to see how one teasing remark from a rather infuriating man had brought back Lamb's fear like tidal wives rushing to the shore. "Just stay close to us," Merula assured her. "It will be fine."

Raven took them down the terrace to where a few other people stood talking. The men were well dressed and the ladies decked out in silk, satin, feathers, and pearls. They cast curious looks at Raven and Merula, quickly assessing their social station. In these rural surroundings the guests seemed less certain of whom they'd be spending the evening with than they would have been in London.

Relief was almost tangible when Raven introduced himself as Lord Raven Royston, a natural historian from London, and Merula as his fiancée who also had an interest in the nightly phenomena. "Especially if we can study them à la belle étoile."

An elderly man with white hair and a short beard shook his hand amiably. "Morehead. Professor Morehead. Mathematician. You might be aware that there is a lot to be calculated about the skies?"

Raven acknowledged that there probably was, and Morehead launched into a long and difficult explanation about the distance between the earth and the moon.

Merula shifted her weight restlessly, spying around as far as she could without appearing too obviously bored with the subject. She used the first short silence to tell Raven she was getting herself some punch from the buffet and took Lamb with her, going through the wide open French doors into a room lit by a chandelier overhead. A sofa lay to the left along with some chairs with delicately twirled legs and a cabinet full of precious china. A long table held silver platters with food and a crystal punch bowl. A footman filled glasses and handed them out to the ladies.

Lamb accepted hers with trembling fingers. As they stepped aside to look at the china cabinet, she whispered to Merula, "I've never drunk punch before in my life."

"There can be alcohol in it, so better make sure you don't drink too much too quickly," Merula warned her. "Just a sip can be very refreshing."

Lamb tried it carefully. "It stings my tongue."

"There must be champagne in it, or some other drink that fizzes."

Lamb giggled. She stared into the cabinet. Merula thought she was admiring the fine patterns on the china cups, but then she realized Lamb was looking at her own reflection in the glass in the doors. She suppressed a laugh of her own.

On the other side of the room was a door that led into a hallway, and as it stood open, Merula assumed she was allowed to go through. She touched Lamb softly on the arm and nodded toward the door.

While the footman was busy serving punch to other guests, they crossed the room and went out, standing in the hallway.

A chandelier burned here as well, illuminating a towering flower piece on a wooden chest and a set of broad carpeted stairs leading up. Merula's heart was beating fast. She had a feeling that, being inside Bixby's house, she should do something to find out more about him and his connection with Oaks, but on the other hand, she realized it would be extremely impolite to just wander off and explore his rooms.

If only she had a reasonable excuse to go somewhere . . .

"What is that?" Lamb asked. She pointed up the stairs. Across the railing they could just see something dark and fluffy.

"It's a beast, staring at us," Lamb whispered. Her face was pale now, and she clenched her punch glass. "Mr. Bixby said something about animals that might bite us."

"Nonsense," Merula said. "He said they would *not* bite us. And if it is indeed a beast, it's mounted and can't stare. I'll go see it up close."

"I'm not coming." Lamb planted her feet apart as if she was digging her heels into imaginary sand.

"Fine with me. I'll just run up and be down again in a few moments." Merula transferred her glass from her right to her left hand and used the right to firmly clench the railing as she walked up. Her courage was sinking fast under the ominous creaking of the wooden steps under her footfalls. It seemed to be so silent here, as if all the guests outside were miles away.

The dark, fluffy thing grew larger as she approached, and her heart jumped around in her chest. What on earth was it? She had never seen anything quite like it.

The head was attached to an enormous body that stood in an upright position on its hind legs, its front legs with sharp-clawed paws up as if lashing out at the beholder. The mouth inside the huge head was open, showing off vicious teeth. A card on the wooden platform the beast was mounted on read URSUS ARCTOS.

"A bear," Merula said out loud. "I had no idea they were so large."

Standing in front of it, she had to look up, as the bear's gaping head was well over her own. She reached out a tentative finger to feel the fur on the chest. Suddenly there was a sound down the corridor. A click as of a door closing.

Her heart seemed to stop for a moment, then thunder on. Sweat broke out on her back. She wasn't supposed to be here. What could she do?

On impulse, she dived into the shadows beside and half behind the bear. Its fur tickled her arm as she pressed herself close to the wall.

Voices approached.

Merula held her breath, fighting the urge to close her eyes, as if this would make her invisible to the people drawing near.

"I'm sure," a male voice said, "that we can find a solution for it."

"It should have been taken care of," another replied, apparently irritated. "Bixby assured us he had it all worked out."

"He has. We can trust him."

"I hope so. There's a lot of money involved, and we can't afford to make any mistakes."

The men passed her hiding place and went down the stairs. She didn't dare peek out at them and just caught a glimpse of dark figures and the whiff of a spicy scent. Then they were gone. She exhaled and moved out of her hiding place.

In her haste and confusion, she had held her punch glass to the side, and some liquid had spilled across her dress. She pulled out a handkerchief and dabbed at the wet spot, which was fortunately not too visible on the dark-purple fabric.

A sip or two of the remaining punch revived her spirits, and having put the handkerchief away, she went down the stairs. Her footfalls were quick and light, relief tingling like the punch upon her tongue. *Find Raven and stay with him for the rest of the night. Take no more chances*, she vowed to herself.

Merula froze on the last step of the stairs. Lamb was nowhere to be seen.

Taken aback, Merula looked about her for a moment, expecting the girl to materialize.

Had she heard the voices of the men about to come down and hidden herself?

"Lamb?" Merula whispered. She went to an alcove and swept the green velvet curtain aside, intending to laugh with Lamb at their fright over the suddenly appearing men.

But the alcove was empty. The air that wafted out of it was stale, moist as if the back wall was damp and moldy.

Wrinkling her nose, Merula dropped the heavy curtain back in place.

The door leading to the kitchens, then?

Merula tiptoed over, called out for Lamb softly, tried the door. It opened, but there was no one in the dim hallway behind it.

Merula turned and looked around her, then went to the door leading into the room where the dutiful footman served punch. Enough people were present, talking, laughing, but there wasn't a trace of the red costume or Lamb's blonde head.

As Merula craned her neck to look again for the girl, fresh perspiration broke out on her brow. Where had Lamb gone? She had said she didn't want to be alone. Why would she have wandered away?

Merula put her half-full glass on a side table and rushed outside to look for Raven. He was still deep in conversation with the professor—that is, the professor was explaining something and pointing up at the night skies while Raven nodded and smiled in appreciation, his eyes betraying that he wanted to get away but saw no way to achieve it.

Merula marched up to them and put her hand on his arm. "My dear, I have something to show you. Excuse us, Professor. I'm sure we will hear much more about your fascinating theories later tonight."

She dragged Raven away, who sighed in her ear, "At last. I thought I would never get away from him."

"I intervened for a reason. Lamb is gone!"

"Gone? How do you mean? I thought she followed you like a shadow."

"Yes, but . . ." In a low voice, Merula quickly explained what had happened. "I don't understand where she went."

Her voice faltered, and she swallowed hard. "I can't help thinking something might have happened to her."

Raven tilted his head. "A tentacle came from the woodwork and grabbed her?"

"Bixby said there were animals here. What did he mean?"

"He also said they don't bite. He was just riling us a little. Come, we'll find her." Raven strode ahead, looking around him as if he expected he would see Lamb standing somewhere and could simply present her to Merula.

Knowing she had already looked in all the likely places, Merula followed him with an anxious flutter in her stomach. *If something happens to Lamb, I will never forgive myself.* The thought echoed through her head.

Raven and she stood in the hallway looking up to where the imposing bear stood. "Are you sure she didn't follow you? She might have heard the voices and run into the corridor to the right." Raven pointed up at it.

"But why, then, hasn't she come down again?"

"I have no idea, but I'll go and look. You stay here."

Raven rushed up the stairs and disappeared.

Merula turned her back on the stairs and pretended to be looking out through the decorated pane beside the front door. Her mind was racing. Had someone seen her and Lamb go into the hallway?

Had that person waited until Lamb was alone to attack her?

But if someone had jumped at her, she would have screamed. She would not just have gone along, without a fight.

Merula looked about her, and suddenly she saw something that made her heart beat even more. A punch glass abandoned on the floor. Not fallen, not broken. But set aside, it seemed.

Had Lamb seen something suspicious and put down her glass to go explore?

But she had been fearful, so would she go off investigating on her own?

It didn't make sense at all.

"Merula!" Someone touched her shoulder.

Merula spun round. A man with dark hair and lively eyes stood surveying her. His lips seemed to want to curve into a smile; then pain flickered in his eyes. "You look just like your mother."

Merula gasped for breath. "My mother? Did you know her?" Her hand went up unconsciously to where the pendant was hidden under her clothes, the one that had been left with her when she was abandoned as a baby. A pendant with a place name on it, probably here in Dartmoor. And now a man said she looked just like her mother.

"It was a long time ago," he said. "I could be mistaken. But I heard you introduced as Miss Merula Merriweather?"

"That is correct. And my mother's name was Blanche," Merula rushed to say. She didn't know if her father had been called Merriweather, or whether her parents had even been married, so she avoided giving a last name so the unknown man wouldn't get confused. "She was here, in Dartmoor, before I was born. Did you know her then?"

She had always wanted to meet someone who had known her mother, who could tell her something about her. All the things Aunt Emma had never wanted to tell her, saying it was better she didn't know.

"Merula!" Raven's voice distracted her for a moment, and she looked up to where he appeared and came racing down to her. "She is not here."

Merula turned back toward the man who had approached her, but the spot was empty. He had walked away so suddenly that she was not even sure he had been there. She touched her forehead a moment. Was she losing her mind?

Raven stood beside her now. "Who was that talking to you?"

"So you also saw him?"

"Of course I saw him. What did he want of you?"

"He called me by my given name, even though I've never met him. He said I look just like my mother. He must have known her before I was born. But now he's gone, and . . . I wanted to ask him so many questions." Anguish shot through her that a chance to learn about her past had slipped through her fingers.

Raven gestured with a hand. "Back to the most urgent matter. Lamb is not upstairs. Of course, I haven't searched every nook and cranny, but if she just wanted to hide from the men for a moment, she wouldn't have gone far. I don't think she went up after all." He sounded puzzled and worried, speeding up Merula's heartbeat.

"Where can she be, then?"

Raven nodded at the front door. "Outside."

Merula stared through the glass into the increasing darkness. "Alone? But she was so afraid earlier."

"We will just try and follow her." Raven opened the front door.

Merula glanced back at the room where punch was being served. She wanted to talk to the man who had known her mother. She wanted to learn so many things that had been in the back of her head all her life, pushing to the fore at times, only to retreat again as Aunt Emma's evasive responses just led to frustration on both their parts. Here was a man who had seemed genuinely pleased to see her, remembering her mother with fondness.

Her head spun at the mere idea of what he could unlock for her.

But Lamb was missing and they had to find her first.

CHAPTER 9

Outside, the cool evening air brushed Merula's face, and the first stars were visible against the skies. The thin clouds Lamb had complained about had drifted away, and it was clear and perfect for stargazing. But Lamb wasn't here with them to look up and see her first shooting star.

Merula wrapped her arms around her. "What if someone wants to hurt her?"

"Why?" Raven gestured for her to follow him across the terrace to go around the side of the house. "No one here knows her."

"One girl has already died. Perhaps it's some maniac like Jack the Ripper."

Raven shook his head. "I'm convinced crimes are usually committed for a reason. Not just because there's a madman on the loose."

Merula hurried after him. "But the villagers are angry. They destroyed the posters inviting people to come here. They attacked Oaks's house. Perhaps it doesn't have to be logical what they do."

"Lamb grew up in Rotherhithe." Raven made an eloquent gesture. "She knows how to handle herself. She won't just be grabbed by a madman."

"Then where is she?"

They had rounded the house and were at the back now, looking out over a formal garden. Down a path strewn with broken shells, they caught a dark mass, apparently the wall of some enclosed garden. Or perhaps a maze? Some country houses drew countless visitors each summer with their intricate mazes in which one could wander for an hour without finding the center or the way out.

Merula pointed at it. "We should look down there. Perhaps Lamb got trapped in the maze."

Raven had already rushed ahead of her. She had to run to keep up with him. In spite of his reassurances that nothing would happen to Lamb, he was hurrying like he was chasing a criminal. As if he was rushing to prevent . . .

Merula's mouth was dry. She should never have gone upstairs alone. Lamb had warned her earlier they had to stay together or one of them might get hurt.

Raven halted and raised his hand. "Listen," he whispered.

The sound was vague at first, then becoming clear. A peal of laughter. Female.

Raven looked at Merula. "Is it her?"

"I don't know. I've never heard her laugh quite like that."

Intrigued, Merula was now ahead of Raven, walking to the dark-green wall of twigs and leaves. It wasn't a maze but a hedge growing around an enclosed rose garden. They came to an entry gate, which was ajar. To their left, a wooden construction arose, heavily grown with yellow climbing roses, and they caught sight of two entwined figures. The man's head bent down over the woman's as he kissed her time and time again.

Whether it was Raven's foot hitting a bit of stone or a blackbird suddenly flying away chattering indignantly, the pair became conscious of their surroundings and broke apart. The man said something and vanished quickly around the construction while the woman stood there, still and amazed, raising her hands to her lips.

Merula pushed the gate open and went in. "Lamb? Are you well?"

Lamb looked at her with dazed eyes. "Yes. I'm so sorry. We were only supposed to stay away for a minute. While you were up looking at that creature."

Merula felt a surge of anger rush through her veins. "We've been looking for you for at least fifteen minutes. You can't just walk off without telling me where you are! And who was that man? What did he want of you?"

"He says he fell in love with me the moment he laid eyes on me." Lamb sighed in satisfaction. "He likes me. Little old me!"

She clasped her hands together and whirled round in a circle. "The stars in the skies must be changing people. How can he like me? But he says it is so. His kiss told me it is so."

She halted and reached up to touch a yellow rose, the

stem of which had been slipped under the lace adornment on the neckline of her costume. "He picked this for me. He said it couldn't compare to my beauty."

Merula shook her head impatiently. "You can't just run off and let Lord Raven and me look for you. I thought you were afraid of the dark."

"I wasn't alone. He would have defended me."

Lamb sighed again, but before she could indulge in more nonsense about her heroic defender, Merula took her arm and dragged her along. "Back to the house."

Her anger was mainly caused by the anxiety and guilt she had felt when Lamb had been missing and the sickening idea she might have been hurt, killed, like the other girl had been. Instead, it appeared Lamb had been courted by some man who . . .

"That rose wasn't even his to pick. This is Mr. Bixby's garden. Or . . . you're not going to tell me it was Mr. Bixby himself, are you?"

"Of course not. He is old!" The latter word carried an intense indignation and disgust.

Lamb extracted herself from Merula's grasp and passed Raven with her head down. He stood at the entry gate and studied Merula's expression. "Are you well?"

"Of course I am well. I could just . . . ." Merula wrung her hands together. "She says she believed she had only been gone for a minute. While I was upstairs looking at the bear!"

"Well, love does seem to have the effect on people that they lose sight of the time," Raven said philosophically.

Merula shot him an angry glance. "Don't tell me you understand her."

"Not at all. Just making a statement of fact."

Merula wondered if Raven had ever been in love and lost track of time when he was with the woman he adored. But she wasn't about to ask him anything about that. Not now, not ever! Feelings were just silly.

"Who was that man anyway?" Raven asked.

"I don't know. I didn't see him properly. You?"

"No. I think he was fairly young, though. For a moment I thought . . ." Raven walked with his hands folded on his back. "That it was our grocer's son. Ben Webber."

"What? The man who is rumored to have wanted to marry Fern? That would be very insensitive."

Raven shrugged. "Or very smart. By going after another woman so soon, he can show people he's not pining for any serious love lost. Rumors that he was snubbed by Fern will die down quickly. And by getting close to Lamb, he can also find out things about us. I'm worried he didn't believe me when I told him I'm a newspaperman."

"That is not the point," Merula objected, but before she could go on, a woman's scream tore the silence in the gardens. It wasn't one isolated cry but kept coming, waves of piercing screaming, as of someone in absolute terror.

Raven broke into a run toward the sound, and Merula followed him without thinking twice about it. She heard footfalls behind her, suggesting Lamb was also coming, not because she wanted to see what it was, probably, but because she didn't want to be left alone.

The screaming had stopped now. The sudden startled silence was even worse, closing in on Merula from all sides like a menacing presence.

Raven lengthened his paces and raced even faster. Merula couldn't keep up with him. Panting for breath, she had to slow her pace, pushing a fist into her side to stop the vicious stabs there.

Holding up her skirts so she could run faster, Lamb passed her and went after Raven. Perhaps her anger about the supposition it had been Bixby kissing her had goaded her?

The breeze coming from the wide open moorland beyond the garden cooled the perspiration on Merula's face, and she shivered, sucking in the air that her burning lungs craved. In the distance she thought she could hear a hound baying, a long-drawn, mournful sound. Hadn't Bowsprit told them about a murderous hound, loose on the moors at night, hunting people? Persecuting them until they died of exhaustion or ran straight into a bog?

What exactly had Bixby meant with his reference to animals that didn't bite?

Where was Raven? Why hadn't he waited for her?

The broken-shell path behind her seemed to creak with stealthy footfalls, and she tried to push herself into a trot again, ignoring her painful breathing. Was that a person up ahead?

"Lamb?" she cried out, half hoarse for lack of air.

But the shape didn't move in her direction. It stood motionless, rooted to the spot.

Drawing near, Merula discerned the immobile features of a female statue, a horn of plenty resting in the crook of a marble arm. An expert workman had crafted the grapes and peaches, the high forehead and delicate cheekbones, the folds of the garb that fell to her bare feet. But Merula was in no mood to admire any art at present. Pushing a hand to her stinging side again, she rounded the statue.

The path turned to the left, but straight up ahead sat a brick well with a brazier beside it. In the wavering light of the flames, Merula spied a collapsed form on the gravel beside the well. Raven had reached the figure and leaned down over it. He said something to a man who stood a few feet away. The man replied, gestured wildly, and hurried off.

Still clutching her hand to her side, Merula reached Raven and gasped, "Is she hurt? Is it serious?"

"She merely fainted after seeing something inside the well, her husband said. I asked him if there was a doctor at the party. He recalled being introduced to one earlier tonight. The village doctor from Cranley. He's fetching him now."

"*Inside* the well?" Merula picked up on the part of the tale that immediately grabbed her. "How can you even see anything inside it? It must be dark."

"I don't know." Raven had taken off his jacket and folded it, putting it underneath the woman's head. A diamond-studded comb in her hair caught the light of the brazier in little twinkles.

Raven muttered, "I hope her husband will hurry up and not just fetch that village doctor but also two footmen to help carry her back to the house. She can't just lie here. The ground is damp."

Only half listening, Merula was irresistibly drawn to the well. To the dark, open mouth of it and the idea that something scream-inducing was hiding inside.

She wasn't quite sure what she expected to see as she approached, her heart in her mouth, but she just had to look.

Her entire body was tight as she stood and leaned over to see inside. It should have been dark in there, but it wasn't. There was light inside the well, quivering and wavering, and on the dark surface of the water . . .

Merula gasped and drew back. She closed her eyes a moment, certain she couldn't have seen that. Her mind was playing tricks on her, just as it had upon their arrival at Oaks's house when that shadow had swooped down from between the gargoyles to unfold into a monstrously big bat.

"What is it?" Raven was beside her, leaning his hand on her shoulder. "What did you see?"

"Go and look. See if you see the same thing I did." Merula drew a deep breath to steady her heartbeat.

Raven went to the well and looked in. She saw the way his head jerked back a little and his arms tensed. He turned to her. "There's a light in the well, and it shines on some kind of . . . creature."

"Alive or dead?" Merula's voice trembled.

"I'm not sure. It seemed to move."

"Exactly. That poor woman must have wanted to look in to see if she could draw an echo. Then she spied that thing and . . . Imagine seeing it when you don't expect anything other than water."

Raven nodded. "I can understand why she screamed."

He seemed to steel himself before he looked in again. He craned his neck, then leaned both of his hands on the rough stone edge of the well.

"Careful," Merula warned him. "The stonework might be poor. You could fall in."

"I don't think so. This stonework is fine. Someone climbed into it to attach a torch to the wall. That is the light. I suspect that same someone of putting the animal inside. I don't think it's alive. The movement is caused by something it rests on." Raven spoke in concentration as he studied the interior of the well. "Something that bobs on water."

"What?" Merula came to stand beside him. "That means it's some kind of . . . contraption? Bixby did warn us about animals, but . . . Is this his idea of making a little joke? Scaring his guests? Look at that poor woman!"

"Indeed." With a worried expression, Raven turned and went back to the fallen form. He crouched beside her and felt her pulse. "Erratic," he called out. "Why is it taking that doctor so long?"

Merula looked inside the well again. Now that Raven had assured her the beast was dead and was some kind of thought-up scene, she dared take a better look at the creature. It was dark, hairy, and fierce-looking. She had never seen anything like it before, not mounted, not in pictures. What on earth was it?

Voices approached, and men rushed onto the scene—the husband, Bixby, another man, two footmen. Bixby spoke to someone he called Doctor, ordering him to examine the woman.

Raven said, "If she suffered anything at all from her collapse, you are to blame, Bixby. You and your tasteless joke."

"Joke?" Bixby seemed confused. "What do you mean, man?"

"That thing in the well. The dead animal you hid there, lit by torchlight so a curious guest who peeked in would get the scare of his life. Cheap, I say, and not the act of a serious scientist. Or a true gentleman."

Bixby flushed a deep red under this attack on all he stood for. "I have not hidden any dead animal in my well. What on earth are you talking about?"

He walked over to the well with large strides and looked in.

With a cry, he jumped back. "What is that? Who did that?"

"You claim to know nothing about it?" Raven sounded dubious. "You did not order one of your people to climb in and light it, hide the creature there?"

"No, certainly not! I deny any knowledge of it. How dare you accuse me in this manner! On my own land!"

"When we arrived, you did speak to us of animals that would not bite," Merula pointed out.

Bixby laughed, an insincere sound. "Yes, I have statues of animals in my park." He gestured around him. "Normally people walk here in the daytime and can see those animal statues from afar. Since we are now going to look at the Perseids in the dark, I thought it wise to remind people of the presence of the statues so they wouldn't bump into one in the dark and think it was something real. I wanted to prevent this." He pointed at the woman. "How is she, Doctor?"

"Coming to," the doctor said. "We can try and lift her between us and carry her back to the house, where I can better tend her."

The husband and the footmen lent a hand, and they carried off the unfortunate guest. Raven halted the doctor a moment. "Excuse me, but I heard you're the village doctor from Cranley. Did you happen to examine the body of the girl who was found strangled by the river?"

The doctor's florid, energetic face assumed an expression of suspicion. "Who wants to know?"

"I'm closely involved with the Royal Zoological Society in London. I want to know if there's any truth in the rumors that her injuries were caused by a sea monster. Did she have unusual marks on her neck?"

The doctor eyed him. "I reported my findings to the police."

"Come, come," Bixby said. "Lord Raven here is an influential man. Surely you can tell him something, Doctor?" He fixed the man with his eyes.

The doctor shuffled his feet uncomfortably under the scrutiny and sighed. "What I saw on her neck, I've never seen before. Not on a live person or on a dead body. And

I've seen quite a few dead bodies during my studies. I can't explain what killed her."

Raven nodded thoughtfully. "Do you happen to know Mr. Oaks?"

"Yes, by sight."

"Have you prescribed him some drops?"

"No. Is he ill?"

Raven made a dismissive hand gesture. "Drops to make him sleep better."

The doctor shook his head. "I never prescribed him anything. But my predecessor might have. The old village doctor died last year. Carriage accident, very nasty. Horse's harness broke, the animal pulled away, tore him right off the box. Fall smashed his skull. He was very beloved around here. Could have worked here for many more years. Sad story. Now if you will excuse me, I have a patient to tend to at the house." And with that, the doctor rushed off after the footmen carrying the unconscious woman.

Bixby remained, shifting his weight uncomfortably. "Why did you ask that doctor about drops? Do you think Oaks is taking medicines that make him delusional?"

Raven narrowed his eyes. "I said they were sleeping drops. Why would you think they'd make him delusional?"

Bixby shrugged. "It would perhaps account for his behavior and his mood swings." He glanced at the well again, his mouth tightening in distaste. "Who would do such a thing to me?"

Raven brushed off his jacket, which had been under the

unfortunate woman's head. "Your poster in the village was also torn up. You must have enemies."

"That thing"—Bixby spat—"is not indigenous. The villagers didn't find a dead animal in the woods and put it in my well to give me a scare. That is some . . . exotic thing. It must come from Oaks's estate."

Merula's mind raced back to the room with the specimens and the empty glass container she had seen there. What had the label said?

"Tasmanian devil," she pronounced slowly.

"Excuse me?" Bixby asked.

Raven looked at her with a surprised smile. "Yes, I wondered if it was that. How did you know? Have you ever seen one in a drawing?"

"No. Lamb noticed an empty glass container in Oaks's room with all the specimens kept in alcohol. The label read Tasmanian devil, along with a Latin name denoting that it is flesh eating. I wondered what it was, what it would look like."

"Well, you can see it down there." Raven turned to Bixby. "Did you take the Tasmanian devil from Oaks's estate?"

"Take it? Why on earth would I take it? I just told you I have no idea who put that thing in my well."

"Your people helped you prepare for the feast tonight," Merula said. "Who put the braziers everywhere?"

"The footmen. And some local people helped out."

"Aha. Who exactly?"

"My keeper will know that. I don't interfere with these . . ."

"Peasants?" Raven provided, smiling sweetly.

Bixby turned red again. "I leave the work to those who are hired for it. That is what they are paid for."

"So someone local might have set this up," Raven mused. "Put the torch inside the well to make sure there was light and then . . . I wonder how the beast stays afloat. Do you mind me climbing in there to have a closer look?"

Bixby studied him as if he were insane. "If you want to risk your clothes and limbs." He turned away. "I'm going back to my guests. We must not let this little incident spoil our evening."

As he walked away, Raven stared into the well. Merula came to stand beside him. "Do you think it's a good idea to go down there? Can't you better wait until the morning and have someone else do it for you?"

Raven glared at her. "I'm an active man. I can climb down a well. Whoever put the beast there managed."

"He might have been shorter than you are and not as broad in the shoulders. What if you get stuck somehow?"

Raven now seemed to want to try even more. "If you don't want to watch, then go back to the house as well." He was already in his shirtsleeves, so all he did was rub his hands a few times and then sit on the edge of the well to swing his legs across.

Merula looked at Lamb, who had watched everything with wide eyes. "Maybe we had better leave."

"You have no confidence in me at all," Raven declared bitterly. "Ah, the stench is terrible. I wonder if it's the beast or decaying leaves in the well itself."

Lamb grimaced at Merula. "Can we go? Please?"

Merula nodded. She wanted to talk to Lamb a moment, ask her about the man who had been kissing her.

Ben Webber, Raven had suggested, but surely that could not be true? Webber was said to have wanted to marry another only a short while ago.

They walked away together, Merula leaning over to Lamb confidentially. "So this man who asked you to come out with him, you must have known him somehow. You would not just go with a stranger into the dark. Where did you meet him?"

"You were there. He smiled at me then, and what a lovely smile it is. Wait until my mother hears about this. She always warns me that I should not look up, be satisfied with a man of my own station. But I want a better life. Imagine what it would be like working in a shop. You can see all the things that come in and try them first. Chocolates and beautiful things and lotions to make your face better."

Merula halted and looked at her. "So it was Benjamin Webber, the greengrocer's son."

"Isn't it wonderful?" Lamb enthused. "The moment I saw him, I took a liking to him. But I thought he would never notice me. And then I was in the hall waiting for you and he knocked on the window beside the front door and gestured for me to come out. I only meant to talk to him a minute, honestly."

Merula shook her head as they resumed walking. "You shouldn't go with a man you don't know. He could have hurt you."

"A nice man like him doesn't hurt women."

Merula bit her lip. They had been told that Benjamin Webber wanted to marry Fern, so what could his interest in Lamb really amount to? A convenient distraction, like Raven had supposed?

How hurt would Lamb be once she found out . . . ?

"I'm not too sure about him," Merula said carefully. "He could be smiling at any girl around. I would be sorry if your first kiss turns out to come from . . ."

Lamb giggled. "That wasn't my first kiss, Miss. I got my first kiss when I was just thirteen, behind Polly's boarding house. He was a young shipmate, only in London for a few days. He told me I was really pretty and gave me a ribbon to wear in my hair. The prettiest blue I had ever seen, with a silvery sparkle to it. I never told him I was just thirteen. He thought I was seventeen at the least. He promised me he'd come back, but he never did."

She sighed wistfully. "I was sad then. Looked out for him for months. But sailors can't be trusted. Polly says they have a woman waiting for them in every port. Benjamin, on the other hand . . . Isn't it odd I can just call him Benjamin? He also asked what my name was. I wish it had been something grand like . . . Theodosia. I don't like the sound of it, but it's a much better name than just Anne."

"Anne is a fine name. You don't have to make yourself different for him."

Lamb made a scoffing sound, as if Merula didn't under-stand any of such things.

And perhaps she didn't. She just knew that she'd like a man to appreciate her for what she was and not try to change her.

"And what else did he say?" Merula studied Lamb's profile.

"There wasn't much time to say anything. He took me into the rose garden, and then we kissed. I guess it was meant to be from the moment we first saw each other. I'll tell it to our children and grandchildren. The scent of the roses as he leaned over to me." She reached up and touched the rose on her costume. "I'll dry this and save it, forever. Imagine him telling me it can't compare to my beauty."

She smiled at Merula. "I would be sorry, Miss, to leave London and leave you. But it will be wonderful here. Mother can live over the shop."

Merula's mind raced to keep up with Lamb's unfolding plans. "Are you sure Webber's mother will like that? You do know she runs the shop and he's just her errand boy?"

Lamb looked hurt at the use of the word *errand boy*. "I don't know a thing about that. I do know he has a store and he told me that he's going to be important in town soon enough."

"Why would that be?"

Lamb shrugged and stuck out her chin defiantly. "I'm not going to tell any more if you think he's just an errand boy." She was silent for a few moments and then burst out, "It's easy for you to look down on him, as you were raised in a fine home and you even associate with lords and all. I'm just a girl from Rotherhithe who has to build herself a better life."

"Of course, Anne, and I'm sorry. I didn't mean to offend you. I honestly hope Mr. Webber likes you and will take an interest in you."

Saying it aloud, Merula realized it was a blatant lie. She didn't believe for one moment that Webber was sincere and she didn't even want him to be. She liked Lamb, and she wanted to keep her with her. Not lose her to some green-grocer in Dartmoor.

Footfalls came up from behind, and Raven overtook them. A weird chemical smell accompanied him. "I couldn't pull out the beast," he declared, "so the police will have to do that tomorrow."

"Police?" Merula echoed.

"Yes, if it's Oaks's Tasmanian devil, the creature was stolen from him. Oaks has to report the theft and ask them to find the culprit. That person has been inside his house. Perhaps we can also argue that that person is somehow responsible for the death of Oaks's maid Tillie. We have to do anything we can to divert suspicion from Oaks."

Merula nodded thoughtfully. "I see. And did you estab-lish how the beast was able to float on the water?"

"Yes, someone had cleverly built a sort of raft for it to rest on. Had propped it up and all. I daresay it was well thought out."

"So not an impromptu action of throwing a dead ani-mal in a well to give a well-bred lady a scare."

"No, cleverly done, I'd say. You must be wondering, as I am, who would do such a thing. It seems now that not only was Oaks targeted, but Bixby as well. Is there anything to unite them?"

"They are outsiders. They both came to live here but were not born in Dartmoor. Perhaps the local people want to drive them away? Bixby spoke in such mocking terms about the villagers associating the meteors with a saint's tears. He tramples what is sacred to them. That won't go down well. They must be ready to strike out at him, like they did by destroying his poster with a pitchfork."

"Yes, that would seem likely, but how does Tillie's murder fit in? Surely they would not kill one of their own girls to achieve their aim, would they?"

Merula had to agree with that. "Besides, if they dislike Bixby so much, why did they listen to him when he told them not to burn down Oaks's house? I had a feeling then that they were in awe of him, perhaps even afraid of him somehow. As soon as he appeared on the scene, their behavior changed."

"True. But the fact that they cower in his presence doesn't mean they wouldn't do something when he's not around. To spite him behind his back?"

"Possibly." Merula inhaled the scents of the garden as she tried to make sense of the latest addition to the series of strange events. "Bixby said locals helped to get the grounds ready for this party. Perhaps they only pretended they wanted to help and put the Tasmanian devil in the well to disturb the party and prevent another one from taking place here? But who could have brought them the Tasmanian devil? Who removed it from Oaks's house? The stable boy did mention he knew where Oaks kept his money chest. So he has been inside the house."

"Ben Webber as well. It also surprises me he was invited as a guest here."

"Isn't he grand enough to be invited?" Lamb asked in a querulous tone. She pouted. "I wager Mr. Bixby sees his talents."

"I wager Mr. Bixby thinks he can use the power struggle between the old elite and the new businessmen like Webber to his own advantage," Raven said. "I wonder who those men were you overheard on the landing. Most of his guests aren't locals. If those men weren't either, then they are outsiders who want Bixby to do something for them here."

"Who says it would be here?" Merula objected. "It could relate to transactions in London. Or Bixby's financial situation. Fern said she believed he had spent a lot of money on the house and might be in debt. She might have overheard rumors to that point at the inn."

"Rumors are not facts." Raven had slipped into his jacket again and tidied his appearance. Sniffing at his hands, he grimaced. "To see how it was floating, I had to touch it. I had better have refrained from that. I should go inside and see where I can wash up a bit."

"Please do." Merula kept her distance from him. "We still have some stargazing to do." As she said it, she looked up and saw a silver flash across the dark skies. "I think that was one."

"Why are they called Per-somethings?" Lamb asked.

"They are called Perseids because they come from the constellation Perseus." Raven held his hands away from him as if he couldn't bear the smell. "An astronomer discovered that, someone who studies the night skies and draws up plans of the constellations. Many places have planetariums these days where they have recreated the solar system on a smaller scale." He nodded to Merula. "We should go to one someday."

"What's a constellation?" Lamb asked.

"A group of stars." Raven halted and pointed up at the skies. "As you can see, the stars form patterns. These patterns all have names."

"Of course. But they aren't called Perseus or something weird," Lamb cut in confidently. "They're called the plow or the swan."

"They all have Latin names as well," Raven explained. "They were discovered ages ago, and then people called them by Latin names or by figures from Greek mythology. Perseus was a Greek hero."

Lamb smiled as she watched another shooting star. "Benjamin is my hero," she whispered. "We will be so happy here."

Raven shot Merula a startled look, but she shook her head quickly to indicate he should not speak. Lamb seemed offended at everything brought up against Ben Webber, and Merula didn't want to alienate her further.

It was painful enough already that Lamb had turned against her because of a few poetic words spoken over a rose Webber hadn't even bought for Lamb but had taken from another's garden. He reminded her of Galileo's chameleon, a creature with a wondrous ability to change his color to blend in with his surroundings.

The wind that blew upon her felt chill, and she was suddenly shivering again.

When Lamb had been missing, she had believed her to be in danger, and when they had found her again, she had believed her to be safe. But perhaps the danger wasn't gone. Perhaps, after tonight, it would be greater than it had been before.

CHAPTER 10

When they came home, there was a carriage standing in front of the house. The lanterns on both sides of the vehicle threw moving shadows on the gravel.

It wasn't like any normal carriage but had a door in the back with bars in it.

Merula grabbed Raven's arm. "The police! They must be here to arrest Oaks."

"How could they do that? He isn't well. They can't simply . . ."

As Raven spoke, the front door opened, and two constables came out dragging a man between them. He was shouting wildly.

A man in a suit followed, speaking with Bowsprit, who seemed to be protesting the course of events: ". . . might be worsening his condition," Merula could hear Bowsprit say.

Raven walked up quickly. "I am Lord Raven Royston from London. What on earth is happening here?"

"I don't care whether you are the queen's own envoy," the man in the suit barked. "I'm arresting this man for murder and other unexplained happenings along the coast. He should be behind bars where he can do no further harm."

"He was found this morning," Raven spat back in the same brusque, commanding tone, "unconscious, and we have tended him ever since. He has a case of brain fever or other illness and can't be moved. You can certainly not lock him up in some damp cell. He might catch pneumonia and die."

"He will die anyway." The man gestured at the constables, who had hesitated at Raven's approach. "Put him inside." To Raven, he added, "If he does die, it saves us the cost of a trial."

"And the effort of even building a case against Oaks?" Raven's expression was grim. "This is outrageous. What evidence do you have that this man is involved in the death of that local girl Tillie?"

The man in the suit didn't flinch. "She was his maid. He had been harassing her, and when she didn't want to give in to him and fled, he pursued her and killed her. You'd be surprised to learn how often things like that happen. Gentlemen and their maids . . ." His tone was mocking as he studied Raven's fine evening attire.

Raven ignored the sneer. "I thought the people claim there are strange markings on the victim's neck. Traces of some sea monster. She was also found beside the river, I heard, her back turned to the water as if she was fleeing something that came at her from the water. If a monster arose from the river and killed her, surely Mr. Oaks is not to blame for the death?"

The man laughed softly. "I don't believe in what these superstitious people say."

"So you are not a local man?"

"In fact, no, sir, I am from London as you are. Scotland Yard."

Raven hitched a brow. "Why would Scotland Yard have an interest in a girl's death in some isolated little town?"

"Strange things have been happening here. Damage has been done to influential names. I'm looking into all of it. Now if you will excuse me, I have a prisoner to transport and question once we've arrived."

"Oaks is in no condition to be questioned. I found drops in his bedroom that he might have been taking."

"Ah, he acted under the influence of some stimulant. I've witnessed my share of violence done in opium dens. What soothes one man can put another in a bad rage, my lord."

The inspector shook his head, his expression softening somewhat. "I'm sorry if he's your friend, but you will have heard of cases where men killed other men as the rage came upon them. Strangling a girl must be easy then. He might not even have a clear memory of it."

Merula swallowed. Their host had been found unconscious and had spoken incoherently once he was in bed. He had mentioned having seen something, a ship not having a chance. He had also cried out about something gruesome. Did fits come upon him in which he didn't know what he was doing?

"If he has no memory of it," Raven said, "then how will

you prove his involvement? You can only accuse him of a crime he cannot recall if you have witnesses who saw him do it. Or found traces of his presence near the body."

"Traces of his presence?" The inspector laughed. "How does this sound to you? We found hoofprints close to the victim's body. Someone drove his horse down the river-bank to the water. The tracks were clearly visible in the soft bank. The blacksmith in Cranley recognized the shoes as having been made for Oaks's horse. He should know, shouldn't he? It's his work. Like it is mine to take this pris-oner along. Now good night to you."

Tapping his hat, he walked to the carriage. The two constables had gone into the back with the prisoner, and the inspector climbed onto the box with the driver. He raised his whip, the horses jumped forward, and along they went, whisking the unfortunate owner of the house away from his possessions.

"I'm sorry, my lord," Bowsprit said, "that I was unable to prevent them from taking Mr. Oaks."

"You did all you can, I'm sure. Scotland Yard, well, well. I would never have guessed. There's more at stake here than just the murder. Mysterious happenings along the coast, he said. Does he mean the shipwrecks we heard about before? Would those be a matter for a London inspector?"

"I took the liberty, my lord," Bowsprit said, "to glance over some newspapers as I sat by Mr. Oaks's bed. I found records of no less than six shipwrecks in just three weeks' time. It struck me as quite a lot, as it's not the season for storms. I put the papers together for you to look at. They are in the bedroom. You might deduce something from the details provided in each instance. Now I must first go see to the horse and cart. The stable boy has already gone to bed."

"Yes, of course. Thank you." Raven directed Merula and Lamb inside. They heard Bowsprit talk to the horse and click his tongue to soothe it.

Lamb said she wanted to go to bed as well if Merula no longer needed her.

Suspecting her of wanting to dream of her newfound love, Merula said she could go. She herself followed Raven up to the bedroom, which seemed suddenly soulless now that Oaks had been dragged away.

The blanket had half fallen from the bed, and Merula put it back in place while Raven gathered the newspapers Bowsprit had put aside for him.

The turning of the pages sounded too loud in the empty room as he read. "Strange indeed. Why would so many ships get into trouble here, in front of this particular coast?"

"There might be rocks underneath the water. A treacherous undertow? A sudden change of wind? There seem to be places all over the world where sailors fear to go."

Raven *hmm*ed. "Perhaps. None of the ships were empty. They were all heavily laden and with valuable goods. I will study this closer. We must now first get some sleep." He looked at the deserted bed. "Poor Oaks. He's not a strong man, and then to be treated like a murder suspect . . ."

"I do hope he will make some sense when he's questioned. Else the inspector might believe he's really guilty.

The mention of the drops he might have taken seems only to have further prejudiced the inspector against him."

Raven nodded slowly. "Unfortunately, but it couldn't be helped. The drops should have reached Galileo by now, and as soon as he knows what they are, he will let me know. It might be something quite harmless."

He bundled the newspapers and held them to his chest, a pensive look in his eyes. "What was that," he slowly asked, "about Lamb and that fellow Webber? She cannot seriously believe he takes an interest in her."

"I think she does believe that. She seems to have the wrong idea of him altogether. Of his prospects and his position at the shop. She seems to think it is his already and it will be hers as well, as soon as they marry."

"Marry?" Raven echoed with a half laugh. "They've barely met. Why do women always immediately assume that one conversation means marriage?"

"This was more than a conversation," Merula said, remembering the entwined figures in the rose garden.

Raven watched her, the paper bundle clutched in front of him. "Have you ever had such an experience? Perhaps at a party as well, a few stolen moments?"

Merula flushed at the direct question. "I can assure you that Aunt Emma would never let me out of her sight. She has friends, too, who would report back to her the instant I was alone with a man. And I can also tell you I'm not interested at all in that sort of thing. I want to pursue my research."

Raven looked down with a frown, as if he was contemplating some problem. Then he muttered, "Yes, of course. Good night, then," and left the room.

Merula stood and wondered whether her declaration had been so fierce that he hadn't believed her. Perhaps she should have explained to him that her research gave her freedom that meant the world to her, while marriage seemed like it would only tie her down. That it was the last thing on her mind to commit herself to some man who would not appreciate her but only expect her to sit at home waiting for him while he was out to his clubs or his dinners.

Even worse, having her own household, she would be forced to entertain other ladies at tea and organize soirees with musical entertainment. Her soirees would be compared to those of others and would probably be found inferior, if only because her piano didn't come from the right piano builder. She could just shudder at the idea of the snobbish attitudes taken by her aunt's acquaintances and the constant struggle to pay for the latest fashions, while actually she cared so little for the trimming on a dress.

Her hands idly rearranged the blanket on the bed. Suddenly she felt something. Hard and square. She pulled it out. It was a small notebook. What was it doing in Oaks's bed?

It seemed to want to open in the middle, and when she let it, she spotted rows of figures that seemed to be part of some calculation. Some parts of it were repeated on the other page. Part of it had been erased again, with wild movements, as if Oaks had acted in anger or emotion. What could it mean?

She decided to give it to Raven to ask for his opinion and left the room quickly. She knocked at his bedroom door, but there was no reply. She listened for sounds indicating he was in there, but it was completely silent. Then she looked down the corridor. Had he gone to Oaks's sanctuary? To the room with the specimens preserved in alcohol?

For a moment Merula recalled the vicious Tasmanian devil staring up at her from the shadowy depths of the well, and she shivered. Then she steeled herself, and clutching the notebook as if it were a weapon, she walked down the corridor.

Boards creaked under her footfalls, and the wind outside pulled at the windows, rattling the panes. A draft seemed to whisper through the corridor, striking cold upon her sweaty face. The door into Oaks's specimens room was indeed half open.

She hesitated a moment, unsure, as if suddenly someone other than Raven could be in there to jump her and hurt her. Were they even certain they were in this house alone? Was there some way in, used by someone who wished to do Oaks harm?

But Oaks had been arrested; he was no longer here. Had the perpetrator's goal been achieved? Would the actions stop here? Or would they go on?

She heard sounds and, curiously, peeked in. The door on the other side of the room was open, and the sounds came from there. Out of the bathroom where the kraken hung on his stand.

Her stomach plummeted, and she wanted to turn away

and run. Her mind raced with images of the creature having come down off the stand, slithering across the tiles, leaving wet traces. His tentacles reaching out greedily for anything that came into his path. She could almost feel the soft wetness on her skin, the suckers spreading their poison.

But she didn't even know if they were poisonous. And dead animals could not move about.

Besides, if she didn't go and look now, she'd never know what was happening in there.

Merula put down the notebook on the floor. From the wall, she took a javelin that was hanging there, one of Oaks's many traveling souvenirs, and balanced it in one hand at shoulder height, as she had seen athletes do. It made a rather clumsy weapon for someone not accustomed to using it, but it was at hand, and Merula didn't want to face whoever or whatever was behind that half-open door completely unprotected. The javelin's pointed metal tip was sharp, gleaming in the dim light.

Holding her breath, she approached the open door, listening to the sounds inside.

The splash of water, a gurgle almost. Ben Webber had said that when the kraken moved about, it made the sound of splashing water. Raven had been on the verge of laughter at the idea, but if this wasn't the kraken, then what was it?

The blood thrummed in her ears, and her knees were wobbly. The javelin almost slipped from her sweaty palm and she had to rebalance it.

She couldn't dismiss the images of gigantic tentacles

coming to grab her and squeeze the breath out of her throat. Perhaps the creature didn't need poison. Perhaps it killed by pure strength alone.

If she screamed, would anyone hear her and come to her aid? Would there be time enough to save her?

But gripped by her fascination with the happenings in the room, she walked on anyway.

Kicking the door open wide, she jumped in, the weapon held high to strike at whatever might be threatening her.

Raven, on his knees in front of the kraken, half turned to her and yelled when he saw the javelin pointing straight at him.

Merula lowered the impromptu weapon with a sigh. She had never been so glad she didn't have to try something new.

"Are you mad?" Raven roared. "You could have hurt me with that thing. Or yourself."

"I heard strange noises. What are you doing?"

"Looking closer at the kraken."

"But what's that gurgle?"

"The bath. I removed the stopper to empty it. I want to know what's in it. The water is so dirty, I can't see to the bottom, and . . ."

He hadn't wanted to put his hands in without knowing what was in it. A wise precaution, probably.

Suddenly light with the nerves of the past tense moments, Merula put the javelin on the floor and came to stand next to him. "What about the kraken? What do you want to ascertain about it?"

"That it is dead," Raven said with a half-mocking grin. "I don't believe in spooky kraken haunting the land, but I'm not enough of a zoologist to be certain an animal can't look dead and still be alive. Some species can go without food for months, I heard. They go into a sort of dormant state."

"And?" Merula swallowed hard.

"It doesn't respond to any stimuli. What's more, one of its tentacles is missing."

"Missing? You mean it's gone?"

"Yes. Cut off with a sharp knife or other blade. It's a very clean cut. I can't ascertain when it was made, but I wonder if whoever took it is using it to strangle girls."

Merula suppressed a gasp. "Do you think it's possible? It seems so soft and pliable."

"Perhaps, but it would explain the strange markings. And someone has been inside this house to remove things, or else the Tasmanian devil would not have been in Bixby's well."

"True." Merula held Raven's gaze. "Who could have done that?"

"Bixby himself, for one. I don't like him, and I think he could be the killer. He encouraged the doctor to answer my questions about the markings on the victim's body. The doctor's confirmation that the markings were unlike anything he has ever seen of course supports the idea that a sea monster is at work here, exactly what Bixby needs to divert attention from himself. He could have put the Tasmanian devil in his own well, hoping it would be discovered during the Perseid watching so it would seem he's also under attack. A victim of strange events, like Oaks. How do you feel about Bixby?" Raven gave her a probing stare.

Merula shrugged. "I haven't had a chance to talk to him. How can I have any opinion about him? Most of all, why would he want to hurt Oaks? What would his motive be?"

Raven sighed as he rose to his feet. "I have no idea, really. But you overheard those men in the upstairs corridor saying that something should be done soon and that Bixby should have arranged for it already. That could be referring to Oaks. Implicating Oaks in murder."

Merula blinked. "But why? Who can they be, and why would they use Bixby to harm Oaks?"

Raven raised his hands and rubbed the palm of one hand with the index finger of the other. He opened his mouth to start into an explanation, then sighed and shook his head. "We can conjecture all night long, but chances are minimal that we'd hit on the right answer. We simply don't have enough information. We don't know who the men are who spoke in the corridor and what their connection to Bixby is. Or how Oaks can even fit in. We can't ask Oaks anymore. He's in the hands of the inspector, and that Scotland Yard man is not going to let us near him. He made it very clear he wants to close this case quickly."

"I did find something." Merula rushed out into the corridor to retrieve the notebook and gave it to Raven. He looked at the numbers with a frown. "Means as much to me as Professor Morehead's endless formulas."

"Hold on to it. It might prove important in the end. Is that bathtub empty already?"

Raven went over and looked inside. "Empty but for a ladle on the bottom."

"A ladle?"

"That's what it looks like."

Merula came to stand by his side. Indeed, on the bottom of the rusty bathtub, a metal object rested, spoonlike with a long handle. It could have come from the kitchens.

Merula turned her head to look at the kraken, then at the floor. "The first time we were in here, there were wet traces on the floor. Perhaps Oaks uses this ladle to spoon a liquid over the kraken? To keep it moist, as a measure to preserve it?"

"I'm not sure that would actually work." Raven cast a doubtful look at the kraken.

"I'm not saying it works, just that Oaks might believe that it does. The use of formaldehyde to conserve specimens is also quite new and not without risk, I heard from my uncle's secretary."

She frowned to recall what Whittaker had told her. "People working with it noticed their eyes and lungs became aggravated, I think. Andrew thought it was comparable to the smoke of burning wood irritating his throat when we went ice skating. They had braziers along the rink, which—"

"Andrew?" Raven interjected. "You were on familiar terms with your uncle's secretary? He even took you ice skating?"

"Julia and me. Aunt Emma considered him a fit chaperone. She knew that Andrew would never take liberties, as his job was at stake. I'm almost certain he was a bit enamored of Julia, but he of course realized that she has to marry a man of her own station or preferably above."

"Of course," Raven said cynically. "But to you no such rules apply."

Crudely put, but true, Merula supposed. As she was just a relative living with the family, the shine of Aunt Emma's title and Uncle Rupert's wealth did little to nothing for her marriage prospects. She would have to be happy if a middle-class merchant came along for her.

Aunt Emma had once even said a vicar might be acceptable, "as a last resort." It wasn't flattering for the vicar or for Merula herself, she had felt. Compared to that, Andrew Whittaker had been a much better choice. The time they had spent together when he had built the pupa cabinet for her butterflies, working from her design, had been quite pleasant.

Still, looking back on it now, Merula felt it had been silly to think shared interests or kindness extended could be anything like love. It had to be bigger than that, stronger, more inevitable, overpowering you even against your own better judgment.

An inexplicable bond that formed between people who weren't even looking for it. Who might never even admit that . . . they felt it?

"Zoologists will always look for ways to keep decay away from their collections," she said, rushing to return to the original topic of the conversation. "A friend of Uncle Rupert's was quite upset when his snow leopard began to fall apart before he had even brought it to England. He suspected one of the natives who had helped him hunt for it of meddling with it so it didn't preserve well. The snow leopard seems to be a character of local lore, sacred even. Much like the saint's tears Bixby mentioned to us tonight."

"Where there are people who believe something, there are also always people who want to keep those beliefs alive for their own gain. I wonder whether that could also be the case here." Raven's gaze wandered to the window with the bars and the darkness stretching behind it, across that lonely land of heather and tors with names referring to strange incidents that had supposedly taken place there.

As the excitement wore off, Merula felt tiredness creep through her body, an overwhelming sense of defeat. They didn't know much, not just about Oaks and the murder, but also about the mysterious man who had addressed her. She had wanted to find him, speak with him, but she had not seen him anywhere among the guests after that. It was as if he had vanished.

"You did see the man who spoke to me? When you came down the stairs? He was real?"

Raven stood in front of her and eyed her. "Yes, he was real. Why do you ask? Do you suddenly think you are a victim of delusions?" He held her gaze, forcing a wan smile. "We're not on a moving train, so it can't be that."

Merula returned the half smile. "No, but . . . I do desperately want to know more about my parents. Perhaps I . . . want it so badly that I'm imagining things. Everything has been so strange since we came here. The grim atmosphere, people's peculiar behavior, the . . ."

"Threats." Raven sighed. "I wanted to take you away from London so you could recuperate from the shock of Lady Sophia's murder and having to flee, hide from the police. I was also not sure if those involved in what they called the butterfly conspiracy would not come after you to take revenge for what you did to them. I wanted you to be away, be safe, have a good time. But now it seems we've only ended up in more deep waters."

"Waters." Merula stared ahead. "It's all connected to water. The wreckmaster and his men on the estuary beach doing something no one is allowed to see. Tillie getting strangled by some monster from the deep, her body found beside the river. The Tasmanian devil hidden in a well. Traces of Oaks's horse left in the soft riverbank. How can it all be connected?"

"Shipwrecks," Raven added. "Don't forget the sudden increase in shipwrecks. Yes, it's all connected to water. You're so right."

His tired expression lit in a smile. "I hate it that our quiet journey causes so much anxiety now, but I can't deny I immensely enjoy sleuthing with you."

Merula stared into his eyes, feeling the same sensation rush through her veins. Suddenly, despite the darkness outside, there came the joy and warmth of being with someone she trusted and with whom she'd be able to conquer any hurdle.

Raven held her gaze as if he wanted to say more, then he suddenly, almost impatiently, averted his eyes and collected the javelin off the floor. Its end clattered against the tiles. He said curtly, "To bed, then. It has been a long day. And we have an even longer one ahead of us tomorrow if we want to save Oaks from the peril he's in. It's obvious he can't save himself, as he's in no state to defend himself or prove his innocence. He has no friends here who will stand up for him, and the local people want to see him hang anyway, so they will tell that inspector from London anything he wants to hear. Imagine that blacksmith declaring that the hoofprints found near the river were undoubtedly made by Oaks's horse. How can he know? To my knowledge, horses' shoes look pretty much the same."

"The blacksmith is the victim's father. If he believes Oaks is to blame, he might have lied about the shoes just so Oaks would be arrested. The poor man already lost his wife, now his only daughter. He must be blinded by grief, desperate to see the guilty party hang. And Oaks is a wealthy man, so perhaps our blacksmith believed he would never get convicted unless he helped the police by providing solid evidence?"

Raven nodded. "Unfortunately, the police are often reluctant to go after someone with status and money, especially if there are other suspects to be had. We'll have to talk to the blacksmith first thing in the morning. He can also tell us more about what kind of girl his daughter was. The picture we might form of her can help us determine what she might have been caught up in. I cannot shake what Fern told us. Tillie's belief she would be rich. Can it be a coincidence that she died so soon after?"

He looked at the dark window again, shaking his head with a grim expression. "It would be a sad story indeed if her shortcut to riches turned out to be a shortcut straight to the grave."

CHAPTER 11

The next morning Merula awoke with a start, her mind full of screaming voices and animals that stared at her with malicious eyes. But it was quiet outside her bedroom window, except for the wind knocking gently upon the pane.

She dressed, lingering a moment as she put on her necklace carrying the pendant that connected her to Dartmoor. At least that was what she had always believed. The pendant formed an odd irregular shape with ragged ridges on the top, and it was engraved with the words HARCOMBE TOR. Merula had always taken it to be a memento of some kind, but as she stood there now, she wondered if the shape of it represented the actual tor it was named for. Was there such a place around here? Could she go there?

As she asked herself the question, she almost had to laugh. Dartmoor was full of tors, of standing stones and other landmarks. How would she ever search out this place?

And even if she could go there, what did she expect to find?

Some clue to the identity of her parents?

That might be found in a church archive, or in a grave-yard. But certainly not on a windswept hill, two decades after her parents had supposedly been there.

She dropped the pendant in place and finished dressing, half angry at herself for the hope she had had when coming here. It was irrational to believe she could find out something about the past. Aunt Emma had often warned her not to, as it would only make her unhappy.

Still, the unknown man had addressed her, saying he had recognized her name as she had been introduced to others. He had claimed she looked like her mother. But Merula didn't look at all like the woman in the photograph on her dressing table at home, the photograph of her alleged parents. Had Aunt Emma lied to her? Why?

Where had the mysterious man disappeared to? Where was he now? Could she find him, ask him about the past?

Coming out of her room, Merula saw Bowsprit carrying a tray with a coffeepot, cups, sandwiches, and boiled eggs to the library. She followed him quickly. Raven had said he wanted to go see the blacksmith, and perhaps, on their way over to the smithy, they could discuss a way to contact the man she wanted to talk to?

Raven stood at the large table in the library's center. He had cleared it of all that had been on it and was now putting books on it here and there, forming some sort of errant pattern. He waved Bowsprit and the breakfast tray to the desk, roaring that he needed space and quiet.

Bowsprit, feigning a hurt expression, deposited the tray on the desk and poured the coffee. Merula approached the table to see what Raven was doing.

On the right he had put several blue books and designated them *the sea*, creating an estuary and a river from more books. Other books formed the houses of Bixby and Oaks and *the village*—with Ben Webber's shop specifically flagged. A house outside the village was marked with a note reading *smithy*. Merula recalled that smithies were often required to stand apart from other houses, as the fire from the forge was a risk to thatch roofs and wooden sheds holding people's valuable livestock.

Raven followed her gaze and gestured. "I sent the stable boy to the blacksmith's with a message that he's wanted here. He must know Oaks was arrested last night, so I trust in his curiosity to come out here and see who asked for him to come. I want to talk to him away from what is familiar. To unbalance him and get some answers as to why he lied to the police about having recognized the hoofprints by the river as belonging to Oaks's horse specifically."

"If he believes Oaks is guilty, he might not be willing to come to this house. And do please be gentle with a man who has just suffered the shock of his daughter's violent death."

Merula felt uncomfortable with Raven's reference to wanting to "unbalance" the blacksmith. Not just because he was a grieving father, but also because he had influence in the village. It was upon *his* signal that the villagers had retreated after Bixby had warned them about the risks of burning down the house. If the blacksmith felt ill-treated, even accused of lying to the police, he might lead the villagers against them anew and this time succeed in doing serious harm.

Raven ignored her request and swept the table with the books and notes with both hands. "This is the scene of our murder. The environment in which it took place. This is also a stage for the key players." Raven pointed at the estuary. "That is the terrain of the wreckmaster. The place where he's in charge and can do almost anything he wants. We know he moves upriver as well and is friendly with tinners, millers, farmers, people who might be part of a smuggling route. He's old elite, so to speak: part of the traditionally influential people on the moors who create the income the villagers have relied on for centuries. Then we have the village where men like Ben Webber try to take control. He told us that, with the railway coming and tourists flocking in, there should be tearooms and souvenir shops. He wants to change not just the appearance of the village but also the way in which money is earned. That means power will shift from those who have traditionally controlled the money sources to new people, like Webber himself."

Raven pointed at other books he had placed in isolation. "And here are the houses of our host and Bixby, which are more or less islands, not just in the wild moorland, but also in the perception of the townspeople, as both Oaks and Bixby are outsiders. They do not fit in and are watched with suspicion."

Merula nodded. "Attacked, even, if Bixby's Perseid poster and the placement of the Tasmanian devil in the well are anything to go by. And where is the inn where Tillie worked before she came to serve Oaks?"

"I hadn't come to that yet. I think it should be . . ." Raven studied his scheme.

Bowsprit came up to him with a cup. "Your coffee, my lord. If I may?" He handed Raven the cup, took a book from a chair beside Raven, and placed it before the village, seen from the estuary. "The inn. And if I may make one further suggestion about your scene?"

Raven rolled his eyes at Merula, but he didn't protest.

Bowsprit walked to one of the long shelves and pointed at some tin soldiers that were standing there. "These could be your key players. You could place them at the various locations. They can also be moved about so you can determine who had access to places or who was familiar with whom."

"Give them to me." Raven accepted the tin soldiers and began to put them on the books. "The wreckmaster and his aide who tore your notebook apart." He threw Merula a quick look from under his lashes, indicating he hadn't yet forgotten her aversion to showing him what she had sketched.

"Here, Ben Webber and his mother. We should not forget about her. She seems to be a force in her own right."

"You don't think," Bowsprit said, "that a decent lady has anything to do with murder? If it had been Fern who had died, my lord, and the means had been poison, I would have agreed that it might have been Mrs. Webber. A drop of something in a cup of tea and the unwanted prospect for the beloved son is gone. But the victim was Tillie, not Fern. And strangulation? Out in the open? I can't see a respectable woman resorting to it. And the strange markings on the neck—how would she have made those?"

"The kraken is missing an arm," Merula said.

Raven walked around the table, as if he wanted to see his tableau from another angle. "Yes, but Ben Webber's mother never came to this house. How would she have laid hands on the arm?"

He threw his head back and stared up at the ceiling. "I don't think she came out at night and strangled that girl, no. But she might be the influence behind it all, the undertow, if you will. Place yourself in Ben Webber's position. He's ambitious, he wants to work hard and get on in life. He has a position to do so as he'll inherit his father's shop in due time. But his mother is watching him, and she can decide about the shop until he turns thirty. She can make life hard for him if she wants to. He likes girls."

Merula felt a moment's stab of sadness for Lamb.

Lamb. Where was she, anyway?

"Did Lamb help you with breakfast, Bowsprit?" she asked. "Is she still in the kitchen?"

"She's in the kitchen, but not cooking or cleaning. She's making a hat."

"A hat?" Merula echoed.

"Yes, she seems to think she needs a better hat and is adorning it with feathers she found."

"Found where?" Raven asked with a suspicious look. "I hope she hasn't been plucking them from Oaks's mounted specimens. Some of them are extremely valuable, but only if they're intact."

"Do you know where she got the feathers?" Merula asked Bowsprit.

The valet shook his head. "She wasn't very communicative about it," he said with a sour expression that suggested he had asked and Lamb had told him to his face it was none of his business.

Merula sighed. "Well, as long as she stays around the house and takes care, it's not too bad, I suppose."

"I assume"— Bowsprit pursed his lips—"that she's making the hat to go someplace and show it off to someone."

"Aha." Merula studied his face a moment, trying to determine whether he was just agitated by Lamb's furtive behavior or worried for her sake.

Raven waved both hands in the air. "Anyway, we were putting together this playing field. I was just saying that Ben Webber likes girls. He was involved with Fern, who worked at the inn. He went there regularly, I suppose. Tillie also worked there, but if we can believe the information given to Bowsprit when he was at the inn, she wasn't as popular as Fern."

Raven frowned. "I wonder if, after Fern snubbed him to his face, he transferred his interest to Tillie. He did seem to know a lot about what stories she told. Of silverware and such. How would he know about that unless he spoke with her, after she exchanged the inn for this house? Can we conclude that he also learned more about the zoological collection? That he knew, for instance, about a Tasmanian devil in it?"

"Would Tillie have gone near the specimens room?" Merula wondered.

Bowsprit made a so-so gesture with his hand. "Webber did emphasize that she liked to make herself important with stories. She might have looked in. Or she was put up to it. In my experience, people who like to tell tales can easily be challenged into doing something by implying they don't dare do it."

"An excellent point. And who would have put her up to it?"

Bowsprit shrugged. "Webber comes to mind. Perhaps Tillie believed she could prove to him she was more interesting than Fern by giving him information about the zoological collection."

"Question is," Raven interrupted, "why Webber would want to know about the collection at all. He is busy with the railway coming, tearooms and toby jugs, and somehow Tasmanian devils and two-headed calves don't really fit into that image. Now on with our little scene. Here!"

With a flourish, Raven put a soldier at Oaks's house. "Our friend Oaks. World traveler, collector of rare animals. An outsider and a man about whom strange gossip abounded."

"You have to place another soldier," Merula said, "for the stable boy. I talked to him and . . . I'm not quite sure what it was, but he seemed to be upset. About the dead girl and about Oaks."

Raven stared at her. "Wait. Wait! Oaks told me that the girl came on to him suddenly when he was coming back from a walk. That she kissed him and tried to coax him into marrying her. What if the stable boy saw that? As it happened out in the open, there's a chance of it."

"Especially if he fancied the girl and was following her around," Bowsprit added. "When he saw her kissing Oaks, he got angry, and later he went after her to kill her in such a way that Oaks would be blamed for it. Then he could punish them both."

Raven didn't seem completely convinced. "Tillie's sudden interest in Oaks never made much sense to me. Why would the stable boy be so mad about it he committed murder for it? Wouldn't he have realized that Oaks would turn her away and it would be an ideal chance for him to comfort her and endear himself to her? No, no, that doesn't fit at all."

He weighed the tin soldier representing the stable boy on his palm. "I think I will have to go out to the police station, to ask for more information. As they've arrested Oaks, they must have something solid against him. Once we know what it is, we can find a way to discredit that information and prove his innocence."

He tossed the tin soldier to Bowsprit, who caught it with one hand and turned away from the table briskly.

"I'll threaten the inspector a little with mention of lawyers and suits if he doesn't tell me what I want to know."

"He didn't look like a man you can intimidate," Merula said doubtfully. "And besides, you invited the blacksmith over. What if he arrives while you're not even here?"

"Then you can try a feminine touch on him. You didn't seem pleased with the way I proposed to handle it. Fine, try it as you see fit. Sympathize with him and his loss and try to build a mental picture of the murdered girl. We must all do our bit." Raven gulped down his coffee, picked up two sandwiches, and rushed to the door. "I'll tell you all later when I'm done." The door closed behind him with a thud.

Merula exhaled. "Brilliant. He leaves to let me deal with the blacksmith. I have no idea how I can face his grief and learn something new. Especially as Fern's story to us in the village church suggested that Tillie wanted to get rich to help her father. If he ever finds out about that, he might conclude that she died trying to help him. That it was somehow his fault. That would be terrible. He already lost his wife and daughter, everyone he cares for. He need not also be weighed down by the suggestion that Tillie took risks for his sake."

"His lordship's idea might not be a bad one," Bowsprit countered. "Assuming the blacksmith believes that Oaks is his daughter's killer, then his lordship's acquaintance with Oaks makes him a natural enemy of the blacksmith. You, however, have nothing to do with it. You were invited here for a pleasant holiday that turned into a terrible tragedy. You are truly shocked by this girl's death, so you need not simulate your feelings. You're not doing the blacksmith any harm." Bowsprit looked her over and frowned. "Before he arrives, you need to eat. You look terribly worn."

Merula flushed. "I did sleep, but I had nightmares about everything that happened. I kept dreaming of this deserted beach where in the distance fires burned. I was looking for someone, but the sand dragged me down, sucking me in, first to the ankles, then the knees, then the waist."

She shivered as the terrible feeling of being caught, trapped, enveloped her again, taking her breath away.

With a concerned look, Bowsprit handed her a cup of coffee. "Better drink something hot. And then after you speak with the blacksmith, we can go for a walk? Get some fresh air. See some places."

Merula clenched the cup. "Do you know this area? You've been telling us so much about it. Have you been here before with Raven?"

Bowsprit shook his head. "I haven't been here before with his lordship. But I have been here before as a lad. We played on the moors all day long. Climbed the tors and tried to find a smuggler's hide."

Merula held her breath a moment. "Do you know Harcombe Tor?"

"Yes. Its strange shape is visible from afar."

"Could you take me there?"

Bowsprit narrowed his eyes. "What do you want to do there? It's just an abandoned hill. There's nothing special to see."

"I want to see it and draw it. I'll get my notebook and pencils. We can also take Lamb. We must not . . . indulge her infatuation with Mr. Webber too much."

Bowsprit's brows drew together. "You do not approve of him?"

"I'm merely concerned about her attaching herself to a man in this place where we're staying for a little while. She'll have to come back to London with us, and what then?"

"Perhaps she won't be coming back to London with us."

Merula stared at Bowsprit. "Why do you say that? She

has just met this man. She has worked with my family for over a year. She knows me, us. Why . . . ?"

Bowsprit sighed. "Feelings change people. My captain always warned us when we came to port somewhere not to go with the local women. He said he had witnessed dozens of cases where the locals killed a sailor because they believed he had been too free with their women. Still, the men saw pretty faces and they were lonely, far away from home. I once barely managed to save a lad pursued by an angry mob who wanted to knife him. The experience changed him for a while until another pretty face came along. You cannot help it."

"But I can help it," Merula said firmly, "and Lamb is coming back to London with us. If she believes Webber cares for her, then he must write letters to her for a few months, a year at the least, and then if their feelings are still strong, we can see."

Bowsprit smiled. "You don't want to lose her. You value her."

"I don't want to lose her to a man who may not be worthy of her. Wait. What's that sound?"

Peering out the window, Merula saw a sturdy brown pony approaching the house, laboring under the weight of the blacksmith. Although he wasn't tall, his figure was stocky and his arms covered with muscle cords, probably from the work he earned his living with. "There's Tillie's father," she said to Bowsprit. "I'll go down to meet him,"

"Remember that he was in the crowd who came out here to burn this place down. You never know what he might be up to."

"People are different when they are in a mob. They get pulled along by feelings, without thinking about the consequences. Now that he's alone, I'm sure it's safe to speak with him."

She couldn't be sure at all, but she didn't want Bowsprit standing right beside her listening in as she tried to address the grief-stricken man. She still hadn't made up her mind about the best way to go about it.

Bowsprit followed her and hovered at the front door while she went outside.

The blacksmith jumped off his pony and looked at her with his deep-set, sad eyes. "Is Mr. Oaks around?"

Merula was taken aback by the suggestion that the blacksmith had expected Oaks to be here. And yet he had come anyway? "No, he's at the police station," she said, adding hesitantly, "I thought you knew he had been arrested last night."

"I knew, but when I got the note asking me to come here, I assumed he had been released already. Rich people can get away with anything. They just pay up."

"Mr. Oaks is still at the police station. I'm sure the case will be handled with great care. They even asked a Scotland Yard inspector to come over and lead the investigation."

"What good will that do us? My daughter won't come back."

"I'm very sorry about your daughter's death. I don't know Mr. Oaks well at all, but when we arrived here, he was very distraught about your daughter's disappearance. He seemed to be afraid for her sake."

"For his own, you mean." The blacksmith's eyes flickered. "He bothered her. Don't you think I know? She never wanted to say a bad word about him, but a father knows. First those lechers at the inn, then Mr. Oaks. A fine gentleman from the city, she called him, a real educated person."

He laughed softly and bitterly. "She was always one to believe the best of people. Softhearted, never saw any bad in anyone. She would have gone to meet her killer, never suspecting . . ."

He drew breath, clenching his hands. "She was a silly girl, and some say she deserved to die for being so silly, but . . ."

"Who says so?" Merula asked indignantly.

"Ben Webber, of course. He's telling everyone who wants to hear that my Tillie was too curious for her own good. That she pried among Mr. Oaks's animals and got herself killed."

"How does Ben Webber know that? Has Tillie ever shown the animals to him?"

The blacksmith shrugged. "He's too smooth for my liking. I told Tillie time and time again not to get too friendly with him. But she never could stand him liking Fern. She might have felt that the animals made her more interesting or something."

He studied Merula with his bleak eyes. "Is there a horse for me to tend here? Why did you send for me?"

"I wanted to tell you personally how sorry I am about your daughter's death. I only heard good things about her. How kind she was and how hard she worked, also to support you after her mother's death."

His jaw tightened. "I earn a good living tending to horses, making nails and tools. I didn't need her to support me. She had to save for her own household someday. She'd get married, have children." He wrung his hands. "All gone now. All gone."

Merula swallowed. "I'm very sorry about that."

"It can't be helped. That's what the doctor said when my wife was dying. I begged him, begged him, to stop the coughing and the blood that came from within, but he just said, 'It can't be helped.'"

"Some diseases can't be cured."

"He took all my money," the blacksmith hissed. "Every time, he had another draft she might try. Eat more eggs. Try poultry. Like we could afford that! But we worked hard, Tillie and me, so she would get better. Then she died anyway. Left us behind."

He took a deep breath.

"I'm sure that she didn't want to leave you," Merula said softly. She had assumed that in communities where living conditions were hard, illness and death were more readily accepted, but the man's grief was raw, bordering on anger, it seemed.

The blacksmith stared at the ground. He mumbled something to himself. Merula couldn't quite make it out, but it sounded vaguely like, "Yes, she did."

The pony pushed him in the back, as if to drag him from his sad mood. The blacksmith eyed her. "If there's no work for me to do here, I'll be leaving again."

"I'll recompense you for your time." Merula turned to

Bowsprit behind the door, gesturing at him to produce some money.

The blacksmith seemed to waver between refusing this offer out of pride or accepting some much-needed income.

Merula reached into the open door to accept some coins from Bowsprit, who knew it was better he stay out of sight. Turning to walk down the steps again, she saw the blacksmith had already mounted his pony. She rushed down to give him the money. His hand was trembling as he accepted it.

"Did Oaks's horse really have such distinctive shoes?" Merula asked, standing beside the pony's head. "You stated to the police you were certain that the tracks left on the riverbank beside the body were made by his horse and no other. How could you know?"

The man held her gaze, his weathered face working as if in indecision. "Your fine Scotland Yard detective can work that out for himself. And you can keep your blood money."

He threw the coins down on the ground in front of Merula's feet and turned his pony away from her. Its behind almost knocked into Merula, and she was just able to jump aside.

Bowsprit came rushing down the steps and asked if she was well. Glaring after the rider, he groused, "There was no need for him to be so rude to you."

"He didn't want to accept the money; he called it blood money." Merula trembled as the full force of the situation sank in. "He actually thinks I was offering him a reward to change his testimony about the hoofprints left by the river."

She raised a hand to her face. "If he starts saying that he was invited here and I tried to give him money, people may believe Oaks is really guilty and we are bribing people to get him acquitted."

She breathed deep. "It was stupid of me to bring up money at all. I only wanted to recompense him for his time and effort coming out here while there was nothing for him to do. Raven's idea that he should be away from what was familiar to him so he might open up . . ." She exhaled in a frustrated huff. "It didn't work. Raven and I should have gone to his smithy anyway."

"If you had, some might have argued you went there to put pressure on him to change his testimony." Bowsprit picked up the coins, rubbing them between his fingers to clean them of dirt. "In hindsight, it might have been better if we hadn't contacted him at all. It might give a wrong impression and harm Oaks's case."

Merula sighed. "Indeed. And I didn't even learn much useful about Tillie. Just confirmation of what we already knew, that she was a kindhearted and gullible girl. What I did find odd was the mention of Ben Webber claiming Tillie had been too curious for her own good because she had pried among Oaks's animals. How would Webber know that unless Tillie had told him? Does Webber think Tillie's prying upset the kraken and the monster came after her? Or is there something else she discovered? We assumed earlier that she might have discovered something that caused her death. We thought it might have happened at the inn, where she could have overheard something. But what if it happened here, in the house?"

She stared after the retreating figure of the blacksmith. "He was resentful about his wife's death. It was years ago, I understood from what others said, and still . . . he blames the doctor for not curing her. That must have been the old village doctor who was in practice here. The new doctor said that his predecessor was so beloved—well, apparently, not by all."

Bowsprit slipped the coins into his pocket with a grave expression. "If our blacksmith can carry a grudge like that, it doesn't bode well for Oaks. Even if the police do let him go, the blacksmith will still consider him guilty and might come after him. The old laws of an eye for an eye are very much alive here. The only way to truly clear Oaks's name, for now and the future, is to deliver the real killer and irrefutable evidence as to his or her guilt."

Merula nodded. "Let us hope Raven is making some progress at the police station. But before he's back, we have something else to do. I'll get my things now, and we can set out for Harcombe Tor."

★ ★ ★

The wind was strong across the moors, whirling around them, attacking them now from one side, then the other. Merula's hair, although pinned up and secured under her hat, was being gradually undone, strands pulling loose and sweeping back across her face.

Lamb, by her side, was not faring any better, at times holding on to her simple straw hat with both hands to prevent it from being torn away. The other hat, the one she had been working on, was at the house—fortunately, probably, as Merula doubted the newly attached feathers would be able to withstand this force of nature.

Bowsprit walked vigorously, his bare head in the wind, his arms waving by his sides. His normally florid expression was now even redder from exertion and the cold swept into his cheeks by the wind. He looked about him with a keen interest, as if recalling those childhood adventures he had mentioned to Merula and reliving those summers all over again.

Every now and then he halted to collect a bit of stone from the path and show it to Lamb, who responded without much enthusiasm. Even the heather he picked for her to dry and take home was ignored, forcing him to carry the bunch himself. The wind tore at it, but the flowers were too small to suffer damage.

"That is Harcombe Tor," Bowsprit called through the sizzle of air in Merula's ears. He pointed in the distance. "The locals call it the will in blood."

"What?" Merula queried, certain she had misheard it.

"The will in blood," Bowsprit repeated. "Legend tells of two men vying for a woman's love. They came to this tor for a duel. One of them cheated and turned before he had taken the obligatory paces. He shot the other in the back. But with his dying breath, the injured man managed to hit his cheating rival as well. Shot in the leg, the cheater couldn't get away, so he died a slow and painful death out here on the moors. In the time left to him, he wrote his last will on the tor's rocky face, with his own blood."

Lamb gasped. "Stop this terrible tale. I don't want to hear more."

"He wrote that the tor was the key to his fortune," Bowsprit continued to Merula. "Needless to say, people have flocked here ever since, digging and looking for the alleged riches. As far as I know, no one has been able to unearth anything."

He shrugged. "Just another tale to tell in winter at the log fire when the evenings are long."

"I think mine of the dead coachman thundering through London at night is much better," Lamb said with her nose in the wind.

The tor's distinctive shape seemed to lure them closer. Merula's heart beat fast at the idea that her parents had walked here, hand in hand, had admired the view, had listened to the cries of the birds. Had they been on a vacation here?

Had they eloped here to marry?

Was there a record of their marriage in the archives at the little church? Could she go there and ask the vicar for it?

But was her last name, Merriweather, really her father's name?

And if she had so little reliable information to provide, would the vicar be willing to help her? He might suppose there was some sort of scandal at the heart of the matter and prefer to avoid association with it.

Lamb gave a cry as one foot half sank into a puddle. Bowsprit reached out to help her upright again. "I hate this land!" Lamb vehemently declared. "It's so . . . wide and lonely and it's cold all the time. High summer, clear and sunny, it should be sweltering, but this ruddy wind is just making me shiver."

"Better think twice if you want to live here," Bowsprit said, with a quick look at her.

Lamb gaped at him. "Live here? Whoever put that into your head?"

Bowsprit shrugged. "I don't suppose you adorned that hat this morning to show it off to the larks. But this land is lonely and the word *ruddy* not appropriate for a young lady who's looking up."

"You're a horrible man." Lamb's cheeks were flaming now. "Nosy too. Worse than Heartwell at home."

Merula suppressed a grin. Heartwell was her family's butler and a man who longed to know every little thing there was to know. He listened at doors, held letters over lamps to try to read the contents through the envelope, peeked into ledgers whenever one was left open somewhere. As he had keys to all rooms and cupboards, he could go everywhere and just "happen to notice" something.

In his essence, he was a decent man, who kept a tight rein on the footmen, ensuring they were not dallying with the maids, and seeing to everyone having fair wages and their days off. He never struck out in anger, didn't drink, and didn't threaten to leave as soon as something didn't meet with his approval, as some butlers did to increase their value. His curiosity was his only vice.

"I daresay," Bowsprit retorted, looking hurt, "that I am not at all like Heartwell. I didn't have to spy to see you with the hat. The rest is mere deduction."

"Deduction?" Lamb scoffed. "The whole case with Lady Sophia went to your head. You think you're some kind of detective. But you're all wrong about me."

"Oh." Bowsprit kicked against a stone. "So you're not going to wear that hat while we are here?"

"Of course I'm going to wear it. That's why I changed it." Lamb huffed with indignation. "I can wear anything I want without having to ask your permission for it."

Merula decided it was time to intervene and pointed at the tor. "Do you also see people at the tor? Or am I mistaken?"

Bowsprit reached into his pocket and produced field glasses. He held them out to Merula. "You can have a closer look."

"How did you get those?" Lamb asked with wide eyes. "Did you take them from Mr. Oaks's drawer?"

"Like you took the feathers from his specimens?"

"Not at all. How dare you!" Lamb stamped her foot, dirt flying up at her dress. The mud attached itself to the fabric in several places, forming ugly brownish smudges.

Lamb cried out in frustration. "Now see what you've done!"

She leaned down to brush the dirt away, but Bowsprit grabbed her elbow. "It's wet. First let it dry up, and then you can easily brush it off with a soft brush. If you start rubbing at it now, the smudges will be lasting."

Lamb gave him a look as if she didn't believe a word he said, but still she didn't brush at the dirt again.

Merula took the field glasses and held them to her eyes. She had to adjust them a moment to focus on the tor. Then she saw it better. There were people there. Two women and a man. The man looked like . . .

Her breathing caught. He looked just like the man who had approached her the previous night.

"Hurry!" she exclaimed. "We must get over there as quickly as we can." She broke into a half trot.

Bowsprit came after her at once. "What is the matter?" His voice was tense, having lost the playfulness of his exchange with Lamb.

"That man is the one who spoke to me last night. He seems to have known my mother. He came to Harcombe Tor, so he must know that it's important somehow. I need to speak with him."

"No." Bowsprit caught her arm. "Let's not go farther."

"Why on earth not?"

"His lordship thinks it best if you do not get involved with the past."

Merula halted and gaped at Bowsprit. "His lordship thinks it best? Why? What does he know? My past is my past, and I can get involved with it when I want to. If you do not wish to accompany me, then turn back."

Pulling her arm free from his grasp, she raced on, ignoring his protests.

What did Raven think? That he was her brother or her guardian? That he could decide everything for her? He hadn't even seen the man properly last night. He had not been able to judge what kind of man he was. He had to suppose the man was somehow bad, else he wouldn't have wanted to keep her away from him, she conjectured. But he had no right. This meant the world to her. She would push on now.

She expected Bowsprit to overtake her and argue with her again, perhaps even try to stop her by force. He was a strong man and fiercely loyal to his master, taking his orders and not wanting to fail him. Surely Bowsprit wouldn't want to return to Raven and tell him he had let her go to the forbidden prospect anyway?

Why had Raven even supposed she would meet the man from last night again? Why had he discussed the matter with Bowsprit, who had not been present for the meteor gazing at Gorse Manor?

What was going on?

Merula lowered her speed, if only because she was panting and unable to continue as she had. Bowsprit wasn't coming, and when she looked back over her shoulder, she saw him and Lamb far behind, speaking with each other as if they were still bickering about the hat and Ben Webber.

Merula felt half glad, half disappointed that he was so easily distracted and not further attempting to persuade her to see things his way. But then, she was free now to do what she wanted.

Near the tor, the two women had wandered down a

path, looking at the ground as if they were searching for something. One of them carried a book in her hand. Were they studying the legend of the will in blood, interested in those riches Bowsprit had just mentioned?

The man stood leaning on a branch he had picked up to use as a walking cane. His hat with a small feather was shoved to the back of his head. He looked casual, a tourist enjoying the scenery.

Merula came upon him quickly, from behind, appearing by his side. He turned his head to her, a smile on his lips that died when he saw who she was. His eyes widened a moment, and his nostrils flared like those of a horse that discerns an adder on the path in front of him. "You!" he cried.

"Yes, it's me. I came to see the tor. But you are here as well. You must have known it was my mother's favorite place to come." Merula was just guessing here, but she had to open the conversation and quickly, before Bowsprit remembered his duties to Raven and came after her to drag her away.

"This wasn't a favorite place of hers." The man shook his head. "She never liked this wide open land. She loved the bustle of the city."

"Then why did she come here?"

"Because he was here; for what other reason?" The man held her gaze. "She would have followed him to the ends of the earth."

"My father?"

The man didn't respond. He studied her closely, his eyes

roaming her face with a half-sad expression. "You are very much like her."

"How can that be? I have a photograph of her at home, on my dressing table, and in that she doesn't look like me at all."

The man held her gaze a moment, as if he was coming to some sort of decision. Then he reached into his pocket and produced a leather wallet such as held valuable papers or bonds. He opened it and reached into the depths of it, pulling out something with a careful, almost tender touch.

It was half of a photograph. The woman in the image looked as if the sunlight was in her face: a mild frown across her eyes, her head held to the side a little. Her dress was simple but elegant with embroidery. Light in sharp contrast with her dark hair.

Merula gasped as she saw how alike were her own exuberant hair and strong features. The mouth, the chin . . .

She looked up at the man. "Why are you carrying this photograph?"

"It's a keepsake of happier days."

"It's but a half. Where is the other half? Who was in it?"

He returned the photograph to his wallet and put that in his pocket. "You look like your mother and you sound like your mother. Determined to have things her way. But it ended badly for her, and I do not wish for you to have that same experience."

He looked past her and called out to the women, "Careful, ladies, stay on the dirt path. The moors can be soggy."

Without looking at Merula, he continued, "They're interested in plants. I take them to places where they can see them. In the past, Cranley was hardly a tourist attraction, but with the railroad opening up this area, there are ever more city people eager to explore the moors. Some come for birds, others for old burial sites. There are rumors some graves hold great riches in gold or jewelry."

"The kistvaens?" Merula asked.

He narrowed his eyes. "You're here to look for them as well? You should be aware that it seems to have ended badly for those who have found such graves and appropriated something from them."

Merula frowned. The books in Oaks's room. Had he wanted to find such graves? Or had he discovered that others were after them?

And how might Tillie fit into all of it?

"Looking for sundew, though, should be quite harmless," the man observed. "It earns me some extra money on the side to make it through yet another summer."

"So you've been coming here for a longer time. Ever since you met my mother? Was she interested in plants as well? I love plants and animals. I also love to sketch and draw. Was she creative? Am I like her inside as well as out?"

The questions tumbled out in Merula's eagerness to learn something, anything.

But the man stared at the ground, poking into the sand with his cane.

Merula pressed, "If you say this is to earn money on the

side, it means looking for plants is not your real profession. What do you do, then? Where are you staying?"

He looked at her now and smiled. "No, no. I'm not telling you anything by which you might be able to find me again. It was my mistake to address you last night. You must forgive me for that."

She waited for a further explanation, but he didn't give one. His features were guarded, his mouth a tight line.

The chilly wind still breathed upon Merula, but inside of her a cold fear was much worse, fear that he would disappear again as he had the previous night, taking with him any answers he might have about her parents. She had never been this close to a discovery before. "You were at Mr. Bixby's party," she said quickly. "Are you a friend of his?"

"Hardly."

The bitterness in that one word couldn't be overlooked. Merula stepped closer to him, lowering her voice. "Is Mr. Bixby somehow a dangerous man? I heard of a murder here recently. A girl from Cranley who served as—"

She fell silent as he turned his eyes on her, glaring at her with strange fire. "Murder? What is that to you? Leave this place as soon as you can. It's not a happy place. It never was."

"The man I'm staying with is locked up for the murder. The victim was his servant girl, but I don't think he's guilty. We must help him to get free again."

"We?" the man queried.

"Lord Raven Royston and I. We've solved a murder

before. You may have read about it in the newspapers. The butterfly conspiracy?"

The man studied her with a frown. "Yes," he said slowly. "I remember now. Your mother had a sister who was married to a man called DeVeere. That's why I recognized the name when I read about this conspiracy. I couldn't remember, though, where I had heard it. It's all a long time ago."

Still he carried her mother's photograph in his wallet. The edges were worn, as if it had been handled many times over the years. "Do you know why my mother parted with me? Why she didn't keep me?"

"How could she keep you when she was dead?"

Merula stepped back. Despite having heard all her life that her parents were dead, she had never truly believed it. Because of the secrecy, she had guessed they were still alive and she was just not allowed to know about them. She had secretly imagined herself finding them someday, being reunited with them. Being able to ask them all her questions.

Or just fall into their arms.

And now this prospect was swept away from her, carried off on the violent wind that streaked the moor. Her mother was dead.

The man reached out and touched her arm, supported her. "I'm sorry," he said softly. "I thought you knew. But you stagger as if you're hearing this for the first time."

"It has been told to me. But I never wanted to believe it." She hung her head, her eyes full of tears. "I hoped that . . ." Her voice cracked.

"I'm sorry," the man repeated. "I cannot make it any better for you. She died."

"When?"

"Shortly after you were born."

"Did . . ." Merula's throat constricted, and she could barely speak. "Did she love me? Did she want to keep me? If she had not died . . ."

The man didn't reply. Merula looked up at him, caught the glimpse of compassion in his eyes. She pulled away from him, reeling with this new blow. "She didn't love me. She didn't want me. She wanted to get rid of me. Even if she had lived, she would have sent me to Aunt Emma to care for me."

He didn't deny it.

Tears ran down Merula's cheeks. She wanted to beat this man or beat the ground or run away screaming until the pressure on her chest grew less. Her mother had never wanted a child, had never cared for her, had just thought up a way to get rid of her and live her life again. To follow the man she had loved?

The man spoke through gritted teeth, "I'm sorry that I came over to you last night. I shouldn't have done that. I had drunk too much, and it made me sentimental. Longing for times which are over and done with. It's just that . . . you are so like her."

For a moment, there was a hunger in his face, a need for those old times he referred to, to bring them back to life. "I was selfish. I thought it couldn't hurt to speak with you and see her likeness in your features, the way in which you suddenly break into a smile or look pensive, like you want to understand the workings of the world. She wanted to understand them too. A party like the one last night would have been perfect to her mind. Stargazing, discussing the infinity of the universe."

The bitterness returned to his expression. "She was always walking with her head in the clouds. Ignoring the reality of life. She believed things had a way of working themselves out. Well, they did, but not the way she had hoped for."

He clenched the cane he held. "I shouldn't have approached you. Or, just now, I should have denied being the same man you talked to last night. In a way, I am a different man. My head was light then and my heart full of the colors she painted for me when she was still alive."

The breathless quality of his voice touched Merula deep inside, conjuring up images of wonderful artwork created by the mother she had never known. Her own sketches were tolerable, perhaps even showing a bit of talent. A link with the past?

The man said, "But this morning I am sober, and everything inside is gray and stone cold like this barren land." He gestured around him. "That is what is tangible and real. No fantasy induced by too much good port."

He focused on her with his flaming eyes. "There's no happiness in this encounter, Miss Merriweather. Either for you or me. I shouldn't have told you *anything*."

"On the contrary," Merula managed to say. "This is a good day for me. Now I will learn to embrace reality. To accept that my parents never cared for me and abandoned me. To accept even that Aunt Emma was right when she told me, over and over, not to ask questions and not to seek out the truth about the past. She said it wouldn't make me happy, and she was right."

Wistfully, she added, "She usually is."

Dear Aunt Emma, who always imagined that the worst would happen. Who wanted to wrap her daughter, Julia, and Merula in tissue paper to keep them away from all the hardship in the world. From even knowing about the darker sides of life.

Merula wasn't sure Aunt Emma's attitude was the best to take. But at least it came from a good heart.

The man didn't respond. He took deep breaths as he stood there quietly beside her.

She looked at his face through her tears. "You are angry," she concluded, half surprised. What had seemed bitterness at first, or regret, was now something different altogether. "You are so angry that if there was something here you could throw and break, you would do it."

As he kept silent, she continued, wiping at her tears impatiently, "Why are you angry? At me? My mother? Aunt Emma, perhaps, for telling me what she has? It has not been much."

"At myself." He smiled sadly at her. "I was the one who wrote the letter to your aunt."

"What letter? There was a letter?" Merula's head reeled. "Aunt Emma only ever told me I had been left with them and that the pendant . . ."

"The pendant?" His eyes flashed. "You saw the pendant? Of course. That brought you here. To this tor." He spat the last word as if it was utterly despicable. As if he carried a deep-seated hatred against this very place.

Merula reached up and produced the pendant from under her neckline.

He stared at it. "You are wearing it? Why?"

"Because it is all I have of her. Of them. A connection to them, to the past."

As Merula spoke and saw the confusion in his eyes and a new flash of anger, she continued, hesitantly, feeling her way into this new thought that had struck her. "But you just said to me that she didn't like this land. She didn't like this place, so why would she have made a pendant of the tor and worn it and . . . This was never hers."

The women who had been studying the ground came walking back, waving at the man.

"I have to leave," he said. "I must guide them further to look for the rare species they are after. I don't even know all of their Latin names, only the places where they are likely to grow. I'm not as educated as they are, perhaps not even as you are. I wager you know the Latin names of plants. If you solved this butterfly conspiracy . . . Were there not members of the Royal Zoological Society involved?"

"Tell me what the pendant means." Merula grasped his arm. "It refers to this tor. To this place. Did they meet here? Were they married here?" It seemed unlikely, as the tor didn't have special meaning for couples. It was the place of a duel between two men vying for a single woman who had both died. "Please tell me anything," she pleaded desperately. "Anything other than that . . ."

My mother never loved me. She never wanted me.

He shook his head. "I cannot change the past. I did then what I believed was right. I wanted you to be happy. I believed that a family life would be best for you, not this . . . wandering existence. Perhaps I was wrong. If so, forgive me."

He held her gaze a moment, and his smile became deeper, warmer. "Forgive me."

Then he pulled himself away and went to meet the women. The one with the book held it out to him, open at some page on which she wanted to point out something to him.

Merula stood, the tears cold on her cheeks under the wind that raced across the moors and hit into the tor as if trying to beat it to the ground. The man met the ladies, spoke with them about the book, then gestured at the tor as if explaining something. Was he a local guide, an expert on Dartmoor lore? But he had said this work was extra. To get him through another summer.

What had he meant about a wandering existence?

Why had he been angry, and why did he still carry the photograph of her mother in his pocket? After so many years . . .

"There we are." Bowsprit stood beside her. He wanted to say more, but his eyes narrowed as he studied her face, detected the tears on her cheeks. "His lordship was right," he said tightly. "This can only make you unhappy. I should have stopped you."

"No!" Merula almost struck at him. "You're all the same. Men trying to decide what is best for me. Because I am a girl, weak, fanciful, not able to fend for myself. But I do want to know the truth. Even if it hurts."

She pushed past him and walked back in the direction from which they had come. There was no point in going after the man, as he was with company and he wouldn't tell her any more anyway. He had been so emphatic about already having said too much. But she now knew a few things. These women were here to study plants. They had to be staying somewhere. At a hotel? With friends?

Whatever way, she would track them. She would track *him*.

Via Bixby, who had invited him to his party. That meant he knew who the man was.

She didn't care what others thought. What Raven thought. If he approved. If not, then so be it. She wanted to know more. Needed to know more.

If she didn't discover the full truth about her birth, her mother, father, the abandonment, she'd die inside.

She felt like it had started already.

CHAPTER 12

"I told you not to let her go after that man!" Raven's voice carried through the door into the corridor.

Merula stood motionless, fascinated by the intensity of the anger quivering in his words.

"I tried to stop her, my lord, but she would not listen. I could hardly have slung her over my shoulder and carried her off."

"That is exactly what I would have done, had I been there."

Merula clenched her hands, nails biting into her palms. Who did he think he was? Why could he decide about her?

"What did this man tell her?" Raven roared. "What did he want?"

"I have no idea, my lord. She walked off ahead of me and spoke with him while I was not there."

"And what good is that to me? I want to know what they spoke about. I told you to keep an eye on her. You didn't do what I asked."

Merula strode to the door and opened it. "What are you

going to do now?" she asked, jutting her chin up at Raven. "Dismiss Bowsprit? He's your valet, not mine. I told him I wanted to speak with this man, and he accepted my decision. He also accepted that he had no part in it and kept his distance. I value his discretion."

"But I do not. And like you said, he is *my* valet. He must obey my orders."

"If you wanted to know what I talked about with this man, you could have asked me."

"And would you have told me? No. You keep secrets from me. Even in a small matter like your notebook and your sketching. You act furtively, and you don't talk to me like you used to. You've changed, and I don't like it."

There was a sudden deep silence.

Bowsprit retreated to the door and slunk out. Raven didn't seem to notice. He stood in the room, his hands by his sides, clenching and opening again.

Merula stared at him. Raven, a man she called her friend, never to his face, of course, but in her mind. A friend because he had shown himself to be one in her time of need when she had been fleeing from the police. He need not have helped her, risked his already damaged reputation for her, but he had. Raven had come to natural history to regain respectability, not throw away the final shreds of it by involving himself with a murder charge. He had taken risks; he had not cared for the consequences.

And now he said he didn't know her anymore because she had changed. As if he was hurt by it.

She looked down. She sought the right words. But she didn't know what to say. Had she changed?

Raven said softly, "I'm sorry, Merula. I just . . ."

The silence lingered, uncomfortable, widening the divide between them.

Searching for something, anything, to say and change the topic, Merula tapped her foot on the floorboards. "Did you find out something worthwhile? From the inspector?"

"If by 'worthwhile' you mean 'good for Oaks's case,' then no. But if you mean 'interesting in the light of things,' then yes."

She began to pace. "Why so cryptic?"

"Straightforward, then." He sounded challenging. "The girl who died, the maid who served here—she was with child."

Merula halted abruptly and looked at Raven. She should probably be shocked at addressing such a topic, as it was hardly ever mentioned, even when a woman was married. There were all kinds of terms to cloak the condition and the eventual childbirth. And this girl hadn't been married, so that made it all even more improper to discuss.

Still, a murder case left no room for such sensitivities.

"With child?" she repeated. "By whom?"

"The police believe by Oaks."

"Oaks? But he said that he had never . . . that she just kissed him once when he came back from a walk and she accosted him to talk him into marrying her."

"Yes, he acted like it was all her idea. But the police

believe that Oaks harassed her, also because her father told them that. They believe that his tale of her having kissed him was made up to explain kisses that someone might have observed."

"The stable boy? Were we right in thinking he saw something? Did he report to her father?"

"The inspector didn't say that, but he firmly believes Oaks was pursuing Tillie and wanted favors of her, and now that she turns out to have been with child, they believe he forced himself on her and then killed her to cover up his acts. If she had told her father she was with child, the entire village would have come out to the house roaring for Oaks's head."

"But Oaks is an intelligent man." Merula tried to see the case coldly and the consequences that might ensue. "He could know that, if he killed her, the body would be examined closely and it would be known she was with child. That would not have helped him at all."

"The police argue that he didn't believe he would be accused. That the killing would be ascribed to the monster that also caused the recent shipwrecks. The inspector heard tales of it left and right. The villagers seem to strongly believe this monster exists."

"What does he think of these tales?"

"He laughs at them, telling me he knew Dartmoor was full of lore and that they could add this kraken to the tales of the hound and the white women on the moor."

Merula nodded and sat down on a chair. Putting her hands on the table before her, she stared at the markings left on her palms by her fingernails. Her head spun with the realization that her mother had never loved her, had wanted to part with her whether she lived or died and that it might have been better indeed never to have known this for sure.

Raven walked over to her. He came to stand behind her, but he didn't touch her. He seemed to want to speak but not know what to say. Then he continued walking up and down the room. "Tillie's condition does provide an important clue for us. If Oaks told us the truth and there was nothing between him and the girl, then who can be the father of the baby?"

Merula sat up and tapped the table. "More importantly, why would Tillie suddenly turn to Oaks, pressing him to marry her? She must have known she was with child and wanted to have a father for the baby. A marriage, shelter, a safe future for herself and the child. That suggests that the real father couldn't or wouldn't take care of her."

"Our stable boy?" Raven asked. "He's young and doesn't have money of his own. He lives here in the attic and he is—I'm sorry to say so, but it seems true—not very emotionally mature. Not a man who can take care of a family."

"Still, if he's the father and he saw Tillie trying to get Oaks to marry her and provide for her in a way that a stable boy never could, then he must have been angry and hurt. He could have killed her."

"Yes, but why lure her to the river and kill her there?"

"Perhaps they always met there and it was, to him, fitting to kill her there where their love had begun and she had spurned him."

"And the weapon used?" Raven stood with his feet planted apart, looking at her as if he was trying to fit everything into a single framework. "The inspector confirmed to me that the strangulation had not been done with bare hands but with some kind of implement or tool."

He scoffed. "As a man of reason, our dear inspector refuses to accept it might have been a tentacle, of course, so he calls it a tool, like a rope or a belt. But the traces didn't suggest that. There were round discolorations on the skin, a number of them over the length of her throat and in the neck under her hair. Like something was wrapped around it which had small round items on its surface. Not a smooth leather belt, not a rope . . ."

"The kraken's arm with its suckers? I still doubt it can be used to strangle someone. I doubt you could really cut off breathing with it. But the body was found near water." Merula pointed at his reconstruction of the area. "Have you learned anything more from the inspector?"

"Just that Oaks refused to say anything. It might be better that way, as he is not in a right state of mind to make much sense. I asked the inspector to have a specialist look at him, and he told me that he had already agreed to have one in."

"Agreed? With whom?" Merula sat up, suddenly alert. "Who suggested that a specialist should be brought in?"

"Bixby. He has been there . . ."

Merula jumped to her feet. "But that's all wrong! Remember how earlier Bixby wanted Oaks to see a specialist on mental abnormalities? He was the one who told us that Oaks was on the verge of a nervous breakdown, the morning he managed to disperse the angry mob. He claimed Oaks's wanderlust stemmed from childhood trauma. If Bixby suggests a specialist and the specialist that is called in is an acquaintance of his, there might be some kind of . . . ruse behind it. A way to incriminate Oaks even further."

"But why?" Raven didn't seem to follow her reasoning, or be convinced that Oaks was in danger. "What advantage would that give to Bixby?"

"I have no idea, but we mustn't lose another minute. We must go out to the police station before this specialist comes in and declares that Oaks is mad."

CHAPTER 13

Bowsprit drove them out to the station, and Lamb had said she also wanted to come to do some shopping in the village. Judging by the feathers on her hat, she knew exactly where she wanted to go. Bowsprit muttered that he'd keep an eye on her, so Raven and Merula went together to see the inspector.

Merula still felt anger as an undercurrent in her veins over Raven's interference with her past, her life, her decisions to make. But she had to focus on other matters now and help clear Oaks from the murder charge that hung over his head.

Inside the station, they heard raised voices. The inspector was standing looking into a corridor, out of which a high-pitched voice called, "I'm not seeing him. If he comes in, I'll attack him. I'll chew off his ear."

"The man is clearly raving," another voice, dark and booming, tried to cry over the protestations. "I need not even go in to examine him. I can proclaim him mentally unbalanced right away. I'll write up a declaration to that point. You can then move him to the nearest asylum. This is not a case for the police but for a psychiatrist."

"Inspector!" Raven went up to the Scotland Yard man, ignoring a constable who called that he couldn't just go in there.

The man turned to them. "You again!"

"Yes, I have to speak with you urgently."

The inspector shook his head. "I don't have time for you now. Don't you see the whole thing has come to a crisis? Your so-called reasonable friend is threatening to chew people's ears off."

Ignoring these protests, Merula passed Raven and said to the inspector, "This doctor you called in, is he a specialist you worked with before?"

The inspector took a deep breath, as if he wanted to tell her it was none of her business, when he seemed to change his mind. Perhaps he understood that without giving them some information, they might never leave?

"No." The inspector rubbed his hands. "Mr. Bixby knew him from a lecture he attended in London, on the effects of childhood trauma on the adult individual, and invited him to give us his assessment at short notice." He sounded as if they should be grateful to Mr. Bixby for this.

"And have you checked his credentials?" Merula asked. "Are you certain that he truly is a specialist?"

"What are you saying?" The inspector's eyes narrowed. "That he is not?"

"In zoology, every expert has his field. Some study birds, others mammals or spiders or butterflies. They know everything about their own species but not much about other species. Perhaps they have some general knowledge but not the detailed experience that an expert would have. I'm just asking if this man here is really fit to judge whether Oaks is mentally unbalanced or not."

The inspector studied her. "And why would he not be fit?"

"Earlier, before the murder of this girl took place, Bixby already tried to force Oaks into seeing a specialist on mental abnormalities."

"So he was already worried about him then, and justifiably so. He has now turned to killing girls. If the specialist had seen him earlier, all of this might have been prevented."

"Not necessarily. Bixby might have wanted Oaks proclaimed unstable for another reason."

"Such as?"

"I don't know that yet. But if you grant us some time . . ."

"He tried to bite me! He is insane!" A man came hurrying over to them, clutching a leather bag in his left hand. He held out his other hand to the inspector. Merula could see nothing special about it, certainly no bite marks or blood, but he cried as if he were severely injured. "I suggest you notify an asylum and have him brought there at once. A very serious affair. He needs to be kept in a straitjacket."

Raven pushed forward, his face pale with anger at this suggestion. "May I ask what your name is and how you happen to be so conveniently around here?"

"I was on vacation in Torquay. I love the sea air. And I

do not see"—the doctor scowled at Raven—"why I should answer inquiries from gentlemen or young ladies who have nothing to do with the police. Inspector . . ."

The inspector gestured at Raven and Merula. "If you will excuse me."

"No, we will not." Raven blocked the doctor's path. "I want to know who he is and if he is really qualified to do this. He wants to have my friend committed to an insane asylum."

With a sigh of frustration, the doctor produced letters from his pocket and handed them to Raven. "There."

Merula leaned over to see what was written on the envelopes. They were all addressed to a Dr. Twicklestone and came from research institutes all over the world: Vienna, Washington, Paris.

The inspector looked duly impressed with the long names and Latin mottoes worked into the emblems used on the envelopes. "May I invite you to come into my office, Doctor, where we will discuss this case? I'm honored, honored indeed, to work with you in this matter. Please . . ."

He gestured and proceeded the doctor into his office, simply leaving Merula and Raven behind.

Raven turned to her. "How convenient that he was carrying all of his correspondence from foreign institutes with him."

"While he's on vacation," Merula added.

Raven nodded. "Exactly. Like he knew he might need them to impress people with. And what do we know now? Merely that he has some letters on him that are addressed to a real doctor. But do we know he is this Dr. Twicklestone? No."

"We have to send Bowsprit back to get the stable boy. He saw a man with a very nice carriage coming for Oaks. Tillie took his card up to Oaks, but Oaks refused to see him. I asked the stable boy what the man's name was, but he didn't know, as Tillie hadn't been able to read the card."

"We can simply ask Oaks." Raven glanced to where the constable was sitting. "Can we speak with the prisoner? Through the door. We need not go in."

"I wouldn't advise it, as he's violent. You won't be giving him anything, will you?"

"Watch us and see for yourself." Raven strode into the corridor. "Oaks! It's me. Did you bite the good doctor?"

"No, of course not. The gall to turn up here! He came to my house earlier, asking for an interview. I refused to let him anywhere near me, even dropped his card in the fire. I was livid at Bixby, convinced he had sent the fellow to me. Bixby claimed, when I asked him about it, how this doctor had seen me when I visited Gorse Manor and that he had noticed there was something wrong with me, with my nervous system, and that I had to move to warmer climes. That he would recommend me to friends of his so I could find lodgings and that Bixby would take care of my house while I was away. That he was even willing to buy it so I would be rid of it and could settle anywhere in the world I would like. But I do not wish to leave Dartmoor and told him so. I've traveled quite enough; all I want now is peace and quiet to study my collection and read books. He insisted I was hazarding my health. Now he shows up here again and . . ."

"Thank you, we know enough," Raven said, and while Oaks banged the door and cried that Raven had to stay and help him and the bewildered constable asked if that was really all they wanted, he strode off.

Merula rushed after him, not understanding his brusque departure. "Oaks is desperate," she pleaded. "We should help him. Being locked up with false accusations of madness and threats of an asylum hanging over him has to be terrifying."

"We *are* helping him. What he just told us made me see the light. Bixby wants the house."

"What?" Merula stared at Raven.

"Bixby wants Oaks's house. He sent a doctor to give Oaks a scare about his health and suggest he move away from here. Bixby would then tend the house or even buy it off him. Bixby probably believed this would work because Oaks had traveled widely and might long to return to this adventurous life. When Oaks denied any such wishes, however, Bixby turned the villagers against Oaks, making them afraid of him and his animal collection. I wager he was the one telling them repeatedly that the creatures can escape from the jars they are kept in and roam the land. Then the murder happened . . . Now Oaks is in a cell and might be locked away forever. Then his property will be sold off, and Bixby can buy it. As the house is rumored to be full of murderous beasts, there won't be any other interested buyers, so he can probably also get it at a low price. It's brilliant."

"But does that mean Bixby murdered the girl Tillie? Isn't that going a bit far just to get your hands on a house?" Merula couldn't help the doubts echoing in her questions. She could follow Raven's reasoning, but the ultimate consequence seemed too far-fetched.

"That depends on what you want the house for. How much it's worth to you." Raven waved both of his hands in the air for emphasis. "We have to go back at once and search every nook and cranny to find out what Bixby is after."

★ ★ ★

Merula stood in the doorway and watched while Raven knocked on the walls of one of the upstairs guest rooms, dropped himself to his knees, and crawled across the floor, looking for hidden space underneath the floorboards. He disappeared half under the bed.

"Nothing," she could hear him exclaim in frustration. "Again, nothing."

A bang resounded, followed by a sharp cry of pain. He came out from under the bed and rubbed his head and neck. "This is not exactly working."

Merula suppressed a laugh at his disheveled figure. His clothes were full of dust and cobwebs and his hair was standing straight up. They had gone through every room from the cellars and pantry to the bedrooms on this top floor, searching for hidden passageways, space behind the walls, stashes of something. Raven had been certain the house had a secret that would deliver the key to Tillie's murder.

But they had found nothing special so far. Walls seemed

solid, cupboards held no secret doors, chimneys were empty but for an occasional bird's nest if the room wasn't used regularly and the animals had been able to get in and settle at leisure.

Now Raven stood dusting off his clothes and looking thoroughly chagrined that his brilliant idea had proved fruitless.

And with that, the chance to clear Oaks was gone.

Merula said softly, "Perhaps the value of the house is not in the house itself but in something inside it. Something Oaks brought with him from abroad."

Raven stared at her. Then he clapped his hands together. "Yes, of course. You're so right. Why didn't I think of this myself? If Oaks had left to recuperate abroad when Bixby first suggested it, he wouldn't have taken all of his belongings. Bixby could have gone through them at his convenience and remove things he wanted. That must be it. Up, up into the attic!"

He raced ahead of her, unlocked a door at the far end of the corridor, and went up creaking steps. They were so steep that Merula had to cling to anything she found for a hold to dare to go up.

It was dim there, light coming only through a few small windows in the roof. She had to keep her head down so as not to knock it on the rafters. "Why would it have to be up here? Oaks has countless travel souvenirs hanging on the walls. When Bixby visited him, Oaks might have taken him to the library, in which case Bixby would have walked right past them. The weapons, the hand-drawn maps, and the skulls. He might have recognized a valuable object among them."

Ignoring her suggestion, Raven began to look through boxes and open up suitcases, raising clouds of dust in the process.

Merula covered her nose and still had to sneeze constantly. She blinked as her eyes became irritated as well.

"We should have asked Oaks." Her voice had assumed a nasal tone, as if she had a terrible cold. "He knows what rooms Bixby has been in. What he might have seen or heard about. Oaks could have bragged about something he acquired on his travels. It could be anything. How will you even recognize it when you find it? It could be papers, a statue, a vase holding something. It could be as small as a precious coin or stamp. I heard that some stamps are so rare they bring in a fortune when sold at auction."

Raven didn't reply. He was fully focused on tearing the lid off a crate.

Reluctantly deciding she also had to make an effort, Merula pulled at a crate in the corner. "This is marked *Canada*, so it must be from the travels in which he found the kraken. Do you know if he caught it himself?"

"Oh, no, he bought it from someone there."

"Perhaps he bought other things from the same person. Shall I see if anything worthwhile is inside?"

As Raven *hmm*ed, all caught up in other boxes, Merula lifted the loose lid. It felt awkward going through someone else's things. Aunt Emma had taught her that it was improper even to entertain the wish to see what another kept, let alone pry among it.

Reluctantly, she pulled out some woolen clothes, a book about botany, a small framed painting of a seaside. Stacks of letters lay to the side, and a brass candelabra was half wrapped up in old rags.

Raven got up and grunted. Careful not to hit his head, he stretched and rolled his shoulders. "You're right." It sounded begrudging. "We have no idea what we're looking for. It could be anything. Bixby could be related to Oaks and think that if he dies, he will inherit everything. Or they could be old rivals. Or Oaks bought something Bixby also wanted, at an auction for instance, or via a mutual acquaintance, and it's somewhere in this house. It could be a valuable book, for all we know. The library is full of them."

"But if Bixby took the Tasmanian devil," Merula argued, "he had access to the house somehow. Why not look for what he wanted at that time and take it? Oaks never missed the Tasmanian devil. He might not have missed the other thing either."

"Unless that thing was in an inaccessible place." Raven pointed a finger at her. "That's it! It must be in Oaks's safe. Valuable papers, gems, perhaps. Or letters seeing to some matter. Oaks might know a secret about Bixby which Bixby is determined to keep hidden."

"Blackmail? Wouldn't Oaks have told us?"

"Oaks might not even realize what he knows or how hurtful it might be to Bixby. Bixby could be acting for another. Remember the men at Bixby's party saying Bixby should have taken care of it by now?"

Merula nodded, her heartbeat speeding up again as she recalled the uncomfortable moments she had spent half hidden behind the mounted bear, fearing discovery and humiliation. "Do you know how to open the safe?"

"No." Raven sighed, his shoulders slumping in dejection. "I thought we would come here and hit on something right away. A secret passageway leading to some underground hiding place of contraband. Smuggling, like Lamb suggested. This house the ideal hideout for the wreckmaster and his men."

"The wreckmaster? But what would Bixby have to do with them? Bixby tried to get Oaks away from here, not the wreckmaster. They can't all be tied up in some giant conspiracy."

"No, I suppose not." Raven lowered himself to perch on a crate. "I guess I have no idea what we are after, really."

He studied his hands and picked some dirt from between his fingers. "It could even be in the collection."

"The collection?" Merula repeated, not understanding.

"Yes. Oaks might own something valuable without knowing it. Or someone might have hidden something in a mounted animal or among the specimens in alcohol."

"That would mean we have to check them all." Merula recoiled in horror at the memory of the Tasmanian devil in the well. In the flickering torchlight, it had looked menacing, ready to jump at her and eat her alive.

Raven sighed. "We can't do that. It's not without danger, and besides, there is no time for it. I should have known better and done something else. Like send telegrams to find out more about this mysterious Dr. Twicklestone. I will go and do that right away. Galileo should also have sent some information about the drops I sent him to analyze."

He jumped up and made his way to the steps. "You stay here. Bowsprit and Lamb should be back any moment. I can't believe I let them keep the cart for this shopping Lamb wanted to do and hired one to get back out here in a rush. But I really believed we could find something significant. Well, I'll return the hired cart while I go send the telegrams. Then I might walk back here. I feel like I need the exercise."

"But it's miles away. You might not even make it before nightfall. Remember how hostile the villagers are. What if they come after you to attack you?" Merula shivered at the idea of Raven's injured body being left along a lonely moor road.

But Raven waved off her concern and disappeared, his careful footfalls creaking on the steep steps.

Merula stood and stared up through the narrow window at the cloud-swept skies. The search had engaged her for a while and made her believe they could find something, achieve something. But it had also exhausted her, and now she felt completely empty and aching for her bed. She wanted to fall into a deep dreamless sleep and wake up to be Merula again as she had been weeks ago.

Merula, who lived her life not knowing much about her past and fantasizing that she would one day meet her mother or her father or even both. She had imagined them somewhere, happy together, doing some grand work they had not been able to do with a baby. They had to have sacrificed her, the possibility of family life, for something great and worthy. A cause that justified it all. They would explain it to her, and then they would be together anyway. She was all grown up now; things were different.

Oh, yes, things were different indeed.

How incredibly, painfully different.

Her mother had simply not wanted her. And how had her father figured in all of it? She had no idea. She didn't even want to know anymore. Enough was enough.

Still, her mind was already working on a way to discover who the man was who carried her mother's photograph. How to get in touch with him again. He couldn't leave her with partial answers like this. She needed so much more.

With a sigh, she rose and went to the steps, taking her time to figure out how to descend them without falling and breaking something. At last, in the corridor where the bedrooms were, she heard Bowsprit's voice talking to Lamb. ". . . to be careful."

"And that is for me to decide." A door banged.

Merula appeared and smiled at the valet, who seemed to be bristling as he faced her, arms up as if to pounce at someone.

"How was your time in the village?" Merula asked.

"Is his lordship out?"

"Yes, to send some telegrams. Our search was fruitless, I'm afraid. If this house has some secret, it is not willing to show it to us just yet."

Merula walked to the library, where the scene was laid out on the table, and studied it, pacing around it slowly. She picked up a tin soldier that hadn't been placed yet and held it up. "Dr. Twicklestone. Should I put him with Bixby? They seem to be in a league. But why? I assume it won't do any good to go ask Bixby. If he has designs on this house, he won't just tell us."

"There must be deeds to this house," Bowsprit mused. "Maps of it or old documents about it. Have you looked at those?"

"No. I have no idea where they might be."

"Here?" Bowsprit went to the desk and sat down, rummaging through the contents of drawers. "I resent Lamb's remark that I am in any way like Heartwell, but this situation calls for unusual measures."

"I suppose that we can assume that with the threat of a straitjacket against him, Oaks gives us implicit permission to do anything we can to save him from it." Merula sat down and picked up a piece of paper to write. *Tillie with child. Father: stable boy? Oaks? Bixby?*

She added the last name without even thinking about it.

Staring at it, it seemed to make sense. The girl had believed Oaks would be interested in her. Why would she believe that unless she had already received attention from another older, well-to-do man?

But how had a country girl met a scientific mind like Bixby? At the inn? It didn't seem like the kind of establishment for his refined taste. Consider his house with the carefully constructed arboretum and garden, his interests in psychology and astronomy, his learned friends like the mathematician. What would he do with himself in an inn where the ale was watered down and the card games crooked?

But, on the other hand, Bixby had a strange command over the villagers, and how could he have accomplished that but by associating with them? Buying them ale, telling them stories, showing off how much a man of the world he was?

All the while turning them against Oaks to get his hands on the house and the secret it contained?

Tillie had worked at the inn serving before she had taken up her position with Oaks. It was not uncommon for men of repute to believe they could use serving girls if they wanted to. Bixby might be no different.

"When you were at the inn," she asked Bowsprit, who was going through all the papers he had unearthed from the desk's drawers, "did you hear anything about Bixby going there?"

"It seems he played cards there a few nights. He was good and won, emptying the pockets of the villagers."

Having just assumed that the card games there were crooked and that the locals who played were in charge of the win/loss division, Merula was surprised at Bowsprit's revelation. "So people owe Bixby money?"

"Yes, in particular the blacksmith. Seems he lost a hefty sum. The man who told me sounded both sorry for the chap and a bit resigned. Seems the man has been getting himself into trouble ever since his wife died."

"Tillie's father is in debt to Bixby?"

"Indeed."

"So Bixby might have enticed him to testify that the hoofprints found at the river could only have been made by Oaks's horse. In exchange for forgetting about the debts? Tillie's father believes Oaks is guilty, so he'd be more than willing to testify, believing it might get his daughter's murderer convicted."

"Here." Bowsprit held up a paper. "Deed of ownership of the house. Including a plan of the grounds that go with it."

"Can those be somehow valuable? Is there a mine on them? Old graves? Remember the books about kistvaens and grave robbery Oaks had in his bedroom."

"Yes, hmm." Bowsprit studied the plan. "Nothing I can see at first glance, but I doubt a mine would be marked. And besides, if Oaks had something valuable here that he was aware of, he would have mentioned it to us or to the police, you'd think. It has to be something he doesn't know about. A hidden treasure only Bixby realized was there."

"But if Bixby knows and nobody else does, how will we ever find out about it?"

Merula threw herself back against the chair and closed her eyes. She was weary to the bone. There seemed to be too many loose ends here and no rhyme or reason to them. In the case of Lady Sophia, the murder method had baffled them for a long time, but the suspects' motives had become clearer as they went along.

Here there were people involved in so many things—fishing, beachcombing for the cargo of wrecked ships, struggle for control of a village, people who clung to tradition and those who wanted progress. Outsiders coming to live in big houses and changing things. Planting trees and filling gardens and inviting city people to come gaze at the stars. Calling them Perseids after a hero from Greek mythology while the villagers believed them to be the tears of a revered saint.

She suddenly had a feeling someone was watching her and opened her eyes. Bowsprit had come to sit on the other side of the table. He looked her over with a frown, as if he was making up his mind about something. It was difficult to stand his probing gaze and not ask him what was wrong, but Merula didn't want to stop him from speaking his mind.

At last he said, "You feel strongly about this man you met on the moors."

"Not in any personal sense. He is a link to my past, my parents. He has answers I want. Need, even."

"Are you certain about that? His lordship seems to think you should not know."

"And how can he decide about that? Yes, he's my friend, but he doesn't . . . he can't . . ." Merula looked for the right words.

"Are you resisting because he is telling you what to do?"

It was a direct and honest question, and Merula blinked a moment to find the answer deep inside her. "No. This is not about him at all."

"But he's worried about you."

Merula's throat constricted for a moment. "He shouldn't be. I can take care of myself. I know what I am doing."

"Do you?" Bowsprit's eyes kept searching her expression. "After the man walked away with the ladies he was guiding, you were left crying."

"Yes, but . . . what he told me is the truth. If it's a hard truth to learn, then I must learn it nevertheless."

"How do you know it is even the truth?"

Merula blinked. "Excuse me?"

"How do you know that what he is telling you is the truth? He could be lying about everything."

"No. Of course not. He knew my mother. He even showed me . . ." Merula realized she was about to tell Bowsprit about the photograph and checked herself. She felt caught out, exposed almost, as if Bowsprit's kind questions had lured her close to an edge she had wanted to stay far away from. "Has Raven put you up to this? Has he asked you to speak with me while he is away and get things out of me?"

Bowsprit rose to his feet. "I serve a master and I listen to him. But I don't let myself be used to trick people."

The anger bristling from his posture was genuine enough.

"I'm sorry," Merula rushed to say. "Please sit down again. I'm just so very confused."

Bowsprit seated himself again with a sigh. "I know. And that is why I wanted to ask you. Raven doesn't know about this."

It was the first time Merula had heard Bowsprit call his master by his first name. As if suddenly formalities didn't matter and he was opening up his innermost feelings to her.

"He wouldn't approve, either," Bowsprit said. "But I follow my own path. I saw you with the man and I saw you crying. I don't want you to be hurt by this man. But if you are determined to learn about your past and this man knows things, this may be the only time you'll ever have to learn them."

"I know. That is exactly why I'm so confused and frustrated. I want Raven to understand and . . ." *Support me. Be there for me.*

"He is afraid, and I can't blame him. This man holds all the answers you want, or so he makes you believe. You're not just confused, you're desperate for what he can tell you. That is dangerous."

"I will not agree to anything . . . untoward." Merula flushed.

Bowsprit shook his head. "I'm not afraid of that. I'm afraid of what the truth will do to you. Or his version of the truth. It was a long time ago, and there will be no way of checking upon the things he might tell you. Do you really wish to know them?"

"Yes." Merula leaned on the table. "Why are you asking me all of these questions? Why does it matter so much to you? Apart from your allegiance to Raven, of course."

"Raven has nothing to do with this." Bowsprit rubbed his bare arm. "Of course he'll be mad when he finds out what I told you, but it's my decision to make. I just want to be certain that I'm not hurting you. Raven would not forgive me if something I said hurt you, and he would be right, too. I wouldn't forgive myself either."

Merula blinked a moment. She wanted to know what Bowsprit could reveal to her, but she couldn't lie to him by assuring him that what he was about to say would not hurt her. She had no idea herself.

If she said so, would he refuse to tell her?

But he had been so honest with her. She had to be honest with him.

"I can't be sure it won't hurt me."

"Because what the man told you has hurt you already." Bowsprit stood again. "We must not speak of it again."

"But we must. I can't bear to think this man knows things that I do not, and now it seems you know things and . . . Why am I not allowed to know? You're all claiming to protect me, but . . . ."

"*He* is claiming to protect you? He must be a better actor than I thought." Bowsprit stood and flexed his hands.

Merula watched him, pleading with him with her eyes.

He sighed and sat down again. "I know nothing about your parents or your past. How could I? When you were born, I was at sea, far away from here. But I do know something about this man whom you met."

"You know him? You've met him before?"

Bowsprit shook his head. "He was at the inn when I was there in my disguise to find out things about the murder and Oaks. He was with other men, and because I was unaware who knew things and who didn't, I asked the man I was talking to who those people at the corner table were. He told me they were traveling actors who come to these parts every summer."

Traveling actors! That fit with the wandering existence the man had mentioned to her.

Bowsprit continued, "They perform their plays out in village squares or at country houses if the owners want to hire them."

"Have they performed with Oaks? No, he's a hermit, so . . . Bixby then?"

"Indeed. I learned they've been coming here for many

years. In fact, some of them've been coming here for decades. This man I spoke with at the inn told me he watched their plays when he was just a boy."

"So it's possible that this man was here and met my mother that one summer when she was here as well."

"It's possible. But how much will he remember of it? It is long ago. He might make more of it and . . . I've seen deceit everywhere, all over the world. People claiming to have information about loved ones who went missing or who died. To get money, to get attention. It is sad, but it happens. I don't want you to become a victim of this."

"If he had wanted to abuse my interest for money, he would have asked for it already." Merula didn't want to say he could easily have done so in exchange for showing her her mother's photograph. She would have eagerly paid for that. "Where are these traveling actors staying?"

"There are some abandoned cottages that used to belong to shepherds who took their sheep out on the moors. They are now rented to the actors. They keep to themselves mostly, forming their own small community around those cottages."

Merula's mind raced. "Can you take me there? Now that Raven is not around?"

"I don't know if that is such a good idea." Bowsprit frowned at her. "An actor is used to playing a part. Why would he be honest with you? What is there for him to gain?"

"What is there for him to lose if he's honest? I think he really knew my mother. He . . . had her photograph with him."

"You're sure that it was your mother in the photograph?"

Merula wanted to open her mouth to affirm, then realized she didn't know for sure because she had never actually seen her mother. She had been gazing at that photo Aunt Emma had given her and stood on her dressing table at home. But who was the woman in that photograph?

"They've all lied to me." Her voice was bitter. "You ask me how I can trust this man, but my own family lied to me. Aunt Emma, Uncle Rupert. Julia I don't blame because she was a toddler when I came to live with them. She grew up with the stories Aunt Emma told us. But Aunt Emma herself and Uncle Rupert . . . There was also a letter they told me nothing about. They lied for all those years!"

"For a reason, I'm sure. They know something about your mother's elopement, the circumstances . . ."

"Why do you call it an elopement? She might have married, she might have . . ." Merula swallowed as she realized the man had told her that her mother was dead. She had not become happy. She had not found whatever she had wanted when she had gone away from home.

Bowsprit continued, "Your uncle discussed this journey with Raven, and he demanded that we take good care of you. I'm sure he never meant for you to get involved with people who come from your mother's past. Raven promised he would watch over you."

"I don't need watching over." Merula clenched her hands and winced as her nails touched the markings already embedded in her flesh. "I only want to use this opportunity. You just said yourself I might never have such a chance again. Nothing will happen to me, I'm sure. Just take me to where the actors live. Let me speak with this man one more time."

"He walked away from you. He didn't want to tell you any more." Bowsprit grimaced. "Either he is sincere, or it was a ruse to lure you to him. Neither of these is a pleasant prospect. He either wants to protect you against the truth, which means it is bad, or he is after something, like a predator after prey. How can I go with you and put you in peril?"

Merula considered this for a few moments. "I want to know. Raven once said to me that not knowing is the worst thing." They had talked about his mother's death, the questions surrounding it, the fear that had grown over the years that her drowning hadn't been an accident but rather that she had been driven to death by some malicious person.

Raven blamed himself that he hadn't been able to protect his mother, and that he hadn't looked into her death more closely when papers suggesting she had been murdered had come into his hands upon his eighteenth birthday. The weight of that guilt pressed heavily upon his life, darkening his future. "I'm sure that if he had a chance to find out about . . . things from his past he wants to know, he would do it. No matter what the risk."

Bowsprit thought about this. He threw his head back and stared up at the ceiling. The silence seemed to grow heavier as it stretched before them. Then he looked at her again. "I'll do it. I'll take you. But we'll tell Raven about it when we are back. You need not tell him what you learned if you like. But we'll tell him that we went there. I don't want to keep secrets from him."

Bowsprit hesitated and then added, "You have the advantage of me, Miss Merriweather. You know things about Raven that he never told me. Apparently he puts much faith in you. You must not damage that faith. You understand?"

Merula's eyes pricked with tears unshed. Bowsprit had every reason to be mad at her because she had become Raven's confidant about matters he himself knew nothing about. He had every reason to be mad at Raven for treating him the way he had, yelling at him for having allowed Merula to meet that man at the tor.

Still Bowsprit was loyal, to both of them.

She was very lucky indeed to know such people. To be able to rely on them.

CHAPTER 14

When Bowsprit had mentioned abandoned shepherds' cottages, Merula had imagined low gray stone buildings with a thatch roof and mud all around them. Not these cheery little homes with slate roofs and wooden benches in front on which women sat sewing colorful costumes and doing each other's makeup.

An elderly man played on a violin, a strangely haunting melody that seemed to mix with the wind whispering across the moor.

There was a table with glasses of wine, cheeses, and cold cuts, and a cute little spaniel lounging underneath in the tall grass and weeds, waiting for a bite to come his way.

Two men in costumes were fencing with each other, the steel of their épées glinting in the light of the sun high above. When one of them attacked and stabbed the other, Merula gasped, raising a hand to her mouth, expecting to see blood stain the man's shirt. But the épée's point had slid back into the handle and the victim wasn't hurt at all.

"A stage prop," Bowsprit explained with disgust in his voice. "Nothing real."

She glanced at him. "Do you not like the stage? Acting? I think it's such an exciting world. I'd like to know more about it." Had her mother been to the plays? Had she met the actors and then struck up a friendship of sorts with the man who still carried her photograph?

Bowsprit shrugged. "It's all a game. Deception in their masks and the trapdoors they use to whisk players away from the stage or have them appear out of nowhere. Nothing that you see is real."

The women who sat sewing looked at them with sharp interest, and a man with a shiny high hat came over and made a mock bow. "Welcome to the Moorland cottages, our humble abode for the summer. How may we help you? Are you perhaps looking for a night's entertainment? We perform several plays, from the lofty Shakespeare to something more . . . may I say, risqué?"

He grinned mischievously. "In present company I will not mention details, but gentlemen will very much appreciate the novelty and wit."

"We're looking for someone," Bowsprit said quickly. "I saw him recently at the inn. He mentioned the name of a communal acquaintance, and as we apparently have friends in common, I thought I'd look him up to talk some more. Unfortunately, I didn't ask for his name, but I do know he lodges here."

"That is unfortunate indeed." Distrust sparkled in the

man's eyes. "We are a large party here. I can't call them out one by one to present them to you so you can see if your drinking mate is among them. But thank you for coming by, and if you'd care for a glass of wine, you're welcome to help yourself to it."

Brusquely, he turned away to go.

Bowsprit said, "There has been a murder in this region. Not just any murder—a man getting stabbed after a loss in a card game, or a wayside robbery gone wrong—but a deliberate gruesome matter. A girl strangled when she was alone by the river."

The man froze. Without turning to them, he asked, "And?"

Bowsprit leaned casually on one leg. "Well, you know how it is when people in small towns start talking. They blame outsiders for all of their problems."

The man turned back to them, his eyes now hostile. "Especially when someone points them in that direction. Is that what you mean?"

Bowsprit didn't deny or confirm.

The man narrowed his eyes. "You must have urgent business with the man you seek."

Bowsprit smiled. "Let us just say he owes a debt."

"I see. That can be urgent indeed. I suggest you look around and find him for yourself. I'm no debt collector. And I want no trouble either. We're hardworking people who earn an honest living with our performances."

"I'm sure of that." Bowsprit gestured for Merula to

follow him past the table with the playful dog and the fencing man to where a large barn was. Voices resounded inside.

Merula whispered to Bowsprit, "Why did you have to threaten him? I don't want to alienate these people."

"Because he wasn't going to help us. Like the villagers, these actors form a closed group. They've been together for many years. They're like family. They don't betray one another."

They came to the open doors of the barn. Inside, two men stood on a makeshift stage of wood and hay bales, and a woman was just reciting her lines, raising her hands to the ceiling as she wondered why on earth fate had sent two men her way, both of whom she loved.

A fourth was watching their performance, his arms crossed over his chest. Merula's heart skipped a beat when she recognized the man she had spoken with earlier at Harcombe Tor.

"No, no," he called out, stamping his foot. "You're making it all sound far too trivial. You need to use your facial expression more. Like this."

He came up to the actress and raised his own arms up, twisting his face into a look of utter despair. "By the time we get to this part of the performance, most spectators will have drunk so much they're barely following along. Exaggeration is the way to go, my dear."

He gave her a playful pat on the back and then turned away, suddenly spotting Merula and Bowsprit. He froze a moment, his eyes betraying a flash of anger. Then he came up to them with a smile. "Welcome, welcome. You want to hire us? I'll step outside for a moment to discuss the terms."

"Especially the money," one of the men shouted after him. Roaring laughter accompanied their exit.

Outside the man drew them behind the barn, out of sight of the women sewing and the table with the dog. He walked fast, muttering to himself. Then a safe distance away, he stopped and hissed, "What on earth do you think you're doing? Do you want the others to recognize you as well as Blanche's daughter? You should never have come here."

"Do you care so much for Miss Merriweather?" Bowsprit asked. "Or for your own hide? I mentioned the murder of a local girl to your leader, and he about fainted away."

"Murder?" the other breathed. "What has that got to do with . . . ?"

Bowsprit planted his feet firmly apart. "Nothing. For the moment."

"Is that a threat?"

"I'm not sure. Do I need one?"

The man exhaled. Then he half laughed. "You're a most chivalrous gentleman. But you're barking up the wrong tree. I've done Miss Merriweather no harm." There was a hint of amusement in his pronunciation of the name.

Merula said, "Why do you find my name amusing?"

"Because it was made up, of course. For our plays, the ones we wrote ourselves, we always made up names. Blanche laughed at our more daring creations. She always used to say, why not choose something straightforward and happy like Merriweather?"

"But my aunt and uncle didn't know that, did they? How can they have . . . ?" Merula stared at him. "Did my mother name me?"

"To her dying breath, she believed that the man she had given up everything for would come and make everything right. She had not registered your birth yet because she wanted you to have his name. But I knew he would never agree to that. Besides, it wouldn't have been a good thing. So when she died, I registered you. I chose Merriweather, as she might have liked it."

"And Merula?"

"That was her choice. She loved birds. She could sit outside and listen endlessly to their singing." His expression was soft and his eyes had a faraway look, as if he saw Blanche sitting and listening to her feathered friends.

"And what about the pendant?" Merula touched the place where it rested under her clothes.

"I don't know where or how she got it. But she clutched it in her hand when she died. She whispered that he would keep his promise to her. But he never did."

"So it was a gift from my father? Did you know him? Was he an actor too? Was he here with this group?"

The man shook his head. "Merula . . ." His voice shivered a moment on her name. "You ask too many questions. It has been twenty years. It's over and done with."

"Not for me. I've never known anything. I've been fobbed off with a photo that is not of my parents, with lies about them having been married. They never were, were they?"

He said nothing.

Merula's voice rose. "Were they? Tell me!"

"What is the use of it?" The man grabbed her arm.

Bowsprit seemed to want to come between them but hesitated as the man spoke pleadingly. "Leave it be. It was my fault for coming up to you at Gorse Manor. For a brief moment I thought it couldn't hurt to speak with you and ascertain that you were happy like I had hoped you would be when I sent you to live with your aunt and uncle. I'm a sentimental old man. But I meant you no harm. Go away from here, cherish that other photograph and whatever your aunt and uncle told you. They love you, you can believe that."

"But what they told me were lies. I suspected that already and now I know for certain. I can't go back to believing what they said. I need to know the truth. Whatever it may be."

The man sighed. "The truth?" He sounded wistful. "What is the truth? You should have asked Blanche's friends at the time, the girls she confided in, the ones she whispered to when they stood around the campfire and toasted each other with the wine."

Merula stared at him. "She was with the actors? Part of your group?" Had Aunt Emma felt ashamed to admit that her sister had run off to be an actress? "Was my father an actor, then? Did she follow him? Or was it her own idea, and did they meet out here?"

"He brought her to us and we took her in. She needed a new family, having abandoned the old." His lips tightened. "How she needed family."

"Did she miss her parents and her sister?"

"She pretended not to. She wanted to show him a happy face. But he was away for days on end, and she pined for him. She only lived when he was around. Like a flower opens up to the sunshine. I once told her she had to leave, go back home. But she just scoffed at me, blamed me for having said it. She avoided me from that day forward. Nobody took much notice of me back then. I was just a stagehand. And a fool."

Merula studied his features. Was he sincere? Or playing a part like Bowsprit had warned her? Was he simply exaggerating like he had just told the actors to do?

"Every summer we've come back to this region. And every summer I've asked myself if it could have been different. If she could have survived. If we could have had a happy ending. But it could not have. I know that. And you must believe it as well. She loved a man so blindly and devotedly that she gave up everything for him. The safety of her home, the prospects she had. She threw it all away with a smile, for love. It sounds so grand, but in the end it was all but grand when she died, alone."

Merula clenched her jaws, her heart breaking for this life-hungry, wide-eyed girl who had grabbed for happiness and lost it all. Had she regretted it on her deathbed? Had she blamed the man who hadn't even come to be with her?

She managed to say through gritted teeth, "And what about my father? Where was he when she died?"

The man looked past her. "He is dead. As he should be. He deserved no better."

"So both my parents are dead. I really am an orphan."

Putting it into words, Merula felt like the world grew wider around her, expanding into an enormous open space without cottages and music and laughing people and sweet little dogs, a space in which she was all alone. No parents, no siblings, no past, no future in which her mother would hug her on her wedding day and her father would give her away. Nothing.

"I'm sorry I can tell you no better news." The man smiled at her wearily. "But in a way, I'm glad you came here and forced me to speak with you and clear things between us. I think you've turned into a lovely young woman. Someone your mother would have been very proud of."

It seemed poor consolation, and Merula resisted the urge to hug herself. She vaguely remembered thanking him and walking away with Bowsprit beside her. The fencing men they passed, the violin player, it was all a blur. She had waited for this chance for so long, believing she could learn something better about her past than the half-truths she had grown up with, and now the moment had come and gone and left her empty.

Heartbroken.

★　★　★

"Merula!" Raven rushed into the room, halting beside her chair, looking at her closely. She felt his scrutiny but didn't look up. She just wanted to sit like this forever, all marble inside and cold.

Raven crouched down. He caught her hands in his and held them tightly. "Bowsprit told me where you've been. I told you not to do it and . . ."

He fell silent. Even without looking at him, Merula could sense the emotions rushing through him. Anger, disappointment . . .

Clutching her hands, Raven muttered, "Why can't you ever listen? I knew no good would come of it. Just look at you now. Oh, never mind. This will never do. Come here."

He let go of her hands, wrapped his arms around her, and pulled her to him. Her head fell to his shoulder, and her cheek touched the warm skin of his neck.

Raven patted her back, saying things that she couldn't even understand but were soothing, like the rain against the window when you're curled up in front of the fire and everything is at peace within.

Then he released her and placed her back in the pillows, shaking his head at her. The sadness in his eyes struck her like a dagger to the heart. He wasn't angry or disappointed like she had suspected. He was . . . hurt. Because she was?

Raven turned away from her and paced the room. "I waited at the telegraph office for replies. They came speedily enough. This Dr. Twicklestone does exist, but he is not in England at the moment. He is on the continent, traveling from society to society to speak of his latest research results. I have no idea how this man we met at the police station got his hands on some private correspondence, but he's not this specialist, and I assume not even a doctor at all."

He drew breath. "I've told this to our good inspector,

who was none too pleased about it and immediately invited the impostor over for another chat. I urged him to take fingerprints and see if the crook is known to them from other cases of impersonation. It's conclusive to me now this is some kind of scheme between him and Bixby to defraud Oaks of his house or something in it. But for what purpose, I still can't understand, and that is the key to the whole thing. Without a reason, there is hardly a case against them for anything other than fraud. How can we ever connect it with the murder? We can hardly assume that Tillie discovered the good doctor was a pretender. How would she have known that?"

Merula listened, registering what he said but not really feeling the need to respond and conjecture with him. Bixby and his fellow conspirators seemed to stay just outside the light she and Raven were trying to throw on them.

Raven continued, "Galileo wrote that the drops we sent are a mixture he had never seen before, having both sedative and nerve-stimulating properties. He suggested it works the same way as a large amount of alcohol, making a man wild and unreasonable, then letting him collapse."

"But Oaks told us it was a harmless sedative he had been taking for some time."

"Yes, I thought about that on the way back here. There are two options, as far as I can see. Someone must have added to his drops or even replaced the liquid inside his bottle with something else, without Oaks noticing. The bottle stood beside his bed, so who could have done that?"

"The stable boy claimed to know where the money chest

is. He has been inside the house. A bedroom is a very private place to go, but the boy might have been curious."

"But"—Raven pointed a finger at her for emphasis—"how would a simple stable boy have access to a medicine he could add to Oaks's sedative? We'd have to accept that he did it for someone else. Someone who provided him with the liquid to put into the bottle."

"Yes, probably. Bixby? He did start talking about delusions as soon as he heard you ask the doctor about the drops."

"Exactly. And think about this: Oaks was most likely under the influence of these drops when he rushed out into the night on horseback and then later collapsed by the river. His horse has been found and captured. It came to no harm. It is hard to decide, though, whether Oaks really collapsed by the river or somewhere else and was then taken to the river to suggest he had returned to the place of his crime. If Bixby came across him when he had fallen off his horse and the horse was still there, Bixby might have slung Oaks's body across the horse and led the animal to the riverside where he wanted Oaks to be found."

Raven seemed to wait for her to discuss this theory with him, but Merula's head felt empty and her interest in the case had almost disappeared. She was just so tired. Even her ribs ached again, as if the old injury was now fresh.

Raven stopped his pacing and looked at her. "Bowsprit told me that you met with this man, but he didn't tell me what he said. He even said that he would never tell me, as it was up to you to decide whether you wanted to say or not. I must confess I hated him for one brief moment, for knowing what I might never know, and also for having gone with you while I should have been the one to do that. I was a fool to think I could keep you from discovering the truth. You had to. I understand now."

His eyes darkened, and he drew breath slowly. "I want you to know one thing. You need never tell me what the man told you. You can keep any secret you want from me. But promise me one thing. If there is something that puts you in danger, something that might . . . take you away from me, then tell me. Because I couldn't bear to find out later that I might have . . . helped you, saved you, and that I didn't, that I failed you. I couldn't live with . . ."

His voice broke, and he walked to the door quickly.

"Raven!" Merula lifted her hand to stop him before he could rush out. "I promise."

He turned to her in a jerk, his eyes surprised and slightly doubtful. "You do? Just like that?"

"Yes. Of course. I know your story and . . . I would never want you to blame yourself."

A slow smile spread across his features.

As it appeared, it brought some warmth back into Merula's cold insides. Like a ray of sunshine streaking through the darkness, a soft touch upon her face. The man had said her mother had died all alone. But Merula herself was not all alone. She would never be.

No matter how hurtful her past was or how sad she was for the mother and father she'd never know, her quick judgment had been rash and wrong. She did have a future. Because she had friends.

Raven came back to her and sat down opposite. "I know you probably do not feel like it, but I could use your help. We need to go over every little detail of what we've heard and seen since we got here. There might be something in it that can help us solve the case. Tillie's murder. Not just for the sake of Oaks. Also for the sake of all the locals involved. When I was in the village, I felt this atmosphere again of fear, like a cloak hanging over the place, suffocating people. Even the young doctor who came to settle here with his family is thinking of leaving again. I stopped by his house to ask if he had known about Tillie being with child before she died, if she had been to see him. He laughed and said girls didn't come to a doctor for that. Especially as he was considered an outsider. The old doctor had been born here, lived here all of his life. But even then girls sooner confided in older women who knew herbal remedies. He couldn't point me in the direction of one particular woman who might have been Tillie's confidant. He kept repeating that he didn't know the people here well yet."

Raven shook his head. "It took them quite some time to find a replacement for the old doctor after his carriage accident, and now he's already thinking of leaving. Country life just doesn't agree with him, he said. But I wager it's this atmosphere of gloom and doom that is driving the poor man away. Proving Tillie's death was the act of a mere mortal might help change things for the better."

"Well, if you're right in assuming that the house is hiding some secret, it seems significant that a local girl came to work here and was then murdered. Fern's remarks about Tillie believing she would soon be rich could be connected to that."

Raven narrowed his eyes. "You mean she might have been sent to work here to discover more about the house's secret?"

"Yes. Everybody assumed she quit her job at the inn because of the men leering at her, but perhaps someone *asked* her to work for Oaks and explore the house. Didn't Webber say she had all these stories about valuables in the house? That suggests she was looking around in the rooms, perhaps even in the cupboards and drawers."

Raven nodded enthusiastically. "That makes perfect sense. But for whom was she working? Bixby? If she was working for him, he needed not kill her."

"Unless she became too talkative. And if she did talk too much, she might have let something slip to someone who used her and then disposed of her. The father of her child?" Merula considered for a moment and then continued, "Both the stable boy and Fern told us Tillie couldn't read. That means that if she needed to look into books or through paperwork, she'd have to ask someone for help."

Raven stared at her. "Merula, you're a genius. That must be the answer. She came to work here to discover something, but in order to do so, she needed help. And once the two accomplices had discovered whatever they were after, the other party killed Tillie so he could have the reward for what they had discovered all to himself."

"Or *herself*. We shouldn't forget Fern. She claimed not to know how Tillie had wanted to get rich, but she could be lying. You said yourself she was unnaturally nervous when we suddenly came upon her in the church."

"Yes, but Tillie's accomplice has to be able to read. Can we assume that Fern can?" Raven asked, doubt in his voice.

"We should find out. It might have been Fern's plan to begin with. She might have overheard something at the inn and then asked Tillie to go work for Oaks."

"Why wouldn't she have gone to work for Oaks herself? If she's the one who can read and write, that would have made much more sense." Raven sank back in his chair again. "Not that anything in this case seems to make sense. It's all like that white woman on the coastal path Bowsprit talked about. Just wisps of fog moving on the breeze. You think you see something, then it's gone. Nothing material."

He leaned back against the headrest and stared up at the ceiling. "Material," he repeated, sounding almost dreamy. "Material."

Merula was sure that he was so physically and mentally exhausted from running to and fro all day long that he was drifting off to sleep and she would soon hear him snoring, when he suddenly flew to his feet.

"Of course," he shouted, slapping his fist into his open palm. "That's it. I should have realized before. Sirens! Bowsprit mentioned sirens on that first day."

He ran to the table and studied the scene.

Merula followed his movements, her mouth agape. Was he succumbing to the strain? Sirens? Those creatures from Greek mythology holding a clue to a case in Dartmoor?

"Yes, of course!" Raven cried. "That must be it. That must be the reason they didn't want us to look too closely, and certainly not to draw things or . . . It must be a trap somehow."

He looked at her. "I can't be sure until I have discussed this with an expert. I don't want to look like a fool, especially not with that Scotland Yard inspector. But think about it. Shipwrecks. Unusually often. The wreckmaster living off the finds. Deriving his power from his position, his success, the money he can acquire. Being in a struggle as the ways of the town are changing. People like Ben Webber taking charge, talking of tearooms and tourists, of selling toby jugs instead of tinning and farming. The wreckmaster is losing control, even to an outsider like Bixby, who can bluff people with his scientific knowledge. Who comes here changing the landscape around his house and bringing in his rich city friends to study the movements of the heavens."

Raven gasped for air to continue his excited explanation. "Now the wreckmaster is a specialist in his own field. The sea and her secrets, her loot. What if he could cause the shipwrecks, to bring fresh spoils to fill his coffers, keep the village dependent on him?"

"But how? Not with a kraken? Surely not with one cut-off arm?"

"No. He wouldn't need one. If he could lure ships to the shore some other way. I read about it. I think they did it in medieval times. You create a beacon on the coast that is not steady but moving. Sailors get disorientated by it and the ship crashes on the rocks. They take the spoils. Perhaps our wreckmaster even saves the sailors so no lives are lost. He may be ethical like that."

Merula tilted her head. "Can you prove it?"

"Only after I've talked to an expert about undertows and wind and everything this coast is subject to. But I think it must be true. Remember how Oaks mentioned having seen something at night? Danger to a ship, something gruesome? Perhaps he knew something about a false beacon luring ships into disaster, and the wreckmaster tried to get rid of him because of what he knew."

"But in that case, the wreckmaster could have killed Oaks. He could have lain in wait for him somewhere along the route Oaks took when he went horse riding. He need not have killed a local girl. I don't think the wreckmaster would. You just called him ethical, in a mocking tone, no doubt, but there is a big difference between theft of ships' cargo and cold-blooded murder of a completely innocent girl."

"Perhaps." Raven waved at her. "I have to go send more telegrams."

"You're completely wearing yourself out." Concern for him filled Merula, pushing her sad thoughts about her own past away.

Raven shrugged it off. "Oaks is locked up. So far we

have made it a little better for him by exposing this so-called doctor as a liar, but we need to do more. Keeping busy is sort of invigorating, if that makes sense."

It made perfect sense, but that only increased her worries for him. Raven's need to engage his thoughts and crack cases was just a way to prevent himself from dwelling on what he could no longer change. No matter how many people he might manage to save from wrongful accusations, he could never undo his mother's death. She was beyond saving.

Already at the door, Raven smiled at her; then his expression sobered. "You take care now."

"I will. You know that. And . . . I never break a promise."

Raven's smile returned. "Thank you."

CHAPTER 15

When Merula heard the sound of hooves outside, she believed it was Raven coming back after having sent the new flurry of telegrams. She was glad for it, as the silence in the house quivered across her tight nerve endings. She knew that with Bowsprit and Lamb around, she was hardly alone, but still there was something about the place that unsettled her. Perhaps it was Raven's strong belief that the house held some kind of secret that people had been willing to kill for.

Just as she thought this, a knock sounded at the door, and Bowsprit looked in. "Excuse me, but Mr. Bixby is in the hallway and . . ." He turned round quickly, and she heard him say, "You can't just barge in here. Don't you have the decency to . . . Hey!"

But his figure was shoved aside, and two men entered the room in a rush. The first was Bixby, his face red and his eyes frantic, the second the man whom Merula had last seen at the police station passing himself off as Dr. Twicklestone. He was again carrying his leather bag.

She glanced round for something to grab hold of, to defend herself with, but the poker near the hearth was too far away to get to.

Bixby cried, "Where is Royston? I need to talk to Royston."

"He will be here any moment," Merula said, to impress upon them that they need not try to harm her. "What do you mean by this sudden intrusion? I understand that Bowsprit"—she nodded at the valet, who stood bristling in the doorway—"told you to wait in the hall as he came up to me."

"There's no time to stand on formalities." Bixby's expression was suddenly weary, and he reached up to rub his eyes. "Things have taken a terrible turn. It was never meant to . . . I should have . . ." He drew breath slowly.

The other man urged, "Tell them everything. You assured me that it could not hurt when I got involved. You lied. It can hurt. I want you to explain before the police come to arrest me."

"If there is anything to explain," Merula said coldly, "you should do so to the police. They already know you are not Dr. Twicklestone and probably not a doctor at all. You could be sued for this impersonation. I'm sure that the real doctor will be none too pleased when he finds out about this."

"You said it would never get out!" the doctor yelled at Bixby. "You told me it was perfectly safe."

Bixby threw up his hands in frustration. "I thought these peasants here wouldn't check. That it would all be over soon. I had no idea people would be murdered and an inspector from Scotland Yard would come."

Bowsprit stepped aside to allow in Raven, who eyed Bixby with a murderous look. "What are you doing here? You have some nerve to show up after what you caused. Or do you deny you tried to harm Oaks? That you have worked for weeks on end to discredit him with people and drive him away?"

Bixby sighed. "No, I do not deny it. But you have the wrong view of the entire situation. It has nothing to do with this dead girl."

"Does it not? I was there when you talked to the villagers as they had come to burn down the house. When you threatened them that some evil would come to their village. You've been playing them."

"To turn them away from here. To save this house and you, the guests staying in it. I helped you. You're just too shortsighted to see it."

"My loyalty lies with Oaks," Raven hissed. "He is locked up for crimes he didn't commit. Because of you!"

Bixby seemed to want to protest; then he made an appeasing gesture with his right hand. "Can we just sit down and talk about it? I came here because I want to explain."

"Yes, only because you're in deep now. Your fake doctor has been exposed and the police are after the both of you."

The "doctor" grabbed at his head. "We must flee. Go to France. If we go now, we can reach the coast and be on a ship before nightfall."

"Are you crazy?" Bixby retorted. "Of course we won't flee. Then everyone really *will* believe we killed that girl."

The other man made a whimpering sound.

"Sit down!" Bixby ordered him with a glare. He himself stayed on his feet, eyeing Raven. "I will explain everything to you. Then you will understand that we have nothing to do with the murder by the river."

Raven leaned back on his heels with a challenging look. "This should be interesting."

Bixby began to pace the room. Bowsprit had closed the door and was standing by it, watching the man through narrowed eyes, as if ready to jump him the moment it became necessary.

Merula agreed that it was good to be on guard. Bixby could have brought a weapon, for all they knew. It could be hidden in his pocket or under his coat.

Bixby said, "When I came to live here, I just wanted a peaceful and quiet place. I assure you that I knew nothing of the matters in which I would get involved. I bought a nice house, to decorate and to adorn with an arboretum and a garden. I invested serious money in that, and I invited friends over to discuss science with me. I met new and interesting people and built my name. Through Professor Morehead, whom you have also met, I was introduced to an industrialist. A man who owns factories and railroads, who even invested in hotels and roads abroad. He's a firm believer in the pull of certain places on huge crowds. You know how by the seaside in Brighton, they've been building a new pier, and people flock to it. Now, he believes that such venues that pull in visitors from other parts of the country can be created anywhere as long you have something to sell to these people. He believed that this wild and barren land has an attraction. Natural beauty, he calls it. I can't really see it, but I did see that if tourists came, they might also want to visit my arboretum and my house and pay money for it. As I just said, I paid a lot to have it decorated and . . . I was in a bit of a tight spot financially."

Merula glanced at Raven, and he met her eye with a nod—he was thinking the same thing. Fern had been telling the truth when she had said Bixby was in debt.

Bixby halted and rubbed his eyebrow. "This investor believed that people might come here, but only if the area was easily accessible. It is now quite a journey by coach from the nearest railway station to Cranley, so he wanted to have a railway here. He wanted to put it across the best direct route . . ."

Raven stared at him, his eyes lighting with sudden understanding. "Let me guess. That would be across Oaks's land."

Merula held her breath. They had been so close with their conjectures. Not Oaks's house, not something among his travel souvenirs or his zoological collection, but his land.

"Exactly," Bixby said to Raven. "Now this investor contacted Oaks and asked if he could buy his land. Oaks refused. He believes he has found refuge here, and he didn't want to sell. Then the investor came to me. He said he was willing to pay me handsomely if I could somehow convince Oaks to sell the house."

"Or if you could somehow drive Oaks away," Merula said. "You let yourself be hired to frighten him into leaving." The men she had overheard in the corridor must have been referring to that. They had said Bixby should already have taken care of it.

Bixby shook his head, raising both his hands in an almost apologetic gesture. "It was nothing like that at first. I needed money and his offer was good. I believed in my own persuasive powers. I befriended Oaks, and I tried to get him to move to another place. The Riviera, the Black Forest, places of interest to a man who loves wildlife and rare animals. I also tried to get him into expeditions to explore the Arctic so he would be away from here. But he refused every single offer. By that time, the investor was leaning on me heavily to come through. I had already accepted money from him to pay some of my urgent debts and . . . I couldn't say no anymore. I noticed Oaks was under nervous strain, and I believed that if I could convince him he was ill, he might leave to recuperate someplace. I pressured him to consult a specialist."

"But Oaks didn't want that," Merula said. "That is why he argued with you recently. The stable boy overheard him saying you should stop pressuring him. It was about seeing this specialist."

Bixby nodded. "I had already agreed with this man here that he would play the specialist. An expert in his field who would urge Oaks to take rest in a better climate. But as long as Oaks refused to see him, we weren't getting anywhere near a solution."

"And the handsome amount of money you had been promised if you succeeded," Raven added dryly. "So then you decided to make life hard for Oaks by killing a local girl, his maid, and pointing the finger at him for the killing. Using the superstitious villagers to go after him and drive him away for you."

"No, of course not. I didn't know that girl, and I've never been near her."

"You're lying," Merula said. "You went to the inn to get friendly with the villagers and feed their fears. You played cards with Tillie's father and ensured he owed you money so you could later pressure him into cooperating with you in exchange for clearing his debts."

Bixby shook his head in violent denial, but Merula pushed on relentlessly, "At the inn, you also met Tillie herself before she came to work for Oaks. You suggested she find work here. You arranged everything to ensure that after you murdered her, you could point the finger at Oaks."

Bixby looked appalled. "I did know the murdered girl by sight, yes, but I swear that I never suggested to her that she could work for Oaks. I also never met her away from the inn. I didn't pursue her and kill her. I swear."

"I'm afraid your oaths mean very little," Raven said coldly. "How do we know we can trust a single word you say?"

Bixby licked his lips. "I do realize that what I told you sounds odd and suspicious. But it is the truth. I did conspire to get Oaks away from his house and land, but I have absolutely nothing to do with the murder. I would never have gone that far."

"But you had to. You just told us the investor had already given you money which you used to pay off debts. So you couldn't return his money to him. You couldn't get away from him. You had to do what he asked. However you could."

"Look." Bixby pointed a finger at Raven. His hand was trembling and his voice was hoarse. "I may have been in debt and open to a less than honorable proposition. I may have told lies and bribed other people to become accomplices with me in this scheme. I admitted as much, and I'm not proud of it. In fact, looking back, I wish I could do it all again and tell this man to his face to find someone else for it. But I am *not* a killer. I could never strangle a girl to death. I'm being honest with you now, coming here to . . ."

"Honest?" Raven held his head back and laughed heartily. "You only came because you heard that I had already unmasked dear Dr. Twicklestone as an impostor. You believe I will now put in a word for you with the inspector and get you off the hook. But why would I? You've been nothing but trouble for Oaks."

"But I did save your lives. I came when the villagers were about to attack and plunder this house. Set it on fire, hurt you. I sent them off. I had influence over them that you never had. Never will have, either. I saved you."

"For your own selfish purposes."

"Nevertheless. You're standing here, uninjured, in a house with no damage except for the dents in the front door, all because of me."

Merula stepped up to both arguing men. "Mr. Bixby

does have a point in that he saved us. The villagers were mad with grief and anger and might have done serious damage. No matter whose interests Mr. Bixby had at heart when he intervened, he did save us."

Bixby said with an eager look, "Consider this. If they had burned the house, Oaks would have been forced to leave. Then the investor could have bought his land. That was exactly what I wanted. But I didn't want to take the risk of people getting hurt in the fire. I had heard Oaks had guests from the city, and . . . I rode out here to prevent casualties. That is the best proof I have that I didn't murder the girl. I never wanted anyone to die!"

Raven scoffed, but Merula focused on Bixby as she asked, "This investor you mentioned, is he here in the village?"

"No, he's in London. But I believe he has spies here. Eyes and ears who watch everything that is happening. Who report to him and tell him of my . . . failures."

Bixby laughed bitterly. "I haven't been able to deliver Oaks's house and land. Now I have even admitted to my part in it. I'm ruined, totally ruined."

"I don't feel sorry for you at all," Raven bit. "You are the reason Oaks is locked up. Because you started rumors he was mentally unbalanced, he is now accused of the murder."

"Not just because of me," Bixby protested. "Tillie's father, the blacksmith, has been telling everyone who wanted to listen that his daughter was harassed by Oaks. That Oaks forced himself onto her. He was so angry about that. And he wasn't the only one. The villagers want to kill Oaks for what he did to the girl. It might be better he's locked up now. Else they might come for him and hang him on the highest tree they can find."

"So we should even be grateful to you that Oaks is locked up where no harm can come to him?" Raven scoffed. "You have a strange way of protecting someone." Then he narrowed his eyes. "Do the villagers know about Tillie being with child?"

"Yes." Bixby held his gaze. "On the night she was murdered, she came to bring her wages to her father as she always did. I was playing cards at another table. Some men were laughing and smirking at her as she walked by, asking if she'd be the bride soon and saying she'd better hurry up about it before . . ." He glanced at Merula. "I'll spare you their crude way of alluding to her condition."

"How did Tillie respond to that?" Raven asked.

"She looked mortified and left in a hurry. Is that important somehow?"

"I'm just trying to reconstruct what she might have done after she left the inn. How she might have met her murderer."

Bixby raised both his hands in the air. "I have no idea. Perhaps she wanted to leave the village and asked someone for help in doing so? It could have been that stable boy. They were in on something together.'"

Raven narrowed his eyes. "You told us moments ago that you didn't know Tillie, except by sight, from her days as servant at the inn. How would you suddenly know about her and the stable boy being involved in something together?"

Bixby exhaled in a frustrated huff. "Do I have to explain everything?"

"If you want to persuade us you're innocent, yes."

"One night when I came here to visit Oaks, I took my horse to the stables because that stable boy was nowhere to be seen. As I approached, the girl Tillie ran from the stables shouting at him, 'I don't need you anymore, I found someone else.' The boy followed her all red in the face. At the time, I had no reason to think twice about it. An argument between two servants is none of my concern. But now, I tell you, that stable boy has something to hide. You better ask *him* about the murder."

The counterfeit doctor had sat in a chair very still, listening in on the conversation. Now he said in a trembling voice, "Can we go now? Will you tell the inspector we meant no harm?"

"I will do no such thing," Raven said. "I have no way of checking on your story. You could be lying, and I don't want to risk myself vouching for a pack of liars. And possibly worse."

"See!" The impostor jumped to his feet. "This was no use. We have to flee. The wreckmaster can help us. He can take us on a boat to France."

"So you know the wreckmaster?" Raven asked. "Is he part of your play for the land? Did he also take money to ensure the railway is coming to Cranley?"

"Him?" Bixby spat. "He would rather die than see the railway come. He is a man of tradition, believing everything should stay the same forever. He's afraid of what will happen when tourists come and not for fishing and boating but for the moors and the plants."

"So you didn't work with him?"

"I hope he knows absolutely nothing of our plans," Bixby said emphatically, "or else we will have no chance at all of succeeding."

"So you still believe you can succeed?" Raven asked.

Bixby stood and looked at him, with a slowly spreading smile. "Oaks may be guilty. Even you are not sure of him. You're his friend, so you defend him, but you're not sure of him. He might be guilty, he might be convicted and hanged, and then the house will be sold. The investor will buy it and the railway will come."

Bixby walked to the door. "If Oaks had been smart, he would have accepted the offer right away. Then nothing would have happened."

"So you admit that the murder has to do with the railroad?"

"No. The murder might have happened anyway, but Oaks would have been gone. He would have been in the Arctic or on the Riviera, having a good time with the money received from his house. Now, because he stuck with it so determinedly, he might die. Ironic, isn't it?"

And holding his head high, Bixby tried to leave the room.

But Bowsprit was still in front of the door. "Shall we

keep them here?" he asked eagerly. "I can go fetch the police to arrest them."

"It sounds tempting," Raven agreed, "but I'm afraid we can't detain people against their will."

Bowsprit looked stricken. "If we let them go, they might run, leave the country."

"Mr. Bixby just explained how flight would look like an admission of guilt. I'm quite sure these gentlemen will stay near Cranley. Won't you?"

Bixby shot Raven a dirty look but nodded his assent.

Raven waved at Bowsprit to step aside. The valet obeyed with a chagrined expression.

Bixby left with long strides, the frightened impostor hurrying after him.

"Do you believe one word of what he said, my lord?" Bowsprit asked.

Raven pursed his lips. "I think that most of what he told us is probably true. I've heard of such investments, here in England and abroad. Tracks leading into the Swiss mountains, hotels in places that are accessible only on foot or by special transportation. People long to see unexplored places. To go where not everyone has been before them. There's money in it, and investors come to it. I also believe Bixby when he says that redecorating Gorse Manor and creating the arboretum was expensive and he needs money. In fact, I'm quite sure that if the inspector looked into Bixby's finances, he would discover that he's in debt. No lies in that."

Raven leaned on the table as he continued, "I also readily believe that Bixby would be interested in a way to make money and would have no qualms about lying to Oaks. Especially not if he made himself believe he was helping Oaks, doing him a favor by taking this big bothersome house away from him and setting him up nicely on the Riviera. Yes, I can see Bixby telling himself that Oaks should be grateful for this chance. But Oaks didn't want to leave, and then the trouble began. Bixby had to think up ways to make him leave. He came up with this doctor who had to express concerns about his health . . . It is something that fits with Bixby's character: he is a man of science, a man of brains more than brawn. He is not intrinsically violent."

"That is all speculation," Bowsprit said. "I don't like him. He's cold and calculating, capable of anything."

"Perhaps, but men have their ways. Their code of honor. I think Bixby doesn't mind lies and manipulations, especially if he stands to gain from them. But murder? And not a murder such as shooting someone in a flash of anger. No, strangling a defenseless girl. From behind, even. I don't think it's Bixby's way."

"The stable boy," Bowsprit said, casting off his dejection and looking eager to pursue this new suspect. "If Bixby can be believed, he had an argument with Tillie and she said she didn't need him anymore. Need him for what?"

Raven pushed himself away from the table. "I'm going to ask the stable boy to come in. Perhaps the argument was simply about the boy liking Tillie and her not returning his feelings because she was in love with someone else. But he might know something relevant." He left the room.

Bowsprit looked at Merula. "Do you believe Bixby?"

Merula sighed. "It's hard to judge people's behavior when you have barely met them. Once I know a person better, I can usually tell if his behavior is consistent. But Bixby is a difficult man to gauge."

"Some men are easy liars," Bowsprit said. "Still, when they lie, sometimes they give themselves away. They put emphasis on something where it shouldn't be."

Merula studied him. "You sound pensive. What is bothering you?"

Bowsprit met her eyes. "It isn't Mr. Bixby. It's that man, the actor, whom we met at the shepherd's cottages. Who told you about your parents. There was a moment in the conversation when he changed. When I strongly felt that he was lying."

"One particular moment?" Merula's hear skipped a beat. "And when was that?"

"When he said that your father was dead."

Merula stared at Bowsprit's calm expression. "So you think he lied and my father is not dead?"

"Yes. I wonder . . . if he was himself in love with your mother. If that was his reason for helping her and helping you, getting you to family in London. Getting you away also from your father."

"But that is cruel. My mother expected my father's return. Even on her deathbed. By taking me away, he deprived my father of the baby he could have had." Merula felt anger well up inside her. "I have to go back and ask him to his face."

"No, don't do that. He will have had his reasons for

acting the way he did. I'm sorry I said this to you. Perhaps I should not have. I don't know if he lied about your father. I only had that impression because of the way in which he spoke and averted his gaze."

"There we are." Raven came back in with the stable boy in tow. "I met him outside the front door," he explained. "As he had kept an eye on our visitors' horses. So, my boy . . . what's your name, anyway?"

"Edward, sir. But they all call me Eddie."

"Well, Eddie, why don't you sit down for a bit?"

Eddie didn't seem to hear him as he stared at the scene of the village, river, and sea Raven had built. "What's that?" he asked, going over and taking a closer look.

"Oh, just a little something I enjoy. Building scenes."

"But it's books and papers and . . ."

"Can you read?"

"Yes, sir." Eddie's face shone with pride now. "Not very well, not entire books, if that's what you mean. They're full of long words. But I can write letters. My mother lets me write to my father for her. He's a sailor. He's away for months."

"I see. Do you miss him?"

Eddie shrugged. "I haven't met him much. I've been in service since I turned twelve."

"And now you're here with Mr. Oaks. Do you like it?"

"His horses are very nice."

"And Mr. Oaks himself?"

Eddie's expression turned dark. He picked up a tin soldier and toyed with it. "He's arrested. He must be an evil man. My mother won't want me to keep working here. But I can't leave the horses. They need someone to take care of them."

"Yes, of course. And besides, Mr. Oaks will soon be returning. He isn't guilty. It was all a misunderstanding."

"Not guilty?" Eddie looked up, dropping the soldier to the floor. It rolled away across the boards. "You mean, he didn't kill Tillie? Then who did?"

"Yes, we would all like to know that."

"But he must have killed her. He was angry with her."

"Angry with her?"

"Yes. He said she had been through his things."

"Things? You mean like valuable things?" Raven glanced at Merula. "Mr. Oaks thought Tillie was stealing from him?"

Merula studied Eddie's expression and posture closely. This idea was completely new to them.

"No, paperwork, he said. But that was silly. Tillie couldn't read or write."

Eddie looked down and stooped to pick up the soldier. He wiped some dust off it.

"But you could," Merula said. Her heart was beating fast as a picture began to emerge in her head. "Was that why Tillie let you in here? Not to look at the specimens but to help her make sense of paperwork?"

Eddie flushed deep. "I know nothing."

"I can understand you're loyal to Tillie. Especially now that she's dead. But you must tell us the truth. It can help us find her murderer."

"I know who murdered her." Eddie's eyes flashed a moment. Then the anger died down again, and he stood with his chin on his chest.

"Who then?" Merula asked softly.

Eddie fidgeted with his hands. "Oaks," he whispered.

"No, Eddie, it wasn't Oaks, and you know that. You're lying. Why are you lying? Because you know who did it and don't want to point the finger at him? But poor Tillie is dead, and . . . She must have been afraid when the killer grabbed her from behind and choked the life out of her."

"Stop it!" Eddie cried. "She died because of me. It is my fault. If I had helped her, she would still have been alive!" He burst into tears.

Merula went over to him and stood beside him. "Why is that, Eddie?" she asked softly.

Eddie gasped for breath to speak between sobs. "She asked me to help her read something. But I thought it would just get us into trouble. So I didn't do it. Then later I was sorry and thought I should do it anyway. She had said it was important and could get her money. I don't know why, but I wanted to help her and make her happy."

He rubbed at the tears that ran down his cheeks. "But when I said I'd help her anyway, she just laughed at me and said she didn't need me anymore. She had someone else to do it for her. That man must have helped her and then killed her to take the money for themselves."

Merula's mind raced. Eddie's revelation fit with what they had concluded themselves earlier. That Tillie might have had an accomplice in her plans to get rich. "You say it was a man. So you know who helped her?"

"Not really." Eddie shrugged.

"Come, come," Merula pressed. "I think you know. At least you have some idea."

Eddie swallowed hard. "Ben Webber," he whispered.

"Ben Webber? And why would that be?"

"Because he always acted like he's so smart. And she liked him. When she was still working at the inn, she liked him. But he wanted Fern. He never looked at Tillie. Until she started talking about money. Then he liked her well enough." The boy's anger was tangible, like heat radiating from an open fire.

"So Ben Webber agreed to help Tillie?" Raven asked. "He knew about this . . . money scheme she was involved in?"

"I think so." Eddie rubbed his face again. He seemed suddenly embarrassed about his outburst.

Raven's eyes met Merula's for a moment. She read the same uncertainty there that she felt inside. Eddie had no reason to lie to them. If he said Tillie had wanted to look at paperwork and he had refused to help her, so another might have done it in his stead, it could be true.

But Ben Webber? He seemed so ambitious, always looking up. Why would he listen to a girl he had never noticed before, telling him about some obscure scheme involving money? He had the shop to tend to, his reputation to consider.

Still, Webber was an ambitious man. And if the money scheme had to do with the railroad coming, Webber might have believed it could benefit him. Hand him the power over the village he craved. A new era with tearooms and toby jugs . . .

"And what about those tales her father is telling about Oaks harassing Tillie?" Raven asked. "Have you ever seen anything like that?"

Eddie shook his head. "Mr. Oaks was friendly to us, that's all. I think Tillie would have thought him very old."

Still, Tillie had suddenly kissed Oaks when he came back from a walk one day and asked him to marry her, protect her. Why? Because she had been with child? From a man who would not marry her?

Ben Webber? The greengrocer's son, who had to marry someone of his own class, not the daughter of a blacksmith who spent too much money on liquor and gambling after his wife died?

But Ben Webber was now courting Lamb. Lamb, who was also not of his own class.

Or didn't he know that? Did he take her for a girl from a middle-class family in London who had been hired as lady's maid to the niece of a lady?

Merula bet that Lamb had dropped Aunt Emma's title as quickly as she could to convince Webber she came from wealthy circles. If Webber thought Lamb was a girl he could show off, not knowing one bit about Rotherhithe . . .

Raven said to Eddie, "Is there anything else you can tell us? Anything about what Tillie wanted with paperwork? And what happened when you were inside the house? Have you seen the specimens? Have you been near the kraken? Have you cut off one of the arms?"

Eddie shook his head. "I didn't want to help her because I thought no good could come of it. I just wanted to keep her safe." He gulped again. "I did everything wrong. Now she's dead."

Raven said softly, "We'll find out who killed her, Eddie, you can depend on that. He will be punished."

Looking past the boy at Merula, he continued. "I think we need to speak with Ben Webber. Confront him with some lies he told us."

CHAPTER 16

At the grocery store, they learned from Mrs. Webber that her son was out with the cart delivering goods. That they might catch up with him if they drove out to Leekwood Farm.

"What is wrong?" she queried with a sharp look from her cold blue eyes. "What do you want him for?"

"A party we will be arranging soon," Raven said. "Thank you and good day."

Outside, he hissed to Merula, "The typical overbearing mother. I wager that because she's smothering him so, our friend Ben Webber takes his pleasures where he can."

"You think he fathered Tillie's child?"

"It seems likely."

"But he was supposed to love Fern. He never had eyes for Tillie. Why would he have fathered a child with Tillie? I don't want him to be the father of her child, as Lamb likes him so much."

Raven grimaced. "Lamb's feelings can't deter us from what we have to do. Excuse me, sir . . ." He gestured to an old man carrying firewood. "Where can we find Leekwood Farm?"

Armed with directions, they left the village across a sunny road, the occasional butterfly fluttering by. Leekwood Farm was a beautiful, well-preserved building with stables and shacks, chickens searching for food in the dirt beside their coop, and a scruffy black-and-white dog running for their cart as far as its chain would allow. Then he stood, straining and barking.

No one came out of the farmhouse.

Raven jumped down and helped Merula off. "That must be Webber's cart." He pointed at a vehicle left beside the stables. "Where can he be?"

They walked over to it. The dog had quieted down and sat watching them, his tongue out of his mouth. From inside the stables they heard voices and then a girl's giggle.

Raven put his finger to his lips and gestured for Merula to follow him. Her eyes had to adjust to the dimness a moment, but then they could see the pair sitting on a hay bale. Webber was telling some story about a hunting party, and the girl laughed at each few words he said. Her cheeks were red and her hands clutched a paper bag, probably containing sweets from the grocery store, as she noisily sucked on something.

"Mr. Webber," Raven called out. "I'm sorry to tear you away from your . . . customer, but I must have a word with you."

Webber jumped to his feet, the cap that had lain on his knee falling to the floor. He retrieved it and brushed some dirt off it. "Until next time," he said to the girl, then rushed over to them.

Raven took him outside and then observed, "You must be very popular, Mr. Webber. I assume that the girl didn't pay for those sweets?"

Webber flushed. "She leads a lonely life here, sir, never seeing anyone. Her parents let her do a lot of work and . . . Well, I just like to spoil her a bit, bring her some sweets every now and then. These are new, pink ones, her favorite color. Just a little kindness, sir, for a lonely girl."

"Yes, and as she doesn't get away from this farm much, she can't tell others about you. She can't find out that your . . . uh, kindness isn't limited to her alone."

Webber flushed even deeper. "I don't know what you mean, sir."

Raven laughed softly. "I mean, *sir*"—he put mocking stress on the term of address—"that Tillie had to die because she was carrying your baby and you couldn't afford your mother finding out about it."

Webber's face drained of all color. "No," he whispered. "No. She wasn't with child. She only said so to pressure me into marrying her. She wanted away from that father of hers. Desperately. She would have done anything to achieve that. Slept with any man."

"Did you tell yourself that to hush your conscience?" Raven's voice was loaded with contempt. "Tillie's father might have had his weaknesses, caused by loneliness and grief, but he loved his daughter and wanted the best for her.

You, on the other hand, took advantage of her, making promises you never intended to keep. You're a predator."

"No, sir, I . . ."

"Not another word!" Raven growled. "When I first spoke with you, you said that Oaks had to kill Tillie to cover it up. You pretended you meant that he wanted to cover up their affair, but you referred to her being with child. You claim not to have believed her when she told you, but you're lying. You did believe her. You realized that you were in trouble now. That once your mother found out about Tillie's condition, you could lose everything you have. You had to kill her to remove her threat to you."

Webber, his eyes bulging in his pale face, looked for a defense but didn't seem to find any.

Merula said, "You're friendly with my maid as well. If you hurt her feelings, I will hurt you. You can count on that."

"Just a little kiss; what does it mean? I wager she has been kissed before. She has traveled, has seen the world. She has been with a footman here, a coachman there. It doesn't matter to me. We're just having a good time."

"Until she leaves again." Merula's voice trembled with anger. Lamb believed she would find a home here, a safe place away from the poverty in London, not just for herself but also for her old mother. This man had never meant anything of the sort. Just a short affair, a few kisses. Hushing his conscience with the idea that it was the same for Lamb. Not even having asked her or tried to determine what kind of girl she really was.

"I demand," Raven said coldly, "that you stay away from Lamb from now on. You're a despicable person for what you did. A cold-blooded killer."

"No," Webber spoke with a trembling voice. "Tillie claimed to be with child, that's how I knew, but I never believed her. It was just lies to pressure me into marrying her. But I would never do that, and she knew it."

"She told you," Raven hissed, "and you knew it could not get out. You had to kill her so she couldn't tell anyone that the baby was yours."

"They would not have believed her. They all knew that she wanted to get away from her father."

"Stop using her father as an excuse for . . ."

But Ben Webber pushed on, in a loud voice, "They would have believed me when I said it wasn't mine and she had been with others. At the inn, at the house. Mr. Oaks . . ."

"Leave him out of it. He's a decent man; you're not."

"Just prove it." Webber spat at Raven, his normally nice and friendly face a mask of rage. "Prove it was my child. Or that I killed her. You can't. I never did anything of the sort."

"But you have been in the house. Tillie asked you in. You had to help her with some scheme. It could bring in money. She needed you and you obliged. You want to rise up in the village, be their new leader. Not the wreckmaster, some old man smelling of fish and saltwater; no, you. Younger, cleverer, at least that is what you think. Did Tillie have to die because of what she knew? So the money could be yours alone?"

"No!" Webber's eyes were even wider now, the color of his anger draining from his features, leaving them marble white. "Yes, she asked me to come into the house and help her look for some paperwork, but then she changed her mind again. She didn't want to do it anymore. Tillie was soft like that. She could never hurt people."

"Hurt people?" Merula echoed. "What was it about exactly?"

Webber sighed. "I don't know. I helped her look once, but we couldn't find the right things."

"What things?"

"Something about the house, the land. I don't know the details. She would tell me once it was all done."

"And you agreed to that?"

"I . . ."

"You saw it as a chance to be with her," Merula understood. "In the privacy of the house."

Webber hung his head and shuffled his feet. "I never meant to do her any harm. She told me she wasn't going through with the money thing, and I said she was a fool, and then she said all these nasty things about me, like I had never loved her and wouldn't care for her, and I left. You can't talk to women when they're all hysterical like that. She had to be crazy to let a chance for money go. But I wasn't about to argue with her about it. I had enough of her tales. The supposed baby . . ."

"She was with child. And she is dead now. Probably because she had no one to turn to."

Webber bristled. "I am not some insane killer. Whoever

strangled her must be mad. Have you not heard about the markings on the neck? No human hands can do that. It wasn't me."

"Then who?" Raven pressed. "You spent time with her, you knew whom she might have been afraid of."

"No one. She was nice; everyone liked her. She was very popular at the inn. Well, not like Fern, but nice enough. No one hated her or would have hurt her. We were all sorry for her because her mother died and her father couldn't make ends meet anymore. He blamed everyone for their misfortune, even the doctor who hadn't been able to heal his wife. He said the man had bled him dry, knowing the cures he prescribed weren't going to help anyway."

Raven stood and stared ahead, his eyes pensive. Merula wondered if some thought had struck him, some light in the case.

Webber said, "You won't tell anyone about the baby, will you? I swear it's not mine. And you cannot prove it. My mother would go crazy if she heard anything like that. She might turn me out of the shop."

"Now that might not be a bad punishment for what you did." Raven crossed his arms over his chest. "You will never learn unless you get burned someday."

Webber pulled back his shoulders. "I have no idea what you're talking about. And that maid of yours is just a tavern wench. She threw herself at me. I didn't even want to kiss her."

Merula scoffed. "How dare you twist the truth like that? We can obviously not believe a word you say."

Raven said, "What about the Tasmanian devil, Mr. Webber? You took it, didn't you? Don't try to deny it. You left your fingerprints on the glass of the container."

"That can't be, because I was . . ." Webber fell silent.

Raven leaned over. "Wearing gloves? Ah, Mr. Webber, such an intelligent man, knowing his alcohol and his form-aldehyde. Of course you wore gloves."

"You tricked me into saying something," Webber hissed, "but I will deny everything until my dying day."

Raven clicked his tongue. "If you get accused of mur-der, that dying day may come sooner than you think."

Webber blinked nervously. "You have nothing against me."

"You had access to the house. You could take away specimens, cut the arm off the kraken. You knew about Tillie's money scheme. The land wanted by the railway. They needed Oaks out of the way. You helped Tillie. You had to make sure Oaks went away somehow. Bixby had failed. He wasn't going to get all the money the investor had promised. But you might. If you could solve the matter. Kill a girl who was a problem to you anyway and then . . ."

"That is ludicrous. What railway? I have no idea what you're talking about."

"The Tasmanian devil, Mr. Webber. Out with it."

"Yes, so I took it. I saw it and it looked kind of fierce and suitable to use in a prank. Bixby doesn't want to buy his groceries with us because we are not fancy enough for his taste. I wanted to ruin his party, upset his guests. I took the beast and hid it in the well. Just to have some fun at his expense. Nothing more."

"And the arm of the kraken?"

"I didn't take that. I swear. I've never even seen the kraken. It was not in the room where I have been."

Raven glanced at Merula. That much might be true, as the kraken was kept in a separate room.

"You're far from cleared, Mr. Webber," Raven said in a treacherously soft tone. "I would tread lightly if I were you. Stay away from Lamb and hope that your mother never makes the connection between you and poor dead Tillie's condition."

Webber trembled a moment, his arrogant attitude shaken at the idea of his mother finding out and confronting him. "You're so certain I could be involved. But what about Fern? Did you even consider her?"

"What about Fern?" Merula asked. "You do not honestly propose she might have strangled her own friend?"

"Friend?" Ben Webber laughed, a low, spiteful laugh. "They weren't friends anymore, not after Tillie told her she was expecting. I never believed it was my baby, but Fern did. She hated Tillie. Also because she was always going on about her privileged position at Oaks's. Fern might have killed Tillie believing she could then come to work for Oaks in her stead. Fern always wanted too much out of life. I wasn't good enough for her when I proposed to her. No, she wanted a man with more money, more prospects in life. She was always scheming. No matter what the cost." He spit in the sand and walked to his cart, got on it, and drove off. The dog barked and growled until he was gone.

"Even the dog doesn't like him," Raven scoffed.

Merula shook her head. "Do you believe him when he points the finger at Fern? I can't see one girl strangling another."

Raven shrugged. "Hatred drives people to extreme acts. Fern is a tall, strong girl. Especially when using some tool, she could have strangled Tillie. You said earlier it was odd that a girl would agree to a meeting by the river at night. But it wouldn't be odd if she had been asked to come there by her best friend. Someone she trusted." He rubbed his hands together. "We need to talk to Fern again. Confront her with the knowledge of Tillie's condition."

He led Merula to their cart and helped her on it. She almost lost her balance as she contemplated the implications of Webber's admission that he had been involved with Tillie. "How are we going to tell Lamb what kind of man Webber really is? She will be heartbroken."

"Why? She just met him."

"But he was her hero, her new future! Her chance for a better life."

"Yes, Tillie must have felt that way about the railway coming." Raven grabbed the reins and put the cart into motion. "I wonder who approached her and forced her to look into the papers at Oaks's home."

"And why she didn't want to be part of it anymore," Merula mused. "If Oaks can be believed, she tried to have him marry her. She chose his side."

"Turning against whoever had engaged her to look through the paperwork," Raven nodded.

He suddenly froze. "Betrayal."

"What do you mean?" Merula studied his features closer.

"Remember how Oaks told us a tale about his travels where he wanted to visit a ruin in the jungle and he needed a local guide and one man came forward, and in the night before they left, he was killed because an anaconda got into his room? An animal killed him, but it was believed it had been let into the window by a human hand to punish him? For his betrayal of his people in wanting to take Oaks to the sacred place. What if betrayal is at the heart of all of this?"

"Tillie betraying whoever asked her to conspire against Oaks?"

Raven nodded. "That person killed her." He stared ahead thoughtfully. "It must have been about more than Tillie not wanting to harm Oaks anymore. To the killer, Tillie's change of mind must have felt like a punch in the gut. So it was someone who relied on her, believed he or she could trust her. Someone like Fern? What if the girls originally devised this plan to get money together? After she killed Tillie, Fern then lied to us that Tillie had wanted riches but had never told her what they were. She could easily lie, since she was certain Tillie would never talk again to tell on her."

"But the stable boy could just as easily have devised the

plan and then used Tillie for his own purposes. He was the one who could read and write, but Tillie had to give him access to the house if he wanted to get into anything. He claims she was doing it for someone else, but he could be lying about that."

"True. And what about Ben Webber?" Raven mused. "Isn't he the most likely candidate to support the arrival of the railroad, to be the spy for this industrialist? And with Tillie's condition, he stood to lose everything: his mother's love, the shop. His future as an important person in the village. The new leader, as it were. For him, killing Tillie solved several problems in a single stroke." He glanced at Merula. "If Fern really knew about Webber and Tillie, she might also hate him now. She might be able to tell us something we can use to create a solid case against him."

"But if she hates him, we can't simply accept anything she says as the truth. She will have every reason to lie. Especially if, as Webber suggested, she herself is the killer."

★ ★ ★

They drove out to the inn, where an eager boy of only six or seven years old grabbed the horse by the reins to lead it away. He pointed to where they could go inside, but Raven asked if they could go round back, as they wanted to speak to Fern in private. The boy seemed puzzled, but said, "If you go around the corner, you can see the kitchen door. It's open, and there are lots of pots and pans out to dry. Fern should be about too."

Raven nodded at Merula. "That way, then."

Behind the inn, on a patch of dried-out, yellowing grass, the pots and pans the boy had mentioned lay in the sunshine. Most were dented or chipped. Fern was seated on a rough wooden bench, running a cloth through a pan she held in the crook of her arm. Glancing up, she widened her eyes a moment when she recognized them. "Are you looking for lodgings? We have none available at the moment. You can only eat and drink."

She laughed softly, nodding at the pots and pans. "And not very well either. Not what you're used to, I reckon." She surveyed Merula's dress with obvious envy.

Raven said, "When we spoke at the church, you forgot to tell us a thing or two, Fern. Tillie was going to have a baby. And you knew who the father was."

Fern sat up straight. "I did not. Tillie said whose it was, but I didn't believe her. It was a lie."

"A hurtful lie," Merula said softly. "After all, Ben Webber had proposed to you."

Fern's eyes were wide and alert, darting from Merula to Raven and back. "Why are you asking questions? Are you with the police?"

"No. We came here from London to have a pleasant time in the countryside. Unfortunately, murder is never pleasant." Raven held the girl's gaze. "Although it can be convenient. If you can get rid of the girl who stole the man you loved and then taunted you to your face with the baby she was expecting."

Fern jumped to her feet. The pan fell to the ground and jumped away across the uneven grass, clanging into another.

Fern cried, "I never loved Ben. That's why I refused to accept his proposal. And Tillie wasn't expecting his baby. She just said that to hurt my feelings."

"Why would she want to hurt your feelings if you were friends?"

"Tillie could never stand all the men liking me instead of her. They did paw her, but they never gave her presents like they did me. She wanted Ben, but he never even noticed that she existed."

"Perhaps not at first," Raven said. "But after she came to work for Oaks and could share interesting stories about his house and his collection . . ." He clicked his tongue. "Ben Webber is an intellectual man. Such a house would pique his interest."

"Intellectual?" Fern scoffed. "All men are alike. They only want one thing."

"So you did believe Tillie's baby was Ben Webber's." Raven stood with his feet apart, eyeing the girl with a dark frown. "You lured her to the river at night and you strangled her."

"No!"

"She trusted you. She would have come to you. And you are certainly strong enough to kill her."

Merula looked at Fern's hands, which were clenched together in front of her. They seemed to squeeze and wring. She shivered involuntarily.

Fern said, "No one will ever believe I hurt Tillie."

"They will once there is official confirmation that Tillie was pregnant. There were already rumors at the inn on the night she died. Once it's confirmed during the inquest, everyone will wonder whose baby it was. If they conclude it was Webber's, it isn't hard to see how angry you must have felt. How humiliated that he replaced you so soon."

Fern wet her lips. "Why would anyone want to spread the word that Tillie was pregnant? They'd sooner hush it up. Her father wouldn't survive such a tale. He always thought the best of her. Not that she deserved that. She didn't want to stay with him anymore. She had had enough of his drinking and his gambling."

"But you said earlier," Merula intervened, "that her plan to get rich was a surprise for her father."

"Yes, a surprise it would have been if one morning he woke up and she was gone. She wanted money to leave this place behind." Fern gestured around her. "Can't you see there is no future here? Not for Tillie and not for me either. But she had a plan to get rich and I had nothing."

"Perhaps you killed her, then, to prevent her from getting away like she wanted. Perhaps you wanted her to be stuck here forever like you are."

Stuck in a shallow grave, Merula thought and shivered.

Fern shook her head. "She never told me how she'd get the money. I didn't even believe her. I thought she was just making herself interesting. Yes, I was angry with her, and yes, I could have slapped her or pushed her in the dirt, but I didn't kill her."

She bent down and picked up the pan again, reseated herself, and continued cleaning. The harsh lines around her mouth told of resilience, of being dealt a blow and getting up again, pushing through, as there really was no other choice but to go on, and on, and on.

Sensing the moment of overtaking this girl and achieving anything was gone, Merula gestured at Raven to leave. He followed her with a sour expression. "That didn't deliver a thing."

"She's far too hardened by life to just crack if you push her. If she did kill Tillie, she knows she'll end up on the gallows for that."

Merula didn't want to add that she even felt half sorry for the girl who might have been driven to the edge by her friend's revelations that she was about to be rich and was expecting a baby of the man who had shortly before claimed to love Fern. "I can picture Fern pushing Tillie so that she fell, hurt her head and died. Something impulsive leading to a death Fern hadn't really wanted. But strangulation with an implement suitable for that, brought along for the express purpose of leaving the alleged kraken marks on the victim's neck? That indicates premeditation. A calculated plan to get rid of someone and implicate another. Does that fit with Fern's personality?"

"Ben Webber said she wanted to have money and opportunity. You never know how far a person might be willing to go for that." Raven sighed, rubbing his eyes.

They stood in front of the inn again, waiting for the boy to bring their horse and cart to them.

Raven said softly to her, "Oaks is still behind bars. The

fact that Bixby engaged a fake doctor to commit him to an insane asylum won't convince our inspector that Oaks isn't guilty of murder. We need more than that. But what?"

"A confession of guilt," Merula whispered back at him.

Raven laughed. "Yes, preferably that, but how do you propose to get it?" His tone suggested the question was rhetorical.

But Merula replied, dead serious, "In the same manner as we did last time. By setting a trap for our killer."

"Oh, no." Raven caught her elbow. "We are *never* going to do that again. I don't want to remember how close it was."

The boy had their cart ready and brushed the horse across the neck one last time. Raven gave him a coin, and the boy grinned from ear to ear. "Thank you, sir. Do stop by again, sir. There has been an inn here even before the great conquest. Knights came here to sleep on their way to tournaments to do battle." His excited look conveyed he would have loved to have been a part of that.

"Don't you have to go to school?" Merula asked.

"There's no school in summer." He sounded as if he thought her quite dumb for not knowing this. "We have to help out with the sheep or getting peat. But I don't go to school in winter either. Father thinks it's a waste of time. If you can work with your hands, you'll always have bread."

Raven tossed him another coin, and he caught it with one hand and ran off with it to assist two merchants who were leaving the inn.

Helping her up on the cart, Raven observed wryly, "He's still satisfied with what the passing folks give him.

But someday he'll want to get away from here. I can't imagine spending your entire life here in Cranley."

With a click of the tongue and a slap of the reins, he put the horse into motion, and waited until they had left the inn well behind before he said, "Don't believe for a moment I will agree to setting a trap for the killer." He glanced at her. "I already died inside last time we tried that."

"This time"—Merula held his gaze—"I won't be the bait. I can't be. I'm not in the right position to do it. But Lamb is. She stayed at the house; she can have found things there. She was close to Ben Webber, and he might see her as a threat. She can claim to have papers from Oaks, or my sketchbook, or . . . whatever the killer might want to have. She can tell her tale at the inn. Because she ran away from me. I treated her badly, and she ran away. She's on her own, then, with what she knows and holds. An easy prey. Yes, that might just work."

Raven shook his head. "I have no idea what you mean by all of this, but I'm not participating in any plan to trap the killer."

"Good. Then Lamb, Bowsprit, and I will have to do it without you."

Raven made a disbelieving sound. "Bowsprit is my valet. If I tell him he can't be in on it . . ."

"Then he'll do it anyway. He'll never let Lamb run any risk. You know that as well as I do."

Raven stared ahead for a few moments, then turned his eyes on her with a challenging look. "And you think I would?"

CHAPTER 17

Merula shivered in the deceptively chilly breeze that came whispering through the group of trees that sheltered them. The creaking of the branches overhead jerked across her raw nerves.

The night was full upon them without stars or a moon. They only had the lantern Raven was carrying. He had turned up his collar and stared into the darkness to where the lit windows of the inn beckoned them. Lamb had gone in about an hour ago, carrying a valise as if she were traveling. She had walked with the gait of someone angry and upset, carrying enough coin to buy food and drink for herself and linger to complain about her bad luck to anyone who wanted to hear.

Until it was time to leave. The inn didn't have any vacant rooms, so Lamb would have to go and walk away from it to reach the village of Cranley and find refuge for the night there.

Merula bit her lip. This was very dangerous, and it

wasn't her risking her neck this time but Lamb. Dear, faithful Lamb.

She had been truly mad and upset when they had told
her of Ben Webber. She had said she was sure he was no
killer and would prove it by doing what they wanted. "If
the killer comes tonight," she had said, "and he jumps me
and you catch him and pull him away from me, pull off his
hood, you will see it is not Ben. I know my Ben."

"Psst!" A dark figure came up to them. Bowsprit in his
old sailor's disguise, the limp and the hanging shoulders,
the wild hair and the beard. He whispered to them, "She did
a marvelous job fooling them all with her tale of how you
had turned her out of the house for having snooped among
Oaks's things. She made a show of keeping her valise close
to her all the time, like it contained something of value. She
ate a little and drank two ales. I hope she can stand alcohol
well. It is easy to get intoxicated on an empty stomach."

Bowsprit sounded worried, glancing back at the inn as
if he couldn't stand the idea of having left Lamb behind in
that place, alone.

Merula shook her head. "The ale will be watered down
as it is in most public houses. And Lamb ate bread before
we left the house. She will be fine."

She said it more to convince herself than the others.
Lamb had been upset about their suspicions of Webber and
in a mood to do odd things. Had it been fair to request this
of her? She was brave and strong, but the person they
expected to turn up tonight had already killed one girl.

"There she comes," Bowsprit pointed.

Lamb's figure appeared, her valise in hand. She was carrying a lantern and taking the path that led from the inn to the village. A stretch of a good mile. Hung with shadows. Where would the killer strike?

They had studied the land in daylight and determined how they could keep an eye on the path and Lamb while themselves keeping out of sight of the killer, who would surely follow Lamb or wait for her along the path. Following her was more likely, as Raven had conjectured the killer would have to be in the inn to learn of Lamb's dismissal and the thing she had supposedly found and was carrying off.

They crouched along the brush, keeping their eyes on the figure.

"Someone left the inn and follows her," Bowsprit reported after a while.

The night was dark and restless around them, strange sounds rustling through the brush. Merula wished she was in her bed, trying to sleep despite the wind rattling the windowpane. But this had to be done. For the sake of Oaks and the murdered Tillie, her distraught father, and an entire community torn apart by the strange events.

"He's overtaking her," Bowsprit said softly.

They closed in on the two figures. Lamb was walking fast, determined, not stopping to look about her. The figure following her was just as quick and deathly silent. This path was obviously familiar to him, as he didn't need to watch his step.

Then Lamb suddenly halted and put the valise down, leaning over as if to fasten her shoe better.

The figure closed in.

"Now," Raven breathed to Bowsprit, and the two of them sprinted to the figure just as he lifted his hands, holding something and swinging it over Lamb's head as she straightened up. She screamed, but the sound died down at once in a gurgle.

Merula ran as well, her heart beating fast. How quickly could the killer strangle a victim? What was he using as his weapon? The kraken's missing arm? Surely it was too soft and pliable? Rope, then? Or cloth? What had left those odd markings?

Raven grabbed one arm of the attacker, Bowsprit the other. The two of them had to struggle to break the figure's hold on whatever he had around Lamb's neck. She made sounds again, spluttering.

Merula assumed that as long as she was resisting, it meant the attempt on her life had been unsuccessful. She reached her and grabbed her, asking if she was well.

The figure hissed and cursed. Raven wrenched an item out of his hands, while Bowsprit pushed him to the ground and tried to pull his arms behind his back to tie them together.

"Look!" Raven held up a leather belt. The studs on it sparked in the lantern light. "A special tool made to kill and make it look like some creature from the deep had done it. Markings as if from tentacles."

The figure lay still now, his hands bound at his back. Bowsprit pulled him to his feet.

And the light fell on his face.

Merula gasped. The haggard features of the blacksmith stared back at her, his eyes dead and dull.

"You killed your own daughter," she whispered. "How could you?"

"She wasn't my daughter anymore. She had betrayed me. First she didn't want to live with me anymore. She moved into this fancy house, telling me time and time again how beautiful it was in there. It had a brass teapot as big as she was, she said. As if such a thing can even exist. As if people like us could ever afford such things. Then she refused to help me with the land. If we had given the land to the city people, they would have rewarded us handsomely. We would have had a decent life for once. I could have bought her a dress if she wanted one. A bracelet even. Not a trinket, but a real piece of jewelry like fine ladies wear. Not this constant scraping by. All she had to do was deliver the deed of the house into my hands. I would have passed it on."

"The house wasn't yours to sell."

"But Oaks would leave. That had been told to me."

"And you helped it along by committing a murder that was supposedly done by a monster from the sea."

The old man glared at her. "It would have succeeded if you hadn't come. You are too clever for your own good."

"We can better deliver this man to the police," Bowsprit said.

Merula stood with her arm around Lamb, who was rubbing her throat and coughing.

The blacksmith said, "It need not be this way. We can all share the money. Give me what is in that suitcase and I will deliver it to the railway men. They will give me money and I will share with you."

"We don't want money," Raven said.

"No, you don't *need* money," the man retorted. "That makes all the difference. For all of my life I have wanted to have something, be something. But I never had a son and then my wife had to die, leaving me with nothing but this little slip of a girl. She wasn't winsome either, like Fern was, who could attract good men. Fern might have done well for herself, married above her station, if she had used her assets right, but not my girl. She just got herself into trouble. She never could believe Webber was a bag of wind. She honestly believed he loved her and would make her life better. Ha! All it would have done is make the entire village laugh at me. The men smirked at her already that night. I couldn't believe what they were saying. That she could really be with child. I had warned her often. But she had to be stupid."

Merula glanced at Lamb, who stood motionless, her eyes wide with shock now that the name of her beloved had been mentioned quite so casually. Her hero, her future, wiped away with one brush of the hand.

"Even if she did a stupid thing, that didn't mean she had to die," Raven said, and nodded at Bowsprit. "Let us bring him in to the police. We can show them his belt.

Homemade especially for the purpose. I don't think that even our experienced Scotland Yard inspector has ever seen quite such a thing."

Merula held the blacksmith's gaze, desperate to understand what had driven him to his crime. How he could stand here, facing them, and talk about it as if it had been logical, necessary even.

"Parents do abandon their children . . ." Her voice shivered on the words, the wounds inflicted by what she had discovered still raw. "But to kill them . . . How could you? She trusted you. She came to you by the river that night believing . . ."

"She didn't go to the river." The man's voice was flat and dead. "She went to our house. She had heard the men's remarks at the inn. She knew what it meant. Soon everyone would know it, laugh at her, at *me*."

His expression tightened even more. "I came in. She hadn't expected me back yet. Usually I stayed out late. But I had followed her home. To see what she was up to, if she was going to meet Webber. I could have killed them both, just . . ."

He gasped for breath. "She was going through her mother's things. I saw her and asked what she was doing. Going away, she said. She couldn't stay, she said. She would not deceive Oaks any longer. She felt sorry for the drops I had asked her to put in the bottle beside the bed. She said she would pour them away so he couldn't take them anymore. She wanted to help him, even after he had rejected her. She had tried to throw herself at him, the foolish girl, believing he might wed her and cover up her shame. I told her he would never. Such a fine gentleman, court a girl like her? Then she started screaming at me that anything was better than staying with me. She had the music box in her hand. Her mother's music box. She used to play it at night. It played such a pretty tune. I would never have parted with it. Never. Not to pay whatever debt . . ." His voice faltered.

The lantern light played across his tense features, hovering between the five of them as they formed a small circle in the expanse of the lonely moors.

"She dropped it," he croaked. "It fell to the boards and it burst apart. It made this last sound as if . . . it was dying. Then she had to die as well."

"You strangled her in your home and then you took her out to the river?"

"On the pony. I left it away from the soft bank so it wouldn't leave any tracks. But there were plenty there. Travelers water their horses there. I simply had to point some out and say I recognized them as belonging to Oaks's horse. I knew the police would never go compare the actual horse's shoes to the prints. Why would they? They are of us, and Oaks never was."

"But an inspector came from the city."

"He locked up Oaks, didn't he?" The blacksmith's eyes flashed. "It would have worked if you hadn't interfered."

"If we hadn't interfered," Raven said cynically, "you would have made another victim tonight. You didn't stop. Even after the death of your own daughter, you didn't stop."

"The money was mine," the man growled, his mouth

twisted into a sneer. "I gave everything for it. I deserved to have it. If this girl"—he nodded at Lamb—"had a clue from the house, I needed to have it."

"The scheme has fallen through," Merula said. "Bixby became afraid of the police and confessed it all to us."

The blacksmith stared at her in disbelief. "Some men have no guts," he rasped.

"For some, there is a limit to what they are willing to do," Raven countered. "Bixby shied away from having anything to do with murder."

"But you didn't," Bowsprit said. "You had already created this." He held out the specially prepared belt. The studs gleamed in the lantern light.

For a moment, Merula didn't understand what he was saying. Then with a shock, she realized. If the special belt to use in the strangulation had been prepared in advance, the blacksmith hadn't strangled his daughter in a fit of emotion over the discovery of her condition, the fear of humiliation, or over the broken keepsake, a memento of his beloved wife.

Uncertain what to believe now, she studied the man's weathered face.

His dull eyes flickered a moment. "There had to be victims at some point. Oaks wasn't leaving. Only deaths could convince the people that his creatures were dangerous and he had to be driven away. The drops would make him act like a lunatic. People would readily believe that victims found in the woods had been slaughtered by his sea creature. I never meant for Tillie to . . . But she wanted to leave me. After all we had been through. She couldn't just leave!"

Merula remembered how earlier when she had spoken with him, she had said that his wife hadn't wanted to leave him and he had seemed to whisper in response, "Yes, she did." Had he been thinking of his dead daughter? The unintended first victim of his plan to create deaths and drive Oaks away, complete what Bixby hadn't been able to achieve? All for money, a way out of the debt he had drunk and gambled himself into?

"Perhaps killing was easier as you had already done it before," Raven said softly. "The old village doctor died when his horse's harness broke and he was dragged off the box. Did the harness break by accident? Or had you tampered with it? Because you hated him for being unable to cure your wife?"

"For giving me false hope, making me pay for all his worthless cures which only made her worse. He knew she was beyond saving, and still he kept prescribing new drops. Merely for money. He was a predator and he deserved to die." The old man stared at him with flashing eyes. "No one questioned that it was an accident. And no one questioned that the sea monster had killed my Tillie and Oaks was to blame. Why did you have to come and ruin it all? You're not one of us. You haven't lived our life. You don't know what it's like."

Raven sighed. "What you intended when you made this belt, and whether you planned to kill your daughter beforehand or acted on impulse that night when you found her in your house, is for the jury to decide. I wouldn't like to be in their shoes."

The old man stared at him, as if the mention of a jury made him realize that he would stand trial and would have to depend on the verdict of people to whom his motives would mean but little weighed against the magnitude of his crime.

He lowered his head, and tears glistened in his eyes. They slipped down his cheeks, as his tied hands were unable to wipe them away.

"Stupid girl," he whispered. "Stupid little girl."

CHAPTER 18

O aks sat at the breakfast table with them, blinking as if he had woken up from some strange dream. He absentmindedly plunged his bread in his coffee and, when he noticed, dropped it on his plate. He stared around the room as if he was seeing it for the very first time.

"I don't know how you managed it," he said at last. "I saw no way out of it. I didn't know what to do. Perhaps I was mad? Everyone seemed to think so."

"That specialist Bixby engaged wasn't even a doctor, so you need not worry about his dire prognosis for your health. The drops you took had been tampered with without your knowledge, and they made you restless and caused you to lose consciousness."

Oaks rubbed his face. "I still can't believe Tillie added something to my drops. I would never have believed she could do anything to harm me."

Merula said softly, "She didn't want to harm you. She only worked with her father because she believed that the money involved would solve his debt and change him for the better. When she realized what she had become, she wanted to get away, also for the sake of her baby. But her father wasn't about to let her."

Oaks crumbled another piece of bread, bits raining around his plate and into his lap. "It's terrible. Who can you trust these days?"

Raven said, "You'll have to guard your collection better so characters like Ben Webber don't have access to it anymore. He took the Tasmanian devil but denied having taken the kraken's arm. I'm still not sure who did that or why. The blacksmith had his own killing tool. He didn't need the arm, unless he removed it to make the illusion of a murderous creature even more real. But he was never inside the house, and I can't see a girl like Tillie cutting off a kraken's arm with such skill. It's such a clean cut, one would think it was done in a single movement."

Oaks nodded. "Very astute, Raven. The cut was made by an ax."

Raven tilted his head. "You did it? To study the suckers more closely, perhaps determine if they were poisonous?"

Oaks looked horrified. "I'd never violate one of my own specimens in such a brutal way. The kraken came to me exactly as you can see it hanging on the stand. The tales I heard from native fishermen and resident natural historians led me to deduce that the lost arm must have been cut off by an ax in a direct confrontation between fishermen and the kraken."

"So they do attack boats?" Merula asked.

"Apparently." Oaks looked at Raven again. "I could

have told you so if I hadn't been locked up and treated like a madman. And when you came to my cell door, I didn't get half a chance to tell you anything." The indignation about that was still thick in his voice.

Raven made an apologetic gesture. "There was hardly time to discuss things at leisure. I only wanted to unmask that Dr. Twicklestone as an impostor. Not just to prove to the inspector that he was building a faulty case, but also to show you that you were never either ill or unbalanced. You just need some rest and then all will be well. Oh, now I remember."

Raven reached into his pocket and produced the notebook Merula had found in Oaks's bed. "This belongs to you. It turned up after the police took you away that night. I have to confess we looked inside it, believing it might help us clear your name."

Merula added, "The calculations had us puzzled."

Oaks accepted the notebook from him with a wry expression. "I was trying to work out how to maintain this house on my income. On my travels, I often joined other people's expeditions and they paid most expenses. Some even paid me, for my expertise. Now that I have a household to run, everything became more complicated."

He smiled ruefully. "I was worried that the railroad people might force me to sell, so I wanted to be financially secure. I even read up on graves on the moors where riches were supposed to be hidden. But what I discovered about grave robbers throughout history didn't entice me to try to make my fortune that way."

Merula said, "When we arrived, Raven asked you if you might write about your travels. That could provide some money, especially if you include sketches of the rare animals you've collected on the way."

"Merula can draw well," Raven said. "She might assist you in making those sketches."

Merula was surprised that he had so much faith in her talent even though he had never seen any of her actual work.

"You don't have to expect, though," Bowsprit said gravely, "that people will believe the animals actually exist. Mrs. Merian drew what she herself had seen in Suriname, and still many doubted whether her drawings were accurate. A spider that can grab a bird; how could something like that possibly exist?"

Oaks didn't seem to have listened well to their discussion. He shook his head, the worried look deepening. "Those railway people will want their line to come. They'll keep pestering me about selling the house. They're persistent. You caught the little fish, Raven, but the big ones are still free. The men behind it who caused all of this misery. They only used people like that poor blacksmith and that arrogant snob Bixby to get their hands on my land. They will try again."

Raven glanced at Merula. He could not, of course, deny that or reassure Oaks that it wouldn't be so bad.

"I think," Bowsprit said, "that you must look into the value of the land from a conservational point of view. I read a most interesting little pamphlet about national parks in

America. There they protect nature and preserve it, making it impossible to build there or exploit the land in other ways. If you could make this a national park, there would never be a railway through it."

Oaks sat up. "Could I really?"

"You would be the best person to do it. You've traveled, you value wildlife, you have specimens here that museums would love to have. Get into touch with the right people in London and you will be protected by friends as powerful as these railroad people are."

"Excellent thinking, Bowsprit," Raven enthused. "Let me know if you need introductions of any kind. I happen to know some people inside the Royal Zoological Society."

Oaks seemed shaken out of his dazed state now that he saw a purpose up ahead related to what he loved most in life. "People here are wary of change though. I don't want to upset the locals again."

"Some of them might even want to support you. Ben Webber only favored the railway because he believed it would bring advantages for his mother's shop. If you could convince him that protecting the natural beauty of the land will also bring people here, he might stand with you."

Merula had to admit it was likely that the self-centered Webber would choose to side with whoever had the most influential friends.

Raven added, "And you need not worry about the wreckmaster objecting to change. He'll be busy explaining to the authorities how so many ships ended up in trouble along the coast lately. The expert I consulted is very interested in those events and hopes to prove that the ships were lured to the coast by a false beacon. He assured me it's a very old trick used in ancient times. The wreckmaster should be careful or he'll end up in prison."

"That's a relief," Oaks admitted. "I never liked his arrogance. I wasn't quite sure that the light I had seen one night was real and not a delusion caused by me losing my mind . . . But now that you assured me there was never anything wrong with me . . ." A hesitant smile spread on his features. "You've really done a world of good."

He reached out and toasted them with his coffee cup. "A world of good."

Tell that to Lamb, Merula thought. The maid had played a brave role in their unmasking of the killer, but she was heartbroken over her loss of the beautiful future with a shop, room for her mother . . .

Merula rose and excused herself to go and find Lamb. She came across her sitting outside on the steps leading to the front door. "I just want to say goodbye to the place," she said in a small voice. "Now that we're leaving again."

Merula sat beside her. "I'm sorry we didn't have a better time. It was supposed to be a vacation, but . . ."

"I was just silly believing he cared for me. As silly as I was when I was thirteen and believed that shipmate would come back for me. Just because he had given me a silver blue ribbon."

"Webber cared for no one but himself. You can't help that."

"I know that." Lamb smiled sadly. "It wasn't about him either. I just wanted his shop and the safe life and the quiet village and all I never had in Rotherhithe. I didn't love him either, not one bit, you know."

Merula nodded. "Of course not." She supposed it helped Lamb to see it that way. But her excitement had suggested she had been a little bit infatuated. Ben Webber was, after all, a handsome and dashing young man.

Lamb said, "Oh, well, I suppose it's for the better. Else you'd have to find yourself a new companion. Your aunt wouldn't be pleased. And Mother? She complains about Rotherhithe, but it would have been too quiet here for her liking. She lives for gossip, a little liveliness in the neighborhood. All her friends live there. She would have been loath to go. And you know that old saying about never replanting an old tree. Her heart might not have been up to it."

Lamb forced a smile. "It's not that bad, Miss. We still have each other."

"We certainly do." Merula squeezed her hand.

They sat in silence, staring at the blue skies, both lost in their own thoughts. Merula wondered if there was time left, and if it was even wise to wish for it, to visit the cottages again and confront the man who had shared something about her mother's past with her, with Bowsprit's belief that he had been lying about her father's death.

If he was still alive, she wanted to know who he was, where he was, and how she might reach him. Not that she ever would, perhaps, but the idea that she might be able to, in case of an emergency, or just . . .

She felt restless not knowing, half deceived again.

A boy came running up the driveway. His simple outfit and the stick in his hand suggested he helped the shepherds. He carried an envelope in his hand. "This is for a Miss Merula," he called from afar.

Merula rose to meet him halfway and handed him a coin for his troubles. He stared at it as if he had never seen such a thing, then rubbed it over his shirt to make it shine. Grinning from ear to ear, he bounded off.

Merula studied the handwriting on the envelope. *Confidential. Only to be opened by Miss Merula Merriweather.*

Her stomach squeezed, and she tore it open with her little finger, something Aunt Emma would have frowned upon. But she didn't want to lose time going inside looking for a letter knife. She looked inside. There were two things. A note and . . .

She pulled out the second item. It was the half photograph depicting her mother.

Merula stared almost hungrily at the face, the eyes, the smile, the whole loveliness of that image. Then she opened the note:

> *You have attained justice for a poor deluded girl. For that you should be rewarded. Keep this photograph of a good woman close to your heart. But never look for your father. If he finds out who you are, then he will come for you, and you will become just like him.*

That was all it said.

Merula turned it over and over, desperate for more, but there was nothing.

She reread the cryptic words, open confirmation that her father was indeed still alive.

Still alive but out of her reach, as she wasn't allowed to ever contact him. The letter even suggested she had to make sure he never discovered who she was.

Or that she even existed?

Had her father never known her mother was with child? But how?

She ran inside and called for Raven. He rushed out of the breakfast room to meet her. She explained hurriedly that she had to go somewhere, and could he take her?

Raven took one look at her excited face and agreed. They were on their way in a few minutes. She directed him to the cottages. Her heart pounded; sweat stood on her forehead. She knew what she would find there: the women, the fencing men, the melancholy violin music and the table, not with wine, probably, at this hour, but maybe their breakfast?

She'd spend time with them. She wanted to know more about the man, his life, and . . . Even if he didn't want her to speak of her mother, then she would not; she would pretend to be interested in the acting and . . .

Anything to learn more.

From a distance, Merula noticed something was wrong. The cottages lay there in the morning sunshine, the doors closed, no people moving about. There were no colors, no pillows strewn outside.

As they pulled up, she spotted the long table, but nothing was on it. The playful dog was also gone. The grass lay trampled by many feet, but no one was around.

She clambered off the cart, ran around, peeking into windows and checking the barn where they had rehearsed for their performance. No one, everything gone.

"What are we here for?" Raven asked. "What's wrong?"

Merula just gave him the note. He read it and frowned at her. "Why can't your father know who you are? And what does the writer mean by, if he finds you, you will become like him?"

"I don't know." Merula let her arms dangle in dejection. "I don't know, and now they've left and . . . They are always here for the entire summer, he told me. Why have they left? Where did they go?"

As she spoke, a woman came walking up, carrying a basket. She looked surprised to see no one there. She called out to Merula and Raven, "Where are the actors?"

"We hoped you'd know."

"They never leave around this time. They're always here until September. They must have received word of something to do in another town."

"But you don't know where?"

"No." The woman shook her head in bewilderment. "I was asked to clean here, and I come every other morning. They didn't tell me a thing. I even baked them bread and brought some apples. I don't understand."

She started to do the same thing Merula had done, peek into windows, knock on doors. No response, just silence.

Merula turned to Raven. "They have left, and they don't want to be found, either. This man must have a lot of power within the group for them to just listen to him. I wish I knew at least who he was or what he once had to do with my mother. But perhaps it is better not to know."

She studied the photograph of her mother closer. "He calls her a good woman. And I believe he means that. But why would a good woman fall in with a man who . . . ? There must be something wrong with my father, or he would not warn me so strongly against him."

Raven said, "If this man loved your mother and she didn't love him but rather another who wasn't worthy of her in his mind, that may be his reason for wanting to keep you away from him."

"Perhaps." Merula stood and looked around her at the cottages sitting so lonely in the outstretched moors. She wasn't sure if Raven was right.

She had sensed genuine concern in the man. Would he still be jealous after two decades and try to separate her from her father purely out of ill will against the man who had taken the woman he had loved?

Or was her father truly a dangerous man?

Dangerous in what way?

How could she "become like him"? Why would that be bad?

Raven put his arm around her. He smiled down on her. "We must go now. There's nothing to be found here anymore. At least now you have her picture. You did get on a bit."

Merula nodded. She let him walk her back to the cart.

Dartmoor had delivered something, some clue, a tantalizing glimpse into her past and perhaps even a key to the future. But did she want to unlock that door now marked FORBIDDEN by the man she had met here?

Solving murders had proven to her she had a keen mind and could unravel secrets, and besides that, she had friends who would support her in anything she undertook. But digging into the secret of her birth, her origin, might prove to be something wholly different than investigating a crime in which she wasn't personally involved. Family was an amazing thing, but also a two-edged blade, as she had experienced here firsthand.

Raven helped her onto the cart and sat beside her. "Back then. We did run out on Oaks somewhat unceremoniously."

"Yes, we must celebrate his release with him and plan for his lands to be protected from further greedy prospectors. Bowsprit handed him a really good idea."

"Perhaps we can travel sometime and explore such a national park somewhere." Raven glanced at her as he steered the horse across the road. "Would you want to travel abroad with me?"

Merula sat up at this sudden suggestion. "If Uncle Rupert would let me. I can imagine Aunt Emma would have a thousand objections. She only agreed to this because she thought London wasn't safe for me."

Merula laughed softly. "I better not tell her about what happened here, or she will think I can't be safe anywhere."

As she said it, a cold wind breathing across the moor

caressed her face and put gooseflesh on her arms. She hugged herself and moved closer to Raven.

"I'll talk to your uncle as soon as we're back in London." Raven cast her a look. "The Continent might be best for a start. I don't think South America would much appeal to him or to my purse. It would be best, of course, if we could let ourselves be hired. As specialists of some kind. Then we could travel with all of our expenses paid."

"If only that could be true," Merula said.

Raven grinned at her. "Who knows?"

ACKNOWLEDGMENTS AND AUTHOR'S NOTE

As always, I'm grateful to all agents, editors, and authors who share online about the writing and publishing process and enable me to keep learning. A special thanks to my amazing agent Jill Marsal, my wonderful editor Faith Black Ross, and the entire talented crew at Crooked Lane Books, especially cover designer Mimi Bark for the evocative cover.

★ ★ ★

As a huge fan of *The Hound of the Baskervilles*, I've always wanted to write a mystery set in Dartmoor featuring a legendary murderous creature. As with *The Butterfly Conspiracy*, the first book in the Merriweather and Royston series, the idea for the premise of *Death Comes to Dartmoor* was sparked by watching Sir David Attenborough's *Natural Curiosities*, where he draws on many exciting sources—biographies, treatises, encyclopediae, correspondence, etc.—to explore misconception, confusion, and conscious deceit in the development of zoology. When I watched him speak of the

mythological kraken and the giant squid, the real-life animal that probably inspired the stories and sketches of ships
being dragged into the depths by enormous tentacles, I
knew I had found my killer for the Dartmoor story. Oaks's
keeping it draped across a stand in his bathroom is of course
inspired by the famous photograph of a giant squid draped
across Moses Harvey's bath stand, taken in 1874, and the
missing tentacle followed from an account of a real-life
fisherman defending himself against a kraken, alias giant
squid, with an ax, actually managing to chop off one of its
tentacles.

Oaks's extensive collection of specimens in alcohol,
including deformed animals, reflects collections in museums I have visited ever since I was a little girl fascinated by
two-headed calves. And as I can never resist an opportunity
to look up at the night skies and see something special—
whether a meteor shower, a lunar eclipse, or a planet visible
with the naked eye for one single night—I just had to work
the August Perseid meteor shower into the story, hoping to
entice you to also look up sometime and admire the splen-
dor of the infinite universe.

Other tidbits to enliven the story weren't hard to find.
Often as I researched online, I laughed out loud in surprise
and amusement at what lay ready to be used and concluded
that indeed fact can be stranger than fiction: men going
insane on the train, age-old graves on the moors containing riches, the professional wreckmaster who sees to division of everything washed ashore, and the (im)possibility of

luring ships deliberately onto the rocks by using false beacons, something experts are still divided about.

And of course there was Dartmoor lore, so full of mysterious stories about mayhem and murder. I put my own spin on a few (like my version of the will in blood I devised for fictional Harcombe Tor). In general, I pulled some of the Dartmoor landmarks a little closer together so my characters could easily travel around and enjoy the full array of natural wonders on offer, but still I hope the depiction is true to the wild beauty of the land and the many amazing stories connected with it and will inspire you as a reader to learn more about it or even visit sometime. As Conan Doyle already recognized over a century ago, it is indeed the perfect setting for a great crime story.